DARK PRINCE

PRINCE

A DANGEROUS ROYALS ROMANCE

BOOK ONE

Val -
Dark
Yummy
heroes
forever!

Annika
Martin

Annika Martin

www.annikamartinbooks.com
Cover art: Bookbeautiful
Book Layout ©2013 BookDesignTemplates.com

Dark Mafia Prince/ Annika Martin. -- 1st ed.
ISBN-13: 9781533414120
ISBN-10: 1533414122

To the lost ones

"A breathtaking ride of danger and dark sensuality."

— NYT Bestselling author Skye Warren

CHAPTER ONE

Aleksio

M ost people who see the ancient cigarette burn on my arm assume I got it from somebody who wanted to hurt me. It's natural to think that. But they couldn't be more wrong.

My cigarette burn is all about love.

Still, it starts getting torn up with the kind of hand-to-hand fighting I've been doing. And more guys will arrive any minute. Panting, moving fast in the gloomy nook of the boathouse, I yank the carefully folded handkerchief from my front pocket, loosen my cufflinks, and tie the thing around my forearm, using my teeth to tighten it, making a protective skin.

The burn looks bad, but it hasn't hurt for years. You can poke it, and there's no feeling.

Which goes to show, if you fuck something up enough, it loses its capacity to feel.

That's true of skin, and it's also true of people. Having no capacity to feel is a definite bonus when you're doing the kinds of things I'm doing today.

My phone vibrates. It's my brother, Viktor, giving me the heads-up, as if every molecule in me isn't already on hyper-alert. But Viktor and I are protective of each other like that. We only just found each other last year.

Viktor and I figure Aldo Nikolla and his underboss—his *kumar*—will come down from the main house last, once they realize they can't get ahold of their men. That's when the party really gets started. I almost can't believe the plan is working. Nikolla is one of the best-protected men in the country, possibly the world. An Albanian mafia kingpin ensconced in a summer residence guarded better than Fort Knox.

We shouldn't be able to get to him with just ten guys. That's the magic of planning for you.

I fix my cuffs, let my Sig hang loose in my hand.

Old Konstantin, the hitter who rescued me when I was a boy, never let me forget the traditions—the suits, the codes, cufflinks just so. *The sleeping king*, he always called me. *You will gather your brothers and take back your kingdom.*

I focus on the pile of bodies in the dark corner. Six guys shot up with enough tranquilizer to sleep for a day. Still, I think they might wake up. Because they're Aldo Nikolla's soldiers. Like he's all-powerful.

Which of course he is.

And even as well as this attack is going, I'm holding it together by a hair.

It doesn't help that Konstantin tried to stop this attack. *Don't do it—you're only two brothers. All three brothers must be together.*

All my life, that was the plan—find my brothers so we can take our kingdom, our vengeance.

The three brothers must be together. You are too early.

Well, priorities change.

I move deeper into the shadows behind the boats and the seaplane. This is a place of dark nooks and crannies. Good hide-and-seek spots. This particular one was a favorite of mine, in another lifetime.

The last time I was this close to Aldo Nikolla was the night I got that burn.

I was nine—Konstantin and I had been on the run two months by then. I had a fever. We crashed in an abandoned building—Kansas City, I think. I woke up in Konstantin's arms as he sprinted past caged-up, neon-lit stores and turned into an alley that stank of piss. He had a disguise stashed there—a dirty wig and lipstick and clothes. Konstantin did a quick change into a bag lady. It was a disguise no self-respecting Black Lion clan member would ever adopt—that had been the genius of it.

A few terse words from him and I made myself invisible under the pile of clothes next to him, eyes and lips squeezed tight. Old Konstantin lit up a cigarette as they approached. If you knew him—and these killers knew him well—it was the opposite of his way. He never smoked.

We could hear Aldo Nikolla and Bloody Lazarus and the rest of them going at the bums on the next block. I pressed my forehead against Konstantin's massive thigh, hiding, as the footsteps slowed in front of us. One of Aldo's soldiers kicked Konstantin and asked whether he'd seen a man and a boy. Konstantin screeched back in crazy old lady gibberish—real Academy Award shit.

That's when the old man moved his hand—just enough to press the cigarette to my arm. Just pressed that fucker right in there.

He didn't know he was burning me. He had no idea. He was trying to save us, screeching in that bag lady getup.

I forced myself to stay still—any movement would give me away.

So I let it burn, let the pain turn my brain red with ice. The cigarette had burned through whatever polyester thing I was under, and I'll never forget the smell. I let the ember sink deep into my arm like a blistering sun, praying he'd move his hand on his own, but he didn't. All his attention was on screeching at the soldiers, putting them on the defensive.

Keeping us alive.

I let the pain be my teacher. The pain taught me I could survive, that I could endure anything. That I would endure and fight another day, just like Konstantin always said. *"Mbreti gjumi*—the sleeping king. You live to fight another day."

But that day has never quite come. Konstantin wants everything perfectly in place first. All three Dragusha brothers united. Legions of men behind us. *They will fall into line when they see the Dragusha brothers have made their way back to each other.*

Superstitious old Konstantin thinks we can't attack Nikolla without three brothers together. But we can't find our missing brother without attacking Nikolla—that's the problem.

Our baby brother is out there. And he needs us. I'll burn the world to get to him.

The next guard strolls in the far door, heading for my side of the line of boat slips. This guy's not thinking about who might be lurking in the best hide-and-seek spot in the place—he's thinking about the lunch spread that's supposedly waiting for him on the upper level. Viktor and I took over the texting between the guards as part of the attack. Like taking over their hive brain.

It's true what they say—the fastest way to a man is through his stomach.

As soon as he's in my orbit, I lunge for him and twist away his weapon. I choke him out before he can make a sound, and then I jab the needle into his neck and he's down.

Some of the soldiers are surprisingly easy to take. But then again, all these guys were suckling at the tit of the Xbox while I was getting beaten to a bloody pulp by Konstantin in our endless training sessions.

My guys are up at the house. The idea is to flush everyone my way. We've been silent so far. As long as nobody shouts or shoots, we keep our element of surprise.

When Aldo Nikolla senses trouble, he'll come down with Lazarus and leave Mira at the house, where he'll think she's protected. She's his one weakness. The best way to control him.

I've played this day out in my imagination so many times. The horror on Nikolla's face when he sees I'm back—Aleksio Dragusha, his worst fucking nightmare, all grown up and in his face. The shock when he realizes I've reunited with my brother Viktor. Because hey, you'd think that when you send a toddler off to a shithole of a Moscow orphanage with no identification, he'd stay there, right? Wouldn't you think?

Surprise, motherfucker!

No way will Mira recognize me.

Even if she didn't think we three Dragusha brothers died alongside our parents, she wouldn't recognize me as the boy she goofed off with a lifetime ago. Lying around on a sea of green grass in front of this wedding cake of a castle, clouds like seahorses.

I'm worlds different from the good-natured mafia prince she knew. I'm pretty much a different species. Because when you're hunted every day of your life, fighting for survival like a rat in a pit of vipers, everything inside you changes. You develop weapons and talents no sane person would ever admire. You lose your humanity.

Mira is worlds different too, now—sometimes I can't believe the shopaholic shit she puts out there on her blog and her Instagram and all the rest of it. But she was pretty amazing when I knew her as a kid.

I guess this life twists everyone, eventually.

It's better that she's not the same person. It makes my job easier.

CHAPTER TWO

Mira

My father has a black cellphone that he never uses, but it's always on, always charged, and always within reach, full of dark threat, just like his gun. He's had it for years, and I never heard it ring.

I hear it the week after my twenty-eighth birthday.

It's a Saturday afternoon. We're out on the porch. I came back for a ribbon-cutting ceremony where I put in a rare cameo as mafia princess Mira Nikolla in Oscar de la Renta and Manolo Blahnik. I was so proud that he'd funded the research wing of the local hospital where Mom died—a research wing in her name. Not a lot will bring me back home these days, but a wing in Mom's name? I'm there.

Missing Mom is one of the few things we have in common anymore.

The cynical part of me wonders if he funded the wing just to get a visit out of me. Maybe he did. It doesn't even touch the debt he owes to society.

Do I sound pissed at my own father? I am. Do I still love him? Always.

We're all each other has left. We've had each other's backs since the day Mom died. The day he fixed me with that intense gaze of his and said, "It's us two now, Kitten. It's us two. Two against everything, alright?"

I should be packing—the limo is coming in a few hours to take me to the airport. I'll be back in New York at the advocacy center where I work, back to being the lawyer in jeans and Target tops, like some kind of reverse Wonder Woman—I spin around and turn into a girl you'd forget two minutes after you pass her by.

Which is exactly how I like it. It makes it easier for me to do my job, fighting for kids and families.

We have people thinking I've spent these past years on worldwide shopping sprees, which is embarrassing, but better than having bodyguards follow me around—that would *not* work at the advocacy center. PR people maintain a fake life for me. A sad social media construct that keeps me under the radar. And mostly it keeps Dad safe. I'm his Achilles' heel. A way to make him weak.

There's a type of bird that lays its eggs in other birds' nests. Sometimes I feel like I ended up in the wrong nest like that. But we're family—that's the bottom line.

Dad did terrible things coming up like he did, but we have each other's backs. Even at the age of ten, I understood. Me and Dad against the world. It still means everything that he said that.

So we're out on the porch of the lake residence, me still in my mafia princess pink, when the chirp sounds out. I have no idea that it's that second cellphone. I guess I never imagined it would have the bird-chirp type of ring. I always thought it would be something more ominous. Like a blaring tone.

But the chirp is ominous to my father. His face goes white.

He answers it, and I can tell it's Lazarus. In addition to being Dad's enforcer, Bloody Lazarus is pretty much the worst psycho I've ever met. Even across the large, lavish porch table laden with feta and olives and strong Turkish coffee in priceless china, even with my dad pressing that phone to his ear, I can hear the psycho.

It takes exactly two seconds for Dad to pull me inside and call out for the house staff guys.

"What's going on?"

He just shakes his head and resumes his conversation. "Put Jetmir on it. Fuck! Fuck! Where's Leke? Fuck."

Dad's voice is higher, not in volume, but octave. It's a bad sign.

But here's the really bad sign: Nobody comes. Dad called for staff, and none have arrived. They always appear instantly. "Staff," in this case, is a euphemism for soldiers whose job is to hang around the house and not be seen or heard unless they're needed.

I never see Dad worried. I never see the world not bending to his every whim. My blood races.

There's only one reason dozens of soldiers wouldn't come running when my father yells for them.

He gets his go bag out of the front closet, grabs his headset, and sticks his Luger into his belt. He hands me a small revolver. Mother-of-pearl handle. Loaded. "Down to the seaplane. Now."

"Dad." I hold it like a dead thing, looking up at him, like, *really*? I don't do firearms, and he knows it. But he's completely freaked out. And I'm thinking about his bad heart. I shouldn't add to his stress.

"Got it." I put it in a proper grip like I learned in shooting lessons. Like a dog, fake sitting down. I'll ditch it later.

He throws me the boat and seaplane keychain. The keys are attached to a little buoy that floats if you drop it in the water. "Get that plane out of the boathouse. Now! I'll meet you."

"We're going in the *seaplane*?" The seaplane is a fun-time thing. It's a recreational vehicle, not a getaway vehicle.

He tips his head up at the ceiling, a movement that tells me everything. We're going in the seaplane because somebody might be on the roof, expecting him to go in the helicopter.

It's a takeover.

Shit.

I grab my purse, kick off my heels, and take the stairs to the lower level. I head through the ornate rooms and back through the servant areas, and burst out the side delivery door.

It's a cool autumn afternoon. Nice. Or at least, it was nice.

I run along the perimeter of the estate, where it's shaded by trees and the limestone wall. Less obvious if you're on the roof.

The first few minutes I jog stealthily, grass cool on my bare feet, but then something builds up in me and I'm just running like hell, shoes and satchel in one hand, gun in the other.

I won't use the gun. Dad always says having to shoot just means your threats didn't work. As if I'll even make threats.

I round a tree, keeping to the shadows. I get down to the seawall and run along it, heart thundering, up to the boathouse door. I punch in the combo and pull it open.

It's dark and gloomy inside the boathouse; Just a few high windows let in the sun.

I scurry around the slips past the speedboats to the seaplane at the end. I unlock the lift with the key that hangs from a string, and then I hit the button to start lowering it to the water. Usually the grounds guy does this. Where is everybody?

The motor whines as it lowers the plane, white with blue stripes and blue pontoons. While I'm waiting for that, I go to the corner, lift a panel, and slam my palm onto a button. One of the boathouse doors jerks and squeals as it begins to raise up like a garage door, unveiling the sparkling blue water of Lake Geneva.

Inch by inch, the light slants in.

Movement from the dark side. I'm not alone. A man.

My heart skips a beat as he pushes off the wall, his face in the shadows, dark curls catching the light. His suit jacket hangs open to reveal a white shirt and a black slash of a tie. Slacks cup and kiss his thighs as he moves. Do I know him? I can't make out his features in the gloom.

"Hello?"

He continues toward me, silent as a panther. Power rolls off him, even in the dark.

Then he strolls past a dim slant of light coming in from a high window, like strolling through a hazy spotlight.

It's then that the full force of his dark beauty crashes through me. Sharp hit of a cheekbone. Generous lips that look softer than sin. Predator eyes so dangerous and beautiful, you might get lost in them. You might let him kill you.

His gaze is a dangerous caress. A .357 flashes at his side.

Somewhere in the back of my mind, I think there's something familiar about him.

He moves onward, into the shadows, and I tell myself it has to be an illusion. This is a man you don't forget.

I feel his power in my bones as he nears. I don't like it, but I know to respect it, the way you respect a hurricane.

And the suit. With most Albanian mafia guys my age, the suit is a uniform, something put on in the morning. This guy wears a suit like a Hun might wear fur. It's part of him, molten with danger.

I raise my piece and aim at his chest. My voice is hoarse. "I'll use this."

His gorgeous lips quirk, and he just keeps coming. Is he that stupid? That brave? It's like he knows I won't use it.

He passes yet another shaft of light from a high window. We lock eyes, and again I'm seized with that sensation of familiarity. Something about his dark curls and dark lashes. Or maybe his eyes, so big and deep and piercing. The line of his slightly scruffy cheek.

I can't shake it...it's like when you catch a whiff of something that transports you somewhere, like a half-forgotten dream that's floating away. All you remember is a feeling. The feeling I have of him is nice.

That can't be right.

He's on me in a flash, a massive arm around me, his face in my hair.

"Let's have that, baby, and we'll wait for Daddy together." He rips the weapon from my hand and then yanks me roughly against him, holding me from behind, hard body against mine.

He presses his piece to my cheek. My mind goes blank. One twitch of his finger and I'm dead.

My heart slams in my chest. "I'm not your baby."

"You're whatever I want you to be, starting now." His voice is a velvet glove, the edge of the gun painful punctuation on his sentence. "It's a new day." He starts pulling me the way I came in.

I make out a pair of slumped forms in the corner of the boathouse. Ramiz. Jareki. "Are they…" I can't bring myself to say it.

"Napping on the job?" he supplies in a vicious tone. "That is really terrible. Really outrageous."

My knees practically vibrate as he walks me out of the boathouse to the bench next to the door. You can see the whole lawn from here. He sits us there and pulls me onto his lap, holding my upper arm in an iron grip.

"You're hurting me," I say.

No answer. Economical with his words. With pain. I know a killer when I come into contact with one. I concentrate on my breath and tell myself not to freak out, but this is bad—really bad. He's cool. Competent. Focused.

"Right now, you can still walk out of this," I say. "Whatever you plan to do, you can't get away with it. Just cut your losses."

The killer says nothing, and it comes to me that he's actually gotten away with a lot already. Planned carefully. Even sitting here is a well-made choice: Dad won't see us until it's too late, partly in the shade as we are. He's positioned for maximum shock.

The killer has everything under control. Like he was born to this.

He's hot and hard under me. Pure muscle and steel and man. My belly tightens. I shift, trying to minimize the places my body touches his.

He pulls me to him. "Where do you think you're going?"

I swallow. *Stay calm. Don't let him feel your fear.* I strain to hear the golf cart whir. Dad'll take the golf cart down. But the green expanse of the lawn is empty. Is he okay? What about his heart? The lake sparkles on, soft waves, gentle breeze carrying the faint scent of seaweed. And I realize something strange: No boats.

It's one of the last lovely fall days. Everybody who's anybody comes up to Lake Geneva from Chicago on a day like this. "Where are all the boats?"

He gazes out—wistfully, almost. A dark curl caresses his cheekbone. "Looks like they took the day off."

He's different from the guys in Dad's circle. Contract killer? Lone wolf? "People wouldn't just not come out—"

He smirks. "Message from the mother ship?"

I swallow. This guy did something to make them stay away. I can't imagine what. He has to be somebody, pulling all this off. That kind of thing takes men. Extreme choreography. "What is this?"

"Shhh," he growls into my ear. "Take the strap off your purse."

"You can't—"

"Can't *what?* Tell me what I can't do, Mira Mira."

Mira Mira. That's the name of the fashion blog the PR person runs. The PR person with the greatest gig in the world, running around to Paris and Hong Kong taking pictures of clothes. Like it's me out there, freaking out over the latest couture.

"Tell me one thing I can't do right now."

I can't. He's taken absolute power in a way no other man would dare. It's strangely mesmerizing, the way impossible feats sometimes are. Because nobody is supposed to be able to do this.

"Good answer." His breath is a caress on my ear. "Don't you test me, Mira. You won't like the result." He moves his lips to my ear. "Now wrap the strap around your wrists."

There's something in the way he says it that gets me hot and cold all over my skin. Is he doing it on purpose?

"Make it nice and tight."

With shaking hands I undo the strap and circle it loosely around my wrists.

He puts the gun aside and with a few twists he yanks it tight, tying the knot, so that my wrists are bound in my lap. He settles me in, then takes up his gun. You can see everything from here. Everything that matters.

I've met a lot of scary guys who are full of special mafia snowflake opinions on wine and weapons, but this man is in another class entirely. A barbarian in Armani. There's a dark freckle on his right cheekbone, like a tiny dark jewel. That, too, is strangely familiar.

Heavy pounding on the stairs behind me. I don't have to look to know someone's coming down from the roof deck of the boathouse. The perfect place for cocktails after a boating party. Or keeping watch during a takedown, picking off the chess pieces.

The guy comes into view, huge and dark and Albanian like my captor, though this one is younger—early twenties, maybe—and has a more military look, with short hair and posture like a soldier. He, too, wears a suit and tie.

"Viktor, I want you to meet somebody. This is Mira Nikolla. Mira, this is Viktor."

The man nods curtly. "Lazarus is still in the wind." Viktor speaks with a Russian accent.

Lazarus was supposed to be here for lunch, but he ducked out.

My captor frowns. Whatever he's doing, he wanted Lazarus under control for it.

He's right to be unhappy. If there's one person you don't want after you, besides my father, it's psycho Bloody Lazarus.

"She agrees," he says, reading my expression.

"You don't know what I think," I spit out. The last thing I'm willing to do is help these guys or offer any kind of insight.

"Have every possible resource scouring for Lazarus. He'll be a problem."

Viktor nods and puts his attention onto his phone, fingers flying.

I study the strong, familiar line of Viktor's nose, so like my captor's. Same with the cheekbones, the lips. Brothers. They both look Albanian, but how is one brother American and one brother Russian?

And then I see Dad in the golf cart, buzzing down the lawn.

"Dad! Watch out!"

Dad hears me, but he keeps driving his cart, which looks like a toy against the green. He knows what's happening. Probably understands it better than I do.

"Turn back!"

Dad sees us now. Face grim.

"This is already better than I thought," my captor says. "Such fucking drama." He nuzzles my hair, turning it on for effect on Dad. I'm just a prop. I always have been, in this world.

"You're not going to get out of this."

"I like the way you smell," my captor whispers. My mouth goes dry as he slides a hand over my pink skirt, holding me tight against him. His body is packed so tight with muscles, he feels like stone underneath me—or he would, if not for the immense heat he gives off.

But his attention isn't on me. It's on my father, who's out of the cart now, running, nearing.

Running is bad for his heart. "Daddy," I whisper.

"Shh. Daddy's coming." My mouth goes dry as he slides the barrel of the gun over my cheek in a horrible, gentle caress.

He wants me to look scared, so I do my best to look bored. Probably not pulling it off. I am scared.

My father slows and holds out his hands, a placating gesture. "Please—"

My captor surges up off the bench, taking me with him, practically pulling my arm out of the socket. We head to the center of the green, green lawn. I become aware of a few more men arrayed around the grounds, seeming to materialize from the shadows around trees and outbuildings. A lot of big guns. Assault rifles.

"Whatever this is, leave her out of this." My father keeps his hands up. "I can give you so much. More than you can imagine."

So my dad doesn't know him, either.

My mouth goes dry as my captor slides the barrel of the gun over my cheek, tracing a design over my cheekbone.

I see my father out of the corner of my eye, but I can't keep my eyes off the gun, cool and deadly across my skin.

"Let her go," my father says. "You looking for money, is that it? We could talk about that. Bank accounts. Boats." Dad points at his cherished 1940s mahogany Chris-Craft, moored at the dock. "Beautiful, priceless things. Whatever you want."

I heave a breath of relief when my captor finally takes the gun off my cheek. "Boats are just glorified cars," he growls, "except they don't go anywhere." The next thing I know, he has it pointed at Dad's million-dollar boat. He pulls me to his chest as the gunshots tear out.

Viktor is smiling, maybe laughing—I can't tell—as he shoots the boat, too. I cringe as the assault weapons start. It's a war zone suddenly.

And then it's over. And everybody's attention is on my father's precious boat, half-sunk.

He's made his point. This is a man you don't buy.

"Now for your dear daughter," he says.

My father rushes toward me. Guys materialize from nowhere to grab him. Viktor pats him down, takes his Luger, his phone, his second Luger. He even finds what Dad calls his party favor, the gun tucked in a special pocket at the back of his jacket. They're tight and well trained.

"Touch her and I will kill you," Dad says. "I'll have your balls."

My captor releases me. I quickly work my hands out of the strap and throw it down, but my arm is seized by one of his minions. My captor doesn't look; he knows where his men are. He just strolls up to my dad—*djall e bukar*—a beautiful devil. "Is that so?"

"We'll string you up and—"

Crrrack.

I scream as his hard, cruel hit sends Dad stumbling backward. He falls, blood dripping from his lip to his white shirt.

"Hey, what are you doing?" I say. "Leave him alone!"

"Stand up, Aldo," my captor says.

"One hair on her head," Dad growls. "If you hurt one hair—"

"Please," I say. "He has a bad heart."

"Poor Aldo Nikolla," he says with a mocking edge. Mocking my father. No man would dare. Ever. It's here that I know my world has changed.

I try to pull away. Arms tighten around me.

"Daddy," I whisper, watching him through bleary eyes.

"It's okay, Kitten," Dad says.

"Kitten," my savage captor sneers. I can't tell whether he's mocking Dad's affection or whether it's the name, which, admittedly, I never loved. I always saw it as wishful thinking on Dad's part.

The intruder comes back to me, drapes an arm around my shoulders. The threat hurts Dad more than any blow. "*Kitten,*" he says, pulling me close.

Dad looks horrified.

I twist in his arms and get an elbow out, manage to shove him away.

He stumbles back. "Oh, Kitten!"

Different arms close around mine, new guys holding me from both sides, holding me too tightly. I try futilely to jerk away.

My captor's smile is all brutal beauty. He sparkles with hate, taking pleasure from Dad's pain. This is very, very personal.

"You disgust me," I say.

My captor comes to me, studying my face, my eyes, like he's looking for something. Again I get this hit of familiarity. But how could I possibly know him? I turn away.

"Unh-uh," he says. "You don't get to do that with me." He takes my chin and forces my gaze back to his, holding my jaw in a fierce grip, fingers thick and strong. I can feel his words like a knife in Dad's heart. "You're mine now to use as I see fit."

I suck in a breath. Dad can't take much more of this.

"And when I want you to look at me, you look at me," he says.

I won't go down whimpering.

So I look at him.

And I spit at him—right in his face—shocking myself. Never in my life have I done such a thing.

A bright dime of saliva glistens on the stubble-darkened skin under his cheekbone. It's small—dainty, even—but it may as well be a nuclear bomb for how it silences everyone, stops everything.

What have I done?

The men holding me have gone stiff.

Even the wind in the trees above seems to still. Dad's supporting himself on his elbow, hand at his chest.

The intruder doesn't wipe the spit off—no, he's too cool for that. He lets it glisten in the sunshine as he stares into my eyes.

His gaze is so powerfully intimate, I think I might not be able to move even if my arms weren't being held by his guys.

My belly quivers as he takes a step toward me. One, then another, until he's directly in front of me. His beautiful smile is cold as ice.

"No," my father says from somewhere in the distance. "No."

But I can't look away. Nobody's ever looked at me with such intensity. My heart pounds.

The intruder raises a finger, and I can see the thick pad of it. A white line bisects the inside of the knuckles; *defen-*

sive wound, I think sort of automatically. I see a lot of them in my work.

Slowly he swipes it through the spittle on his cheek, then he holds it up in front of my face so that I can see. He seems happy. A furious angel at full blast, spit on his finger, gun down at his side.

Panic washes over me like a haze. He's going to wipe that finger on my face or lips. Punch me at best. Most likely kill me.

What have I done? Made it easy.

He turns his hand and simply looks at his finger.

My pulse is an ocean in my ears.

He looks back up, invades my eyes with his stare.

And then he does something I never in a million years would've predicted: Looking deep into my eyes, pinning me with his gaze like that, he sucks on his own finger. He fucking sucks my spit off it.

My belly tightens over the dangerous sexuality of the gesture.

But he doesn't stop there. No, he keeps going, pushing his finger in through his thick lips, shoving it in—slowly, inexorably. Eyes pinning me.

The haze intensifies. The moment goes on forever. I stand helpless in the face of all the things he's shoving into my mind with that move.

It's domination, and it's danger. Invisible fingers sliding into me.

Then he starts to pull it out, just a glint of a smile in the depths of his dark eyes. He pulls it out slowly. This guy, he wants to make me feel every second. Every inch of it.

And I do feel it.

I can't look away from this dangerous stranger with just a glint of a smile in the chocolate pools of his eyes.

I understand something in this moment: Nobody gets out of here unscathed.

"Take *me*," my father says. "Kill *me*. It's what you came here for."

I've never heard him so frightened. Dad's strength has always been dependable as gravity. It was dark strength, used in a way I'll never condone, but it was always there. Everything's spinning off its axis.

The barbarian doesn't take his eyes from mine. "Take you? On what planet are you more fun than Kitten is?" Those evil lips form into a diabolical smile. That, too, is a weapon for this guy.

"But there is one thing."

"What?" my father asks.

"Our brother," he says. "You give us the location of our brother, and we'll be in a slightly better mood."

My father looks confused. "And do I know your brother?"

I stiffen as Viktor nears my father. I'm thinking he'll hurt him again, but he just hands my father a paper photo.

My father takes it. Even from feet away, I can see the small white rectangle tremble in my father's hands. He looks from Viktor to my captor. I know him well enough to see the gears turning in recognition...and horror.

"Seems I'm not dead after all." My captor nods his head at Viktor. "This one was to be sent a world away. You'd think he'd be the hard one to find."

'What's going on?" I say. "Daddy—"

My father's lost in this, though. Whatever it is, it's big.

Viktor speaks up. "We cannot seem to find our baby brother. Our *brat*." He pronounces it in an ultra-Russian way, rolling the *r*. It sounds like *brlod*. He snatches the photo from him, and I catch a glimpse. Three little boys. Two of them infants.

Brothers. Something about the picture tugs at the edges of my memory.

The Russian one says, "We get our *brat* back alive, or we kill your kitten, you understand?"

I suck in a breath. I've been around this life long enough to know there's nothing empty about that threat.

"A name and an address," my captor says.

"I don't have that—I swear!" Dad says. And I don't believe him.

When in my life has my father not bent over backward for me?

Cold horror slides through me.

CHAPTER THREE

Aleksio

Aldo Nikolla looked so much bigger when he was slaughtering our parents. But then, I was small. Just nine.

And then there's Mira. I have this weird feeling that she almost recognizes me. It fucks me up a little.

I tell myself to stay cool, stay hard. I take Mira back—she's his weak spot, his only pressure point. I hold her a little more tightly than I should, and she gasps.

It affects him. I see it in his eyes. Good.

I slide my finger back from her chin and down her jawline. Rough, scarred finger over the unbroken creamy expanse of her cheek—a metaphor for the two of us now.

Mira was there in the background of a lot of the surveillance photos over the years, the cherished daughter in the castle her family ripped from ours. We'd been friends before the attack—as much of friends as nine-year-olds can be. I'd study her expressions when new pictures came in. Always smiling.

She smiles, so happy, Konstantin would say. *The slaughter of the Dragushas has been very, very good to Mira. She takes everything while you hide like a dog. She shops with your millions. Of course she smiles.*

Konstantin imagined I hated her for those smiles, but I didn't. I'd wonder how she was doing, what she was thinking. Sometimes I'd enlarge the shit out of the images. I felt bad for her when her mother died. I was actually worried about her. She had no idea that her own father was capable of slaughtering his dearest friends in cold blood. I thought to warn her. It was a childish impulse.

Needless to say, I didn't admit any of this to Konstantin. He was a hardened Kosovo war vet, out for bloody vengeance. He'd say I was fixating on her, obsessing over her. He'd think I couldn't do what needed to be done. But I've always done what I have to.

Over time, those smiles intensified, and Mira appeared to transform into a plastic princess, a black-haired Barbie doll. Meanwhile, I transformed into something cold and dark and barely human. So I guess I can't fault her.

I hold her a little more tightly than I should and slide my finger back from her chin and down her jawline. I always wondered what her skin feels like. Answer: softer than imagined.

I feel her pulse pounding—she's frightened, but she puts on a good front. For him? I continue down to her collarbone, I stop just before the perfect line of it disappears into her filmy white top. I'm scaring her in order to fuck up the old man. A means to an end.

It's not supposed to be fucking me up.

"I'll kill you," the old man says.

I smile. I'm getting to him. He's a gambler. He'll gamble Mira—to a point. I just need to push more. Make it more real for him—and for her. I can't let him set the terms.

"Let her go," he growls.

I point the piece at him. "Mira is mine until we have Kiro back. That's done. What you do now determines how bad it goes for her. That's all that's on the table..." But why am I pointing a gun at him? I put it back on her cheek. That perks him up.

"Take off your panties, Kitten," I say.

Her chest jerks with an intake of breath.

That's right, I think. *I'm the motherfucker who will cross every fucking line to get my baby brother back.* I turn my head and growl into her ear. "Take 'em off."

Viktor shoots me an approving look. He loves when things get really twisted. He and the mafiya guys he brought over, they're all insane.

Daddy speaks up, finally. "I don't know where he is. I have one thing you could try."

"One thing we could try?" Right. Meanwhile, he hunts and kills us. "You think I'm fucking around here? Off, Kitten. Now."

She glares at me. All those hours when I was supposed to be studying Aldo Nikolla and his men, memorizing their names and weaknesses, I would look at her and wonder what it would've been like to have stayed there.

To have all that safety. It comes to me now that I can make her tell me if I want.

I put the gun back on her father. "Your panties or Daddy's kneecaps. Something's gotta go here."

This gets her moving. She reaches under her pink skirt, grabbing at the panties underneath. She starts shimmying, eyes full of fear and emotion.

I look away, reminding myself that she's just a spoiled mafia princess now, not the loyal, happy tomboy pal she once was. She probably has a diamond-studded pink lace thong under there or something. She's not the same, just like I'm not the same.

She leans over and pulls them off her feet. They're blue. Simple. *Laundry day,* I tell myself.

"Toss them on the ground. You won't need 'em where you're going."

Viktor's lips quirk in dark delight.

She hesitates. I feel everybody's attention, wondering how fucked up I can get. But we're running out of time— we won't be in control of this situation for long. We need answers—fast.

Which means I have to get very, very fucked up.

She throws them onto the grass.

"Get them, Daddy," I growl.

"Pervert," she whispers.

"I'm a lot worse than a pervert, Kitten. As you'll soon find out."

She looks disgusted. I tell myself it's good that she's getting with the program. Because I'll be as fucked up as I need to be to get our baby brother back. I'll trash my very soul to save him—it's how it has to be.

"If my dad says he doesn't know anything more, he doesn't know anything more."

"I won't ask again," I say.

He bends and snaps them up from the ground. "Good," I say. "Now. Kiro. An address."

"I only have a name. The agency."

Fuck. I need more than an agency. I slide the gun across her cheek. She stiffens. Her eyes are big and dark and fringed with thick lashes. Holding her now, she seems more like the girl I knew. That's just what the mind does, though. It pastes in what you want over what's really there. "You really don't want to see her again, do you?"

"It's all I have—I swear it! She's not in this. She's innocent!"

"You're telling me you didn't bother keeping tabs?"

"The Worland Agency insists on anonymity. It's where I'd start if I needed to find him."

"What's going on?" Mira asks. "Somebody tell me what's going on!"

Nobody answers her.

"It's all I have," Nikolla says.

"Dad?" Mira says.

Fuck. The clock is ticking. Is he bluffing? Gambling with his own daughter? I close my eyes and try to think, but all I can see is Konstantin in his wheelchair, warning me off of this: *Once you start that fight with Nikolla, it's a fight to the death. Once he sees you're back and that you have*

Viktor with you, all the firepower in Chicago turns on you. Their cops, their made guys.

Only the three Dragusha brothers together can win such a fight.

Except Kiro is out there somewhere, and the only way to Kiro is through Aldo Nikolla. Viktor doesn't remember Kiro, but I do, if only in the barest flashes. A happy baby waving his tiny hands in the air. Big eyes. A sweet nature. Not like Viktor and me.

If Kiro is dead, I will destroy the world. I grab Mira's dark hair and pull her to me.

"Don't touch her."

"I'll touch her as much as I want," I say. "She's mine, isn't she? Didn't you say I could have anything of yours I wanted?"

The old boss's lips move, but nothing comes out. The great boss—the *krye*—of the Black Lion clan, is finally feeling desperate. They say when you have your enemy on his knees, you start to feel sorry for him, but I'll never feel sorry for Aldo Nikolla. No destruction will ever be enough for what he did. And he's as dangerous as a king cobra, even with this supposedly bad heart.

"If she's mine," I continue, "I can do anything I want with her, can't I?" I press my face to her hair. "She tasted so good."

"You're a dead man," Nikolla growls.

What if that's all he knows?

I glance at Viktor. It's time. Viktor and me, we don't need words. We're one mind. Brothers up from the shadows. Viktor gets on the phone. Time to go to plan B.

I slip an arm around Mira. "Probably a good time to adjust your expectations for your weekend downward, Kitten."

She stiffens in my grip—just as angry as she is pissed, it seems. She never did scare easy.

"Kitten." Nikolla gives his daughter a doleful look. "We're okay."

"I might not go with *okay*, exactly," I say.

"His heart is bad, you jerk." She rips away from me and hauls off, like she's going to hit me.

I catch her arms and get her back under control. She's still something of a warrior, a fact that doesn't come through on her idiotic fashion blog. And all this time I thought she'd turned out like the other princesses. A beautiful show horse.

It's not ideal. I didn't plan on her actually affecting me.

I give her a long, hard look that lets her see the cold parts of my soul, and finally I feel her tremble. I flash on what it would be like to have her naked at my feet, trembling like that. I shake the thought out of my mind.

The sound of breaking glass up at the house tells me Viktor's guys are in there looting. Mira looks stunned. "Bind him, gag him, and take him away," I say.

Tito moves on the old man and sticks a needle in his arm. Mira screams and jerks. The old man is out like a light. "Where are you taking him?"

"Don't worry," I say. "We won't let him die."

She looks up at me with something like hope in her eyes.

"For now," I say.

Tito loads him up into the ridiculous golf cart. "Note to self," I say aloud. "Have Viktor shoot me if I ever get one of those things."

Viktor grins.

She follows the golf cart up the hill with a hopeless gaze.

A few more of our guys have arrived, sliding across the grounds like shadows. The Russians reporting to Viktor.

Viktor nods up at the house.

"Come on." I push her toward the house.

She stops and turns. "Just tell me what's going on."

"You don't know?" I'm a little surprised she hasn't figured it out by now, but then again, she thought we died that day, just like everyone. Except her father and Lazarus.

"Tell me," she says.

"Taking weapons, cash, souvenirs. Maybe some of the art. Maybe wreck a few things. I believe the technical term is pillaging. Or is it plundering? I'm never sure about that. You'd think I would've looked into that."

Mira stares at me with a stunned expression.

"What's wrong?" I growl. "I got a bluebird on my head or something?"

"He dies. You die. What's the point?"

Again I hear old Konstantin's warning. *If you hit the hornet's nest, if you show that you and Viktor are alive and together, all of Nikolla's firepower turns on you.*

As if on cue, some windows break. Then gunfire sounds out.

"Antique gun collection, I think," Viktor says.

I push her. "Go."

The princess looks up at her precious castle. Does that house represent a sunny, safe, beautiful life? Does trashing it change that? Does it change something inside her? "Can I keep...one thing?"

I'm guessing jewelry. Something valuable. Shoes, maybe. There are rumors about her shoe collection. "Depends. Can it shoot bullets? Because, lenient as I am—"

"It's just a coffee mug. Nobody'll care about it."

Another window breaks. Viktor's guys'll break a lot of the stuff, but they'll be able to tell what's good to sell. They've brought vans for the loot.

"It's easy to find. It's just a chipped mug with a picture of a cat head. It's in the lower kitchen cupboard. No—it's out on the counter..."

I motion to one of Viktor's guys and send him ahead for the mug. "Mind the time."

I flash on the old Mira, all pigtails and grass stains. Champion of trapped bugs and bullied kids. Everything in the house and she picks a coffee mug.

I snort. Like I think it's stupid. Like it's not a little bit of a knife in my abs when I think what I might have to do to save Kiro's life.

CHAPTER FOUR

Mira

We're up at the drive in front of the house. I hate not having underwear on. It makes me feel vulnerable. Especially in this uncomfortable skirt suit. Not that I don't have worse things to worry about.

I plead repeatedly for news of my father, if only to know he's still alive. My captor just texts.

I can barely watch as thugs carry off the beautiful things my mother collected—the period chairs, the Warhols, the chinoiserie. I stifle a sob as I catch sight of my mother's inlaid harp. Mom loved that harp. It's like they're taking the last little pieces of my mother from me.

A crash from inside. They're wrecking the place.

"This is pointless." When he doesn't acknowledge me, I grab his wrist. "What does this get you? Come on!"

He looks at my hand and then looks up at me. For a moment, I think he, too, senses that weird familiarity between us. As though we knew each other in a dream. He drops his phone in his pocket, and takes my wrists. "You need to stop focusing on your beautiful life in there and start praying that Daddy decides to come through."

"Ow," I breathe.

"Good. That's you getting with the program. I'll do whatever I have to do to get my brother back. Do I want to hurt you? No. I don't. Will I?"

My heart races.

"Will I?"

"I get it," I whisper.

His grip is too tight, his gaze too intense, like he sees everything inside me. People rarely look too hard at me. When they look at me at all, they accept the version of me I serve up to them. The shopaholic mafia princess. The dedicated, lawyer in glasses.

"Dad's innocent. He'd tell you if he knew anything else."

"Wrong, Kitten. *Dad's* playing the odds."

"Don't call me that."

A ping sounds. He lets me go and pulls his phone out of his pocket. A twenty-first-century general waging battle.

Whatever the person on the other ends has texted him, it troubles him.

That's my chance—I take off running, tearing for the trees and the main road.

I get maybe ten feet before guys seem to materialize around me, taking me by the shoulders. I twist and fight. They lift me right off the ground, carrying me back.

The strangely familiar intruder is still on the phone, eyeing me with that intensity, watching me struggle. A model between photo shoots if you didn't know any better.

They put me back in front of him. He lowers the phone and addresses me quietly. "Do it. Go ahead, Mimi, do it again. See what happens."

Mimi.

He blinks, waiting. "Do it, go for it."

Mimi. Only one person ever called me Mimi—Aleksio Dragusha. My childhood friend. But Aleksio and his family were slaughtered by a rival clan back when we were kids. I was wild with grief. They had to sedate me.

Five caskets lowered into the ground. Three small, two large.

I focus on the familiar freckle on his cheekbone. This man is so much bigger. So much harder and meaner. But his freckle...his eyes... "Aleksio?" I say in a small voice.

"Ding ding ding, we have a winner." He says it offhandedly, as though our friendship meant nothing. He simply keeps his eyes fixed on the mansion with its majestic stone wings stretching out on either side. The place where he once lived. Prince of a mafia empire.

"Oh my God. Aleksio!"

Mimi is what his baby brother Little Vik called me. Little Vik couldn't say the *r*. Aleksio would tease Little Vik about it, and the name stuck. A nickname. His brother. Viktor Dragusha.

"We thought you were dead. We buried you!"

"You buried a few rocks. Maybe some boiled cabbages, who knows."

I can't believe he's being so...flip. "Aleksio! We buried you." I'm repeating myself. "I thought they killed you..." If my life were postcards on a bulletin board, the image of Aleksio Dragusha's casket being covered up with dirt would be central, affecting everything around it. He was my best friend. I doubt I was his. Aleksio had lots of friends. Everybody loved Aleksio.

"And Viktor. Little Vik! Oh my God. You're *both* alive..."

He focuses on his phone, running his guys.

"We went to your funeral. It was so, so..."

"Sad" isn't the word. "Sad" barely touches it. He was my best friend in the world. We were adventurers together, bonded together, carving out a sunny niche inside a world of darkness and secrets we sensed but didn't understand. I think that's what made us friends—the feeling of being refugees at the edges of something evil.

"Aleksio," I whisper. I think about his remote control car, Rangermaster. I took it after he died, and I kept it in my room. I didn't have the controller, just the car. I used to talk to it like I could still talk to Aleksio. "I kept Rangermaster. You remember Rangermaster?"

He looks at me like I'm a little bit crazy, but he doesn't fool me. He remembers. "You need to stop thinking you know me," he says. "You knew me once, but I promise, you don't know me anymore. Got it?"

"Why are you so angry at my dad? You were like a son to him. He loved you. He grieved over your death! Aleksio, come on!"

"Did your father look like a man overjoyed to see me?"

My head spins as I replay the horrified look of recognition on my father's face. Dad was holding back. I can always tell. "Well, you weren't exactly being civil," I say. But Aleksio has a point.

"You need me to spell it out? He sent Kiro away. He needs to tell us where he is. And he's going to."

Kiro. The baby.

Why would Dad send baby Kiro away? Did he send all the boys away?

"If he sent you guys away, Aleksio, it was to save your life. To protect you from the Valcheks, coming to finish the job."

"Your dear old dad, protector of defenseless boys. Like sending baby Moses down the river to save his life. You're really going with that?"

"My dad went completely crazy on the Valcheks after what they did to you. He and Lazarus took out half that family. They mourned you. Avenged you. He loved you."
We all did.

"Uh-huh."

"He would've done anything for you."

"He would've done anything for what we had."

Heat rises to my face. "Excuse me?"

"Your father got rid of the Valcheks, an enemy he'd always hated, while he took over the most powerful clan this side of New York. Worked out pretty well for him."

"What the hell, Aleksio? What are you implying here? He loved you. Your father was his mentor, his partner, his greatest friend. He owes him everything—he always says it."

"That's ironic." He looks at a text.

"Wait—remember the old crone? The evil-eye crone, Miss Ipa? Everyone thought she had the evil eye and the sight and all that?"

No answer. I know he remembers. She was a legend—the boogeyman and Elvis rolled into one, come down from the Pindus Mountains in her colorful head scarf. Evil Eye Miss Ipa's words had more power than bosses of bosses.

"Remember how she had that prophecy about you and your brothers? It was at that giant New Year's party, and she kept pointing to you and saying that. *You boys. Together you rule…you boys, you three boys.* Maybe that's why Dad wanted to get you out of there. You were a threat to all of the clans, not just the Valcheks."

I wait for him to look up, needing to see my old friend underneath this cold, dark man.

"Don't you see? If my dad sent you away, it was to protect you from the Valcheks and everyone else who worried it would come true! Because he knew people would believe her crazy shit. People always believed her crazy shit. Don't you remember?"

Aleksio gets another text.

"Look at me!"

He won't.

"You were like a brother to me..." With a thundering heart I picture the way he slid his finger into his mouth. The hot, dark things it put into my mind. Not like a brother.

A stray brown curl falls over his forehead as he does more phone stuff.

I swallow past the dryness in my mouth. "And now you're trashing your own family house? It's *your* house now that you're back. You're alive. You're fabulously wealthy. People will want to know you're back!"

He snorts with bitter amusement. "You think I should've just walked in here? You think that would've worked out for me? Maybe with a fruit basket?"

The ice in his heart chills me. *Aleksio.*

We had a secret fort in the yard that last summer. We'd sit in it and draw while our moms drank and our dads ran their crime empire together. Back then we didn't understand our wealth was built on a mountain of blood and violence—not consciously, anyway. But I think we felt the poison. Aleksio would draw robot cars. Such a stupid boy thing to draw. I would draw horses. Maybe we were both imagining escape.

Our link feels just as fierce now. It's no longer innocent, like something hot got charged up along the well-worn pathways of friendship. But it's still a link.

"You're not going to kill me, Aleksio."

A muscle in his jaw fires.

"I know who you really are. I know your beautiful heart."

"That's not a theory you want to test."

"Maybe it's not a theory you want to test."

He looks at me straight on. So cold. "People change, and sometimes they lose their fucking soul."

The honesty of his words hits me. Being around juvenile court means I've seen firsthand the way beautiful, innocent kids can be robbed of hope, their goodness erased. Made into monsters. Predators. But there's always some sliver of humanity in them left. I have to believe that to do what I do.

We were nine when I watched Aleksio's little casket get lowered into the ground. Not too late to turn a kid dark.

I can't believe he'll kill me—I refuse to believe it. But what about Dad? Whether he finds Kiro or not, he won't have a choice—not after the way he treated him today. You don't take shots at Aldo Nikolla and threaten his daughter in front of him unless you're willing to go all the way.

He eyes our mansion as he talks, like he hates the mansion itself. The muscle guys melt off to the sides, to the cars. He can't possibly think Dad had any involvement in what the Valcheks did. And what's up with Little Vik—Viktor? The Russian accent, the barbarian attitude.

His eyes look even larger when he's looking down. Large lids ending in a line of sooty lashes spearing sideways.

"If Dad had anything to do with sending your brothers away, it was to save their lives. Don't be dense, Aleksio—think about this. Everyone knows it was a Valchek hit."

He says nothing.

I suck in a breath. "Leksio D, Leksio D, slowest runner you'll ever see." I don't know why I say it. A stupid taunt from the cobwebs of my memory.

He spears me with a white-hot shock. Anger, maybe—I don't know. I can't read him anymore. "You need to concentrate on not pissing me off, and you definitely need to stop reacting like I'm the boy you remember." I shudder at the force of his words.

A familiar roar sounds from behind me. I spin around.

Viktor and some other scary guy pull up in Dad's pearl-green Maserati convertible.

From behind me, Aleksio says, "You especially need to be careful with Viktor. He wasn't raised right."

Somebody comes up and puts a duffel into Aleksio's hand.

Aleksio takes my shoulder and pushes me toward the car.

"Did you get my coffee mug?" I ask.

Aleksio turns to the guy. The guy nods.

"Thanks," I say.

"You think I got it to be nice, Kitten?" He yanks open the back door and shoves me in, then crowds in next to me. "You should never let your enemies know what you care about."

I buckle my seatbelt. "You're not my enemy."

His gaze shimmers with heat. He reaches out and sweeps a lock of hair from my forehead, tucking it behind my ear. His touch is electric. His voice is husky. "I'm the most dangerous enemy you'll ever have because every time you look at me, you see somebody who's not there anymore. Because every time you look at me, you fool yourself about what I really am."

My pulse races. My gaze strays up Aleksio's corded neck to the jewel of a black freckle on his cheekbone. The boy I knew never felt dangerous like this.

"What are you, then?"

Aleksio says nothing as Viktor pulls out. He turns to watch our house as we head down the long stately drive. Technically his house, now that he's back from the dead. There's something strange about the way he keeps his eyes fixed there. Then he takes out his phone and pulls up some kind of app. "You ready?" he asks.

"For what?" I ask.

He nods at the house. "Watch."

I twist around. "What am I watching?"

He pushes a button on his phone. There's a loud pop from inside of the house, and then two more, and then a roar and a flash. Instinctively I duck as the place goes up in a flaming fireball—several of them. Heat blasts my face even as far away as we are. I touch my hair to make sure it's not ablaze as flames rage through. Nearby treetops catch fire, too.

"What have you done?" I whisper, horrified. Our beautiful mansion. Destroyed.

"Is that a rhetorical question?"

"Our home."

"Not anymore." There's a note of warning in the way he says it. *Not anymore.* Don't push him.

I'm too stunned to answer.

He holds out his hand. "Purse." I hand it over, and he goes through it. He throws out my phone and my mace, then hands the purse back to me.

Life as I know it burns behind us.

Aleksio puts on a pair of aviator shades, cutting himself off from me there in the windy back seat, dark freckle on his right cheekbone like a tiny dark jewel. He's right next to me, but a million miles away, his curls like dusky flags, slapping in the wind and sun.

I shouldn't want him to look at me again. I shouldn't want to see his eyes, to feel that intensity. He's no longer that boy I knew, seeing impossible things in the clouds—I understand that, now.

We head south on the highway, and I press him about my father. He'll tell me only that he's alive, and that they're planning on keeping him that way.

For now. He doesn't have to add that part. We both know it's there.

Dad.

Dad promised me that he'd gone legit over the past decade, but I'm not stupid. If he's legit, it's only as part of a symbiotic relationship with guys like Bloody Lazarus, who runs the bad stuff now. Less stress for Dad's heart.

Without thinking I turn to Aleksio with the impulse to tell him how worried I am about my father, like we're two against the world the way we used to be. It's so stupid—Aleksio is the whole problem here. He wants to scare my father—that's the mindfuck game he is playing right now.

The wind presses his dark suit to his chest, outlining his muscles, seeming almost to caress them. Now and then he texts.

We're heading for Chicago, right into the center of Dad's operations. Right where Lazarus probably is.

Just over the Illinois line we pull off at a gas station attached to a trucker store, a lone outpost at the center of endless weedy fields. I think about my chances of making a break for it. No way would Aleksio have muscle in this area, ready to step out of the weeds.

Or would he? He's twenty-eight now. He's been off building his army—that's what you do when you're readying to go up against a man like my father.

They all get out. I get out, too, just checking how far my leash extends. Viktor starts filling up the car. Aleksio gives the other guy money and writes a list of things he wants from the market inside.

Tito, they call him. Tito wears a winter-type hat over his hair, which would be jet black if it weren't bleached at the tips.

I slip over to a square pillar that holds up the ceiling over the pumps.

Aleksio comes around to where I am, sunglasses propped up on his head. They may as well be down for all that I can read his eyes. "Going somewhere?"

I back up. Hit the pillar.

"What is it, Kitten?" he asks.

"I told you not to call me that."

He tilts his head. "I'll call you what I want."

"I want an update on Dad," I say.

"I want to know what you're thinking."

Anger flares in my chest. He can't even give me an update on Dad? "You want to know what I'm thinking? I'm thinking that you turned out to be a real fucking bastard, Aleksio. It's sad."

There's a hint of humor on his face as he searches my eyes.

"Am I amusing you?"

"I wouldn't say you amuse me, Mira, no. Not at all."

I can't help but feel like he's looking right through me, reading my secrets like the pages of a magazine. I flatten myself against the cement pillar, wanting, needing to escape his gaze.

"What, then?" I ask. "Do I sadden you, too?"

"Oh, a little. I mean, that blog shit? Mira Mira? Are you fucking kidding me?"

My face goes red.

"You never cared about that shit," Aleksio says.

I plant a finger on his chest. "Step back."

He grabs my finger. "You're not in charge."

"Ow."

He tightens his grip. He bends it.

I get the feeling he's testing himself, seeing how far he'll go. I want to tell him to fuck off, and that he won't do it, that this isn't him. But he never responded well to being defined. So I just say, "Don't."

"Don't what?"

"I'll scream for help."

"You could probably do that," he says. "You could probably make a run for it here. I don't know what kind of runner you are these days. Not fast enough to get away from me, but you could make trouble if you got the right person on your side, couldn't you?"

My pulse races as he lets go of my finger and matches his palm to mine, takes hold of my hand before I can pull it away.

"Are you thinking about it, Mira?"

Yes.

"You could even get the cops involved and tell them the story. They hold you while they call around. The feds get involved at that point."

There's a shadow of a smile in his eyes as he examines our clasped hands. Our hands together like that are a perversion of what we are. What we were. It shouldn't feel exciting.

"But you can't really be sure which people are mine, can you?" he says. "And you gotta think, how concerned are the authorities going to be about some bastard tearing down enemy number one's networks? A lot of them would be team bastard. Because I did what they've been wanting to do for years. So you need to be smart."

He lets go.

My heart sinks. Of course he's right. The cops who aren't on Dad's payroll would probably be amused. They'd help—in the way that cops "help" when they'd rather not help.

I have to get away. Save myself.

A man and a woman come out of the gas station with giant sodas. They smile, and Aleksio breaks out a beautiful smile that's like the sun. He's breathtaking.

It shakes me to see him wield such allure, such wild sexuality, but I suppose it shouldn't surprise me. People were always galvanized by him, even back when he was nine. He was never the star runner or the star ball player or anything, but the kids always wanted to be on his team.

These two coming out of the gas station don't even see me. They would never notice I'm here against my will; all they see is an impossibly beautiful man in a suit at a gas station in the middle of nowhere.

"They look like a nice couple," he says softly, pressing the back of my hand to the rough concrete pillar. "How much would it suck if things got hot? If all of these nice people die because you got stupid?"

He draws nearer.

I hate how intensely aware of him I am. How I feel him all around me—on my skin. I tell myself it's the danger. The mindfuck of him coming back from the grave so dark and twisted.

He's acting like a fucking predator—of course I'd be aware of him. The prey is always wildly aware of the predator.

Another car pulls up. A capable-looking man wearing a T-shirt with what looks like a firefighter insignia on the pocket gets out. Firefighter. That's close to a cop. Sort of.

I gasp as Aleksio cups my right cheek, staring into my eyes.

"You're not playing fair," I say.

"Really? That's your complaint here? I'm not playing fair?"

"One of them." His hand on my cheek feels electric.

He studies my eyes. He thinks I'm fucking with him. "And you don't want to try anything. Not with this guy, either. He'd get involved, and it wouldn't go well for anyone."

I regard my old friend with a steady gaze. Like I don't care. Like I'm not scared. "Seriously, Aleksio, you can't just kidnap the most powerful man in Chicago."

He smiles. Kidnapping the most powerful crime boss in Chicago is exactly what he's done, of course. His smile creates a sparkly sensation that goes clear to my core. It's fucked up. I push him, and he steps back, smiling like we're just playing.

There's a *clunk* over by the car. Gas gun settling back in its place. The clang of the little door to the gas tank.

"Aleksio." Viktor.

The other guy, Tito, arrives with a white plastic bag.

Aleksio takes my hand and leads me to the car like a lover, opening the door for me, so chivalrous. Unless you feel how tightly he grips. "Ladies first."

I get in.

We take off, and Aleksio grabs the bag. He passes around waters and candy. He gives me a bottle, a small baggie of English toffee, and panties.

I hold the stuff, stunned.

"Sorry, Kitten. Made in China was the best designer label they had."

He thinks I'm surprised by the panties, but it's the chocolate-covered toffee that gets me. English toffee is my favorite. Always has been. It's a treat I never let myself have these days, because if I start eating it, I'll never stop.

Did he remember?

He turns to stare out at the cornfields. "Go ahead."

"Thanks," I say, too baffled even to bristle at the designer tag insult. I put down the candy and the water. The panties are the cheap synthetic three-for-the-price-of-one kind attached by a plastic thingy that goes through a cardboard square. I yank them apart and put one of the pairs on, shimmying them up under my skirt. When I look over I catch him watching. With a bored expression, he tears into his Snickers bar.

I pick at the string on the toffee. It's the kind of candy you'd find in the sad little "fancy" section of a rural gas station. "Why'd you pick this?" I ask.

"What?"

"You had him buy me English toffee."

"Beggars can't be choosers."

Right. As if he remembered. I break off a corner, chew it indifferently. I need to get my mind around the fact that I'm in actual danger. I need to be smart. To get the hell away.

I ask a few times where we're going, what we're doing, but Aleksio only talks when he feels like it. He's back to surly silence.

People change, and sometimes they lose their fucking soul, he said. Maybe that's the best he can do, warn me who he is now.

They put up the top of the convertible, and we drive around Chicago a while, staying out of areas my father controls—or controlled. I'm not really sure about the status of the family. But if Lazarus has found out what happened, there's going to be trouble.

It's Saturday afternoon. No rush hour. Aleksio's making phone calls. Marshaling troops.

We eventually pull up in a garbage-strewn alley on the poor end of a business district where a lot of charities operate. The buildings on either side are nondescript office buildings, not old enough to be cool but not new enough to be nice. One of the white vans from the house pulls in behind us. A few guys with assault weapons come around, some of them Russian, some Albanian-American.

I'm alone in the car for a second, and then Aleksio's back with handcuffs. He cuffs me to the door.

"We'll be a few minutes." He pauses, then continues, "You still have a chance to get out of this alive. Don't blow it by hitting the horn or something."

The pack of them are at a shadowy side door. I hear an alarm beep, and then suddenly they're all in and the alarm is off. Tito remains outside, guarding.

I lean all the way over, trying to check where I am, see whether anybody is around to signal. I catch sight of a small metal plate over the door. Worland.

That's the place my father told them about. Worland Agency, he said.

Moving fast—they didn't even case the place. This tells me they think Kiro's in danger. *Obviously.* Why else take a risk like they did today?

And what if they can't find him? Worse—what if he turns up dead?"

CHAPTER FIVE

Alesksio

The adoption agency smells like new carpet and Lysol. There are two rows of cubicles surrounded by meeting rooms and a shitload of file drawers and computers.

The guys are flinging open drawers and pulling the lids off file boxes, packing up everything that could lead to Kiro.

Kiro is vulnerable as hell right now. He could be a guy working in a suburban carwash or college kid sitting in Accounting 101. No idea what's coming at him. And if anybody figures out what we're up to, there are some heavy hitters coming for him.

It's a miracle Aldo Nikolla and Lazarus didn't kill him or Viktor that bloody night, considering the prophecy. My guess is that Nikolla didn't have the balls to kill two tiny kids. He thought he could lose them. Thought they'd stay lost.

And we thought we had time.

Tito and the rest of my tight little crew knew I'd found Viktor, and that was containable, but we recently found out the whole of the Russian mafia has been talking about it. The baby sent away, presumed dead. The brother from America comes to get him. The sleeping king. Heirs to a crime empire in America.

Fucking gangster grapevine.

The guys are taking every file and every shred of paper related to the year our family ended. A few of them are downloading the computer files. We'll take the laptops, too. I help stack the boxes at the door. I get updates from the guys watching across the street. So far, so good.

Worland is a charity that has a pregnancy counseling and adoption arm—I vetted it on the way over. It's the kind of place people bring babies they don't want, no questions asked—that's one of the things on their home page. And apparently it's also the kind of place a guy sends a baby he wants lost.

It really is possible Aldo Nikolla doesn't know anything beyond the agency name. The agency could've set those terms to protect itself.

The files are building up. I have some guys check the basement, and I get others started on bringing the shit out to the van. It's amazing to think the key to finding our baby brother could be hidden in all this paper.

Kiro.

My mom let me hold him when she brought him home from the hospital, so tiny and squirmy. Just so tiny.

And he looked up at me with those big brown eyes, and instantly I loved him.

Viktor wanted to hold Kiro, too, but Mom said he was too little, but more like too reckless. Viktor was a one-boy wrecking crew. So he laid a careful hand on Kiro's little belly.

Kiro needs you to be a good big brother to him, my mom said to me. *Kiro needs his brother to protect him.*

My heart nearly pounded out of my chest—that's how proud I felt when that she said it. I promised that I would.

I hold that promise like a blaze in my heart. The slaughter happened soon after. Did Mom know there was trouble coming?

It hurts to remember her, but somewhere maybe she can see I'm fighting for Kiro. She needs to see I won't let him down.

Little Kiro.

He could be in the army for all we know, though I doubt it. Marching in formation is not in the Dragusha DNA.

Viktor had no idea of his roots, and he grew up from nothing to become a key assassin in the Bratva—the Russian mafiya—in Moscow. Meanwhile I ran my own gang just under the Nikolla radar, developing my clan. It was like Viktor and I were living parallel criminal lives on either side of the world without knowing it.

Viktor comes up, and I clap him on the shoulder. Kiro. Alive. Maybe.

"A lot of paper to go through," he says.

I grumble. It's a lot, but we'll go through it all the same, because they may not have computerized the older files. A low-rent place like this. Half-illegal.

"Good thing we have guys."

Viktor checks a text. "Old man's still out cold." His Bratva guys are holding Aldo Nikolla in the basement of a chop shop.

He shakes his head. He doesn't like it. We were hoping for an address, and this is so roundabout. And Mira's father is not a man you can hold on to long. It's like kidnapping the president of the United States—even if you manage to pull it off, you know you're not keeping him long. He's too big, and there's too much heat.

"All this paper," he says. "I say we send Aldo a finger."

My gut twists. Sending Mira's body parts was a plan we'd made while drunk and full of rage—and fearful for Kiro. She's not a fucking soldier. She's not in this. And the way she looked at me when she remembered…

"Let's see what we get. No need to spill all our jelly beans in the hallway."

"*Brat,*" he says. I never get sick of Viktor calling me that—it's the Russian word for "brother." "You guessed her candy."

"Nah. I already knew. That's the kind I used to steal for her when we skipped out of church choir. As a bribe to skip church choir."

"The fashion princess used to skip church choir?" He snorts.

"She was quite the rebel."

"From rebel to consumer running dog," he spits.

I narrow my eyes, not so sure I like that last part.

"It is even worse that you remembered her candy," Viktor says. "I think it will not be so easy to cut off her finger."

"Have I ever not done what it takes?" I ask him. "I'll cut off my own fucking fingers if it saves Kiro's life."

He grunts and grabs a box. He's right, though. It was a lot easier to talk about sending her body parts to her dad in theory.

A text comes in. Suspicious car circling the block twice. Not good.

Viktor doesn't have to see it to know there's trouble— he can tell from my face. One year together and it's like we were never separated. He's hustling everyone out with the last of the boxes.

Back outside in the alley, I uncuff Mira, pull her out of the Maserati, and shove her into the back of the van with the files and boxes of laptops. Then I grab Tito. "You watch her. No one touches her."

We continue loading up. When it's done, Viktor swings in the front of the van, and I take the wheel. I don't like putting somebody else in charge of Mira like this, but if things get hot, Viktor and I need to run the show. Our fucked-up talents as criminals know no bounds.

Viktor's lieutenant, Mischa, pulls out in front of us in the flashy sports car. If there's someone out there, Mischa'll draw that person away while we get the van full of files out of sight.

By now, Bloody Lazarus and the rest of Nikolla's crew will know there's been an attack, but they won't know who we are or why we came. People will be focusing on the house, combing it for Aldo Nikolla's remains, trying to figure things out, buying us time.

Only Mira and her dad know what's going on, and they won't be talking.

But no plan is foolproof.

"Got something to say?" I ask as I pull out.

"No, *brat.*"

Yeah, right.

We drive in silence.

In books, the feeling of being followed is always a tingle down the spine or your hair standing up on the back of the neck. But for me, it's more of a buzzing in the awareness. So faint you don't notice unless you tune into it.

Getting out of there, that's how I feel—awareness buzzing, even though I turn one way and then another and I can see, technically, that nobody is following us, but there's that buzzing, and I have the sense of eyes on the streets. Could they be after us already? Guessing our purpose? Nikolla didn't get to where he was by surrounding himself with stupid people.

Viktor scowls, but he doesn't question my maneuvers. He just scowls. He's always ready for something to be worse than expected. He was pulled from the orphanage at an early age and raised the way really sick assholes raise kids. I don't know whether he even feels his kills anymore.

When I'm confident we're not being followed, I pull the van into a wasteland area at the edge of the tracks and park in the shadow of some junky abandoned strip mall. A daycare and a bakery used to be here, long closed, but the payday loan shop down the block is still going full blast. We've used this area before. The sightlines and escape routes are killer. Another of our vehicles pulls up.

I hop out and send a few guys to the nearby corners, and then I go around and open up the back.

Tito jumps out. Mira stays huddled in a far corner, glaring, squinting, long dark hair pushed all around to one side, so that it hangs off one shoulder like an onyx waterfall, glinting in the streetlight.

"Everything go okay?" I ask Tito.

"Yep."

I climb into the back and pull out a few files, feeling her eyes on me.

She feels too familiar, like gears clicking into place.

She still looks at me like I'm that kid she knew—I see it in her eyes. Fucking Rangermaster. She even remembered Rangermaster. And yeah, it was stupid to give her the English toffee because God, the way she looked at me.

When she looks at me like that, I want to shake her, because that's a road to a whole lot of fucking pain for her.

I don't need her looking at me like that. Saving Kiro might mean hurting Mira. Bad.

Tito and few other guys and me are in the back with her. I've put myself across from her, far away as possible and separated by boxes of files and stacks of papers, like a signal to myself that she's not mine.

She glares. The glare is good. It's right. Hell, she had the right idea with the spitting, reckless as it was.

A black SUV rolls up with two of my book-smartest guys. They back up and open the tailgate, and between the back of the van and the back of the SUV, we've got a bit of a work area between the six of us guys.

The problem becomes evident pretty fast—all the names of the kids are blacked out. The names of the families, too. File after file has blacked-out information. There are codes and numbers at the top of a lot of them that don't mean much. We trade files, comparing.

"This is bullshit," Viktor says. "If the old man thought we were serious, we'd have a fucking address. He's playing for time."

"Can you uncuff me, please?" she says. "The edges are biting into my wrists—"

"You're lucky they're cuffed in front of you," I growl.

"I could help."

"No."

I don't look at her, don't meet her eyes. I wish I still had the mirrored sunglasses on. My nowhere-to-run, nowhere-to-hide bit at the gas station definitely backfired. I don't know what I was thinking, pressing her against that pillar, watching the fear in her eyes like there might be a little bit of lust in there. It was fucked up that I let myself think that.

Mira is everything I can never have. I'm here for one purpose only—Kiro.

And then I put on that boyfriend act for the civilians, pressing my hand to her cheek like that. I thought I'd combust—literally. The moment I touched her, all the people around there could've decided to rush at me all at once and I would've been no good for stopping them, being that my world had shrunken to the silky space between the curve of her cheekbone and the drumbeat of her pulse in her neck.

I imagined pressing my face there and feeling that drumbeat with my lips, like it was the most erotic fucking thing. She would've let me, too. Not out of desire, but because she didn't want to embroil innocent bystanders in a firefight. Because unlike me, she's apparently still a decent person.

I remember Konstantin and me doing a lot of reading in the run-down hideouts we'd move between. Usually he'd only want me to read shit like *The Art of War*, being that I was to grow up to be a capable killer and all, but sometimes I'd get my hands on regular stories.

I remember reading this one crusty old one—*The Picture of Dorian Gray* by Oscar Wilde. This guy stayed forever young while the painting of him aged.

I would feel like that, looking at the photos that had Mira in them. Like she stayed safe and happy in that mansion or in the Chicago penthouse, while I got hammered into something dark and deadly. Two sides of a coin.

Nothing's on any of the computer files, like we feared.

We go through more paper files. The dead ends have me feeling angry and fucked-up. "What the fuck good are files if everything's blacked out? There have to be the names and addresses somewhere, or why keep files?"

Finally we find some actual names and addresses, but they don't help. They all seem to have a number, more codes. Hundreds of codes, maybe thousands.

We decide we have to start matching things up, and then I catch sight of Mira, following our progress with interest. Like she understands something we don't. She knows. She's listening. Tracking.

"You got some insight here? Something for the class?"

"You want to let my father and me go free?" she asks.

I grab the next sheet. I tell myself it's stupid to think that a mafia princess who's spent the past few years on international shopping trips could help.

Kiro is out there, and as soon as somebody figures out we're going for him, he's fucked.

"Illegal adoption agency," Tito says. "Maybe they didn't keep real records."

"No, there have to be records," I bite out. "The answer is in here."

We go through each file, one reading off numbers, and the other guys hunting. It's like matching serial numbers on dollar bills or something.

We send a guy for pizza.

I can't shake the idea that she could help, that she's not as stupid as she acts in that blog. When the pizza comes, I join Mira on the far end and offer her a slice.

She takes it with both her hands, cuffed together as they are, and thanks me.

"If you can help, you should," I say.

"And I should help you why?"

"Because if this doesn't work, we go to plan B."

She doesn't react. She had to know something would come. She chews, staring thoughtfully out the window. Does she have an idea of what plan B is? I follow the direction of her gaze.

"What are you looking at?" I ask.

"The cartoons of laughing baby animals. Side of that building."

I spot the shitty mural on the side of the old daycare. Smiling cartoon animals half-peeled off in the distance beyond a wasteland of rubble and trash.

"Ugh."

"I like it. It's sweet. Something nice in all this decrepitude."

My face goes hot. Mira Nikolla with her dresses and parties on the boat and sunny smiles. "That's because you never look at them," I say. "If you stare at them too long, happy baby animal cartoons start to look maniacal. Don't you see it? You look at them too long, and all you see is death."

I can feel her eyes on me. "That's nice," she says. "You ruin cartoon baby animals for me? Thanks. Is there anything else you'd like to ruin?"

I'm glad she's annoyed, because I said too much, and I would hate if she gave me sympathy on top of everything else. I take her cuffed hands and turn them over, ignoring the zing of electricity between us. I inspect her fingers and spot a jagged scar on the pinky. "This is a very distinctive scar," I say. "We'll start with this one. Or maybe the one with the ring."

She goes white and tries to take her hand back, but I don't let her. "What?"

"Send it to your father."

"You can't." She tries to pull her hand away.

"This is a very recognizable ring. You think he'd recognize it?"

"You wouldn't."

"If we find Kiro, we won't have to."

She looks over at the files. "If I help you find Kiro, will you let my father and me go?"

"If your help gets us Kiro," I say, "we'll let you go."

"What about my father?"

"Let's put it this way—a lot of people are going to start hunting Kiro. And if somebody gets to Kiro first and manages to kill him? And your father was holding out? If you love him, you don't want to know what we'll do to him then."

"Unlock me."

I unlock her cuffs, trying to handle her as an enemy, but the feel of her skin sends a white-hot flash of desire through me.

She rubs her wrists and motions for a box. I slide it over. She pulls out a folder and opens it, studying the papers inside. She pulls one out. "These parts that are blacked out? That's done as part of a process known as de-identification. These files are de-identified. Anonymized." She stuffs it back in and riffles though.

How the hell does the spoiled mafia princess know this?

She examines a paper. "I don't know what Illinois law was twenty years ago, but there would've been protocols in place to make it hard for people like you to trace these kinds of things. And that's how they did it. They still do stuff like this today, but with computers. They make it so you could never identify families and children from just the files. There's a probably a key to the code offsite, or maybe on a computer. Some trustworthy person holds it. You need both pieces—the key to the code and the file—if you're going to read it."

"Like a fucking armored car?" Tito asks. "Like that? Where you need the two keys?"

"Exactly," she says.

"Who would have the key to the code?" I ask.

"I don't know. Somebody who worked there at the time. Somebody who needed to access the files. Probably not the lowliest person, but probably not the highest, either."

"We don't have time to find people who worked there two decades ago," I say.

"Hmm." She twists her lips, and in a flash I'm back with her in the shade of the fort, watching her draw her horses, lips twisting this way and that. Concentrating.

"I have a man," Viktor says. "His father was a KGB code breaker. He could get his father to look at this."

I turn immediately to Mira, to see what she'll say. Her lips quirk. "A KGB code breaker, you say." She tips her head. "Well...if that's all you got..."

Viktor scowls. "They are masters at code breaking, the KGB—"

"She's kidding," I say. "Let's do it. Quick."

She smiles at me, and I come to my senses and look away. Our connection is too alive suddenly, and it fucking burns. It burns worse than Konstantin's cigarette.

We send a group to make copies of the files and get a set of them to the guy, keeping the other set for us. I send another guy to book a suite of rooms at one of the waterfront hotels. It's not safe for her to know where any of us live, and we need to stay mobile and central to snatch up Kiro.

It's night by the time we reach the hotel, one of many in a row of glittering lakefront establishments. "I've missed Chicago," she says.

"What, Paris and Milan don't measure up?"

"Well, they're not home."

Mira walks through the hotel lobby with me, behaving perfectly, thanks to the gun in my suit jacket pocket. She'll make a break for it soon, but not in a way that will endanger the public. She's a woman with a code, too. She always was. I tell myself it's easy to have a code when it doesn't cost you anything. When your code doesn't push you places you don't want to go.

The first time Konstantin made me kill a guy, I was twelve and shaking like a motherfucker, and I didn't get him square between the eyes with the first shot like I should've; I got him in the shoulder and then the gut, and he was on the ground fucking begging for his life, pleading. He was a killer who deserved to die ten times over, but you don't know what it's like to have a man plead, arms stretched out like you're either God or the devil.

I raised the Glock, dropped out from inside myself—like I wasn't even home—and blew his head off.

Just do it. That's how you do the hard things—you just do them.

The six of us set up in the central suite, which is a kind of generic living room with a great view of Lake Michigan, now appearing as a dark expanse dotted by lights, the moon a crescent with a corresponding streak in the waves.

Stupidly picturesque. Like somebody else's view.

We split up names and start going through Facebook pages, looking at photos. Like we'll get lucky and recognize Kiro. It's stupid, worse than a needle in a haystack, but this is what desperate people do.

Mira wants to help, but there's no way I'm giving her an internet connection. So she sits across the room in an overstuffed chair looking out at the view. Is she looking for a way out? I'd be. If she got a weapon off of one of us now, would she use it? Mira was anti-gun as a kid. But people who are threatened will do a lot of surprising things.

We send guys out to run down leads. It's not looking good. Mira thinks we should try to get the Worland employment records from the year Kiro was adopted out. "We can get the key to the code that way—I'm sure of it."

Yeah, it's the way we'd go if we had all the time in the world. But we don't.

It's just her and Viktor and me when the call comes in. Viktor's man can't crack the thing—something about the code being one-to-one.

My heart sinks.

This means we have to go at Aldo Nikolla with everything. Because Kiro is in some serious danger, and that asshole knows where he is. Even Mira has to know he was holding back.

I look over at her, and she goes pale. Yeah, she knows. Because this is a woman who listens and observes, something the surveillance photos never showed. Something those plastic smiles never revealed.

I click off the call.

She stands. "Dad wouldn't gamble me like that. Play chicken like that." It's more a wish than something she actually believes. I hear it in her voice.

"Kitchen stores won't be open this time of night, but restaurants are." Viktor's talking about getting a knife. A cleaver, probably. He grabs his jacket. Unlocks the door.

She flies for it, but I'm ready. I catch her, fit my hand over her mouth, and pull her onto the couch, keeping her head against my chest, mouth sealed nice and tight. I pull out my piece and put it to her temple. She needs to see I'm serious. "Are you going to scream?"

She shakes her head.

"Go," I say to Viktor.

Viktor leaves. I let up off Mira's mouth, but I keep her there.

"Please," she whispers, looking up at me with those large brown eyes. "You're not a bad person."

She's wrong, but it feels good in a way that's painful, her believing that. Like a good feeling I don't get to have.

"You're a decent person."

"No, baby. Not anymore."

"He told you all he knows."

"I doubt it," I say. "If he has more, this'll jar his memory."

"Jar his memory? Sending him his daughter's bloody finger? All you'll do is kill him."

It's a risk we have to take. Once Lazarus hears that the Worland Agency got hit, he could put it all together about us going for Kiro. He could be closing in on Kiro this very minute.

"Please—he can't handle it. His heart is really bad. Please. Let's just try my way. To find the person with the key. Dad can't handle it if he thinks I'm being hurt. If he gets my finger...he can't handle it."

Right about here I realize she's more concerned about her dad seeing her severed finger than about actually having it *chopped off her hand.* I can't believe she's protecting that scumbag. It blows me the fuck away. He doesn't deserve her.

"You're thinking about it," she says hopefully.

"That's not what I'm thinking about." I stand and set my piece aside. The handkerchief I tied over my burn has long since come loose. I pull it out of my sleeve, stuff it in my pocket, and take off my suit jacket, setting it carefully over the back of the couch.

She watches me wildly.

"You want some booze?"

"Fuck you."

"It'll go easier if you're drunk." I roll up my sleeves.

"Oh my God. You don't want to get your nice coat bloody," she says. "Is that why you took it off?"

I don't answer. The truth is that I can't imagine cutting off her finger.

But that can't matter. I've done a lot of bad things I couldn't have imagined doing beforehand. Like that first kill and all the fucked-up things after. You put one foot in front of another, and you don't stop until it's done.

But this feels different.

"Oh my God," she says. And then she wraps her arms around herself and begins to sob, there alone on the couch.

It fucks me up, so I sit by her and pull her into my arms and let her shake and sob. It's the worst thing I can do. I wish she was drunk. I wish I was drunk. I force myself to think of Kiro out there, unprotected. Innocent. I promised my mother I'd protect him.

It's Mira's finger versus Kiro's death.

"You'll be fine," I say softly, holding her tightly. Comforting her for what a monster I have to be to her.

Mira's his weakness only if he thinks we're serious. If he thought we were serious, we'd have an address right now—that's what I'm thinking. Threats weren't enough. We need to panic him, make him understand. I try to think of any other way to do that.

"Will you take a picture of it?"

"What?"

"Take a picture of it. So I can remember it? I don't have a picture of it."

"Of your pinky?"

She holds up her hand and looks at the back, then the front. "I like how it..." I feel her chest convulse with unshed tears.

Bends, I think, finishing the sentence for her. It bends a little bit inward at the knuckle.

Fuck.

"Fine." I say it like I'm annoyed. I drag her up and over to the window. Beyond her is the moonlit Lake Michigan in all its fake postcard glory. "Which side?"

She looks at her hand front and back. "Back."

"That's the side I'd pick, too," I say.

"What happened to you, Aleksio?"

Your father slit my mom and dad's throats and sent my brothers to the ends of the earth. But I don't say it. We're hurting her enough.

"Tell me—"

"I turned into a real fucking bastard, I guess," I say. "A bastard who'll take this nice picture for you. Press your hand here."

She presses it to the window. Her hair has come loose, dark curls around her face, a face I would hate like the devil if Konstantin had his way. I snap a picture with my phone.

When I show her the photo, she starts crying again.

"Come on." I wrap my arms around her. She's trembling, turning into a total basket case. Finally I just pick her up and carry her to the couch. I sit down with her still on my lap.

Suddenly she stops crying, seems to stiffen. "Did someone torture you?"

"What?" I ask, startled.

She touches my arm, the spot just to the side of the mottled pink burn scar. She turns up to me, eyes shining with tears. Even after a cry she's beautiful. Really beautiful. "This is a cigarette burn."

God, I remember this about her—the one way to stop her from crying was always to show her that someone hurt worse. To give her something to care about outside of herself. But I can't. It can't be me. "It's nothing."

"It's not nothing," she says. "It's a cigarette burn. A really bad one. Somebody would've had to hold it very deliberately to your skin for a very long time."

"You want a gold star?"

"Somebody hurt you."

"Somebody *saved* me."

"Whoever did this to you, Aleksio, that person didn't save you. This is not what a savior does."

I push down my sleeve. I'd rather eat glass than be exhibit A for Mira's sympathy. Even if it's what she needs to calm down. "You say that because you don't know." I adjust her on my lap, let her sit more naturally. I put my gun and my phone aside, just out of her reach. "It was an accident," I say.

"Doesn't look like an accident."

"He didn't know. He was helping me hide. He was playing a part, and I had to stay invisible. Not move." For a moment I'm back there letting my arm burn. Trying to be a soldier for mighty Konstantin, the only person I had left in the world. I'm glad she can't see my face.

"How old were you?"

I don't tell people stories from then—not ever. This isn't even one of the dark stories, the lose-your-faith-in-humanity stories. But if it gets her mind calmed, things will go easier with the finger. I take a strand of hair between two fingers, remembering huddling there next to Konstantin, eyes and lips squeezed tight. "Nine."

"Jesus."

"Shit happens."

"Shit happens? That's your astute commentary? Shit happens?"

"You remember Konstantin? The old bodyguard?"

"They said he helped the Valcheks."

Valcheks were just the scapegoats, but I don't argue with her on that. She's upset enough. "Konstantin saved my life. He got me out of there before they found me. They hunted the two of us everywhere. I mean, we could not stop running. We had no money—we ran with clothes on our backs. I was actually in PJs."

"God—"

"Better than being in Spiderman underwear, right?" I pull her tight to me and put my chin on her head. I shouldn't be doing this tenderness shit. Maybe just for a moment, I think. Just a moment of rest. Of something nice.

I tell her the story. It's like an out-of-body experience, watching myself tell her. Suddenly I don't want to stop. The way she listens is a kind of nourishment.

In those dark days I would sometimes think about her and me stretched out on the lawn under the badminton net, splitting apart blades of grass—it was a kind of happy place, I suppose. The boy I was back then needed the sympathy she's giving me now. But here in this hotel room, her sympathy is hell on the man I have to be.

I have to be that man. That monster. I owe it to my baby brother. To my dead parents.

"You did it. You survived."

"Survival isn't amazing, Mira. People are animals in the end, and you do what you have to do to stay alive. It's built in. Like breathing. You want to believe the best, but it's a fucking lie."

She pushes my sleeve back up and rests her fingers on the burn spot, as if to heal it with her fucking sympathy.

I close my eyes as she moves her thumb, back and forth over nearby healthy skin—absentmindedly, maybe, but it's a caress all the same, and it gets me a little hot because nobody ever touches me like that.

She's warm and soft in my arms, and suddenly there's a kind of wrong energy spinning between us—utterly sexual. Her breathing is even a little ragged. Maybe it's fear or maybe arousal. Maybe both.

My mind crowds with images of her under me. Skin flushed. Hair spread around her head like a dark halo. Pale breasts. That Mira gleam in her eyes. Mira was always up for a dare, to go someplace we shouldn't.

Mira always liked things extreme—it's why we always got along. In a flash of intuition, I know that's how she'd like to fuck. I'd hold her down and do it hard and dirty and connect with that place deep down inside her where she knows her sunny, plastic smiles are a lie.

Stop it.

I shut my eyes and drag in the scent of her hair like a drug. It's all I get. I've threatened to cut off her fucking finger, for Christ's sake. I can't fuck her too, as much as I'm desperate to.

"He must've felt awful when he found out."

"What?"

"When Konstantin learned what he did."

"Oh. He didn't know."

"Afterwards, I mean."

"And why the fuck would I tell him?"

"You didn't *tell* him about the burn?" She pulls away. "What? Like, not at all?"

"He would've just felt like shit."

"So you didn't tell him? It would've been an unGodly amount of pain."

"It wasn't like my leg got blown off. It was war, Mira, you don't stop for something you can handle with a Band-Aid. I grew up different than you. You need to understand that. I'm different. I went somewhere you don't come back from."

She settles back against me, nestling into my chest and starts sliding that thumb back and forth again along the good part of my arm. It's connecting right to my cock.

Her voice is husky. "There's no such place. Where a person can't come back from."

My heart pounds, and the way I'm holding onto her isn't right. Like the twisted fucker I am, I pull her closer, up against my body for maximum control. It's a hold for a hostage. With just a shift or two, it's a hold for a lover.

I look at the spot on her hair where I want to press my face, overcome by the intensity between us, listening to her ragged breathing, feeling her gentle touch. If I were in the habit of lying to myself, I'd say she's touching me because she wants to, like it's not a self-soothing thing—or self-serving.

During those early days when we were on the run with nothing to eat, Konstantin would take me past restaurants and tell me to breathe in the smells. He lied to me and said that smells were just as nourishing as food if you really sucked them in. He actually had me believing it for a while.

We'd stand behind some of the nicest restaurants in the towns where we hid, me like an idiot full of longing, eyes shut, breathing in what I so desperately needed.

It's what I do now. I suck in the scent of her and try to make that enough. I suck in the scent of her when all I really want is to bury myself in her. Lose myself in her.

Instead I'll take her finger. I owe it to Kiro.

"You love the one who protected you," she says. "You wanted to protect him back."

"I would've died for Konstantin," I say, breathing in her scent again.

She pulls away and looks at my eyes. "It's what we do with the people we love." She's looking at me like she really wants me to get what she's saying. "He can't handle seeing my finger, Aleksio. You have to find another way."

I stiffen, heart thundering.

"It'll kill him," she says.

"Are you seriously comparing me and Konstantin to you and your dad? Seriously? Your fucking father?"

She rises off my lap, alarmed. Her knees hit the coffee table. "Whoa!"

I grab her arms to keep her from going over backwards, but I don't let go.

I hold her in limbo between falling backward and falling into me, a little off balance. My cock is raging. My cock likes this.

That's when it comes to me that there's a way I don't take her finger. It's twisted. It's not the other way she would've had in mind.

But it's another way all the same.

I tighten my hold on her wrists.

"What?" she gasps. She senses something.

Slowly I guide her down. Not into my lap this time, but down to her knees in front of me. Because I'm a twisted killer, and fuck if I don't want her mouth more than my next heartbeat.

She watches my eyes as I do it, comprehension dawning.

"You want to keep your finger?"

Her eyes fall to my cock, raging in my slacks. Her chest expands. She lifts her gaze back to mine.

I take it as a yes.

Not once has she thought about the pain of losing a finger; it's all about Aldo not being able to handle it. The man who killed his best friend and didn't have the stones to finish off the babies—not that I'm complaining.

She puts her hands on my knees, slides upwards.

My heart thunders, and my cock strains behind layers of fabric.

"You're thinking maybe there's another way." She's grateful. That'll change soon.

I put my arms out on the back of the couch like she's some whore between my legs. My mouth goes dry as her fingers approach. "Maybe."

This whole power play shouldn't get me off, but it does. I love her on her knees in front of me. I love the wrong energy between us.

Mira's skin looks flushed; for a second, I think she wants me. It's as much of a delusion as smells being the same thing as a big juicy steak and a basket of garlic bread, but I'll take it.

She slides nearer to my crotch. I suck in a silent breath as she makes soft contact with my raging erection. She scratches lightly with her nails and gives me a playful look. I give her nothing.

She cups her hand around it, a half-moon of pressure.

She undoes the button. She's shit at working the zipper, breathing hard, now. She looks up and lets me hold her with my eyes, or maybe she's holding me with hers.

"I knew you'd find another way," she says.

I steel myself as she pulls my shirt up from my belt. She leans forward to kiss my abs, tits pressed on my legs. She's whoring herself for a piece of shit, but the message gets lost in my mind, and all I see is that she's the strong one. Between her worthless father and her, she's the strong one.

She undoes my zipper. I adjust my hips to let her pull me out, making her do all the work. The cool air hits my cock. She curls her hand around my root. Squeezes. It feels so fucking good my eyes blur. I give her a steely look. It's all she gets.

She comes in closer, pushing between my legs. As if they have a will of their own, my hands go to her hair, so dark and silky. She keeps the squeeze on my cock. I want to thrust into her hand, into her face. I want to flip her over on the couch and plunge into her. I want her so bad I think I might implode.

She's breathing onto my cock now. *Fuck.* I close my eyes, tip my head back.

She seems like she wants me.

Just empty smells, I tell myself, but some fucked-up part of me doesn't care. Whoring for her worthless dad, but I don't care about that, either.

"Mira." I stroke the back of her hair. "Grab me at the root. Harder." My voice sounds strangled. I settle both hands onto her hair.

She tightens her hold and licks my cock, ice cream cone style, pushing waves of heat and need through me. I never wanted anyone more.

"I'm not a good person like you remember," I warn.

"But you won't cut off my finger." It's a question.

"If you do what I say."

"Okay."

It's hot. It shouldn't be so hot.

I grab her hair and look hard into her brown eyes. "Look at me when you do it," I say.

Keeping her doelike eyes on me, she takes me in her mouth. Just a little bit at first, wetting the tip. I bite the inside of my cheek, to balance things with a little pain.

I'd be lying to say I never imagined this. There was a certain yacht shot Konstantin got hold of, a bunch of Nikolla's made guys at somebody's engagement party, a picture like all the rest except for sixteen-year-old Mira in the background in a bikini. Let's just say that picture was in my stash. But this is so much better. Full-color, full-blast 3-D, her mouth a hot, silky cave. The pleasure is so intense I want to close my eyes, but I don't, because watching her is so goddamn powerful.

I fight the urge to grab her hair and fuck her face. Not yet.

I slide a finger over her cheek and down her neck. Her skin is perfect. Her lips are twice as beautiful when they're stretched around my cock. I'm taking her now. It's nine kinds of wrong.

I wind my hand through her hair, pulling a little, just enough to get her in an obedient mood. Like reins on a horse.

She grips my thigh with her free hand, heat in her eyes, as if she likes this power play thing, too. I tighten. I guide my cock deeper into the warm cave of her mouth. "Suck it," I growl.

She turns it on—full-blast sucking.

I pull out and go deeper, guiding her head.

She squeezes me at the root like I told her to, sucking me in earnest.

It's not enough yet. This needs to be right. I told her there was another way, and I'm good for my word.

"Mira—" I stroke her hair. "I'm going to twist your hair up in my fist and really fuck your face, now. It's going to feel rough, even. But you're going to let me do it. You'll let me use you like a whore."

Something in her eyes changes. She's scared, but turned on, too. Or maybe that's my imagination.

I push into her mouth, going deeper, testing her.

She takes me trustingly. She's not so sure about where I'm going, but she's the beggar here, not the chooser.

"Have you ever taken a guy rough in the throat?"

Something flares in her eyes.

"Have you?"

"Uh-uh," she grunts. A *no*. Of course not. Who would do that to Mira Nikolla? Me, that's who.

I twist her hair in my fist, giving her a little hurt, getting her ready. "You're going to feel alarmed and choked when I shove my cock down your throat. It's how I need it, though. You're going to relax and let me do whatever I want to you. Got it?"

Warily she grunts her assent.

"It'll feel wild and fucked-up, but you'll see that it's just another thing." I nudge her head, thrusting into her mouth. She gags, and I pull out.

"Close your eyes. Relax." I push in again, slower. "You're gonna take me. Turn yourself over to me."

She relaxes her throat. She's getting it.

"See? That's good."

I fuck her face with more force, making her take me deeper. "That hand, it's a little bit of a cheat, isn't it? You need to let go of my cock now. I need you to take all of me."

She lets go and grips my thighs. I tighten my fists on her hair and plunge in deeper. She makes a little sound, but she's going with it. I'd be lying if I said it didn't feel amazing.

I feel like a fucking animal, animated by some prehistoric madness.

It gets even more intense when she turns herself over to my total control. Like she gives up on dignity, on being anything but a thing for my use. It's un-fucking-believable how hot she is, giving herself over to my control. Trusting a twisted motherfucker like me.

"Close your eyes. Concentrate." I reach over and grab my phone and my gun. The phone is to record. The gun is to make it look good for the camera. To make it look like I'm forcing her.

She'll hate me. But it saves her finger.

I hit record and set the phone on the side table, angled just right to get me fucking her face. "You love it like this, don't you?" I thrust harder, in and out. Tears leak from the sides of her dark lashes.

I'm merciless—I have to be.

I push in harder, hitting resistance. She gags.

"Don't you fucking gag, Mira. Take it like the whore you are." Something in her changes, like energy ramping up, fingers digging into my thighs.

The phone records my hand twisting up her hair alongside the gun. It gets her tears. It gets my cock disappearing through her lips over and over.

"Suck harder, bitch," I say. "You're mine to use however I want. When I say suck harder, I fucking mean it."

She sucks harder. I groan.

It looks fucking violent. Like I'm mauling her, like I'm really fucking her up. What that camera doesn't capture is the energy stoking between us every time I say something. Like she actually likes that. I know I'm getting off.

"That's right, you fucking whore. Take it!" I shove my cock in long and strong. "You'll take it in every fucking hole."

Her fingers tighten some more, tits rubbing hard against my legs.

I keep up in front of the camera, knowing I'm capturing the force, the ugliness, but so much more is happening, like a wave, swelling up, taking the two of us somewhere.

Like we're both getting off on it, like it's real for a moment.

"I'll clamp you open and use you like the piece of cock-flesh you are," I gasp. "I'll fuck everything out of you."

I clench her hair with my other hand. She softens for me like she knows that's what I'm needing now. She's a rag doll for me, letting me have her completely. The feeling of it is un-fucking-believable.

My elbow knocks the phone off the table and onto the floor. I don't care. I don't care about anything but being lost in her, and she seems like she's lost in me. I don't care if it's an illusion.

"Take it, bitch."

I splay my non-gun hand over her head, stroking her, needing to touch her as much as possible, fucking her face, moving with her, breathing with her, both animated by the same wild energy.

My eyes are watering from the power of it. I won't say it's crying, but I won't say it's not.

She's amazing and beautiful and everything I lost.

CHAPTER SIX

Mira

The way he uses me is violent. Primitive. Demeaning. And all I can think is, *don't stop.*

He warned me he was going to be rough. He warned me I'd feel alarmed when he shoved his cock all the way down my throat. I was ready for that.

I wasn't ready for the names he would call me.

Or to be so wildly turned on by it all.

It's as if we crossed over to the right side of wrong, and everything is too hot, and his cock is too huge, and I have too many clothes. I want him to lay me out and use me. I want him to do anything to me. Everything to me. I want him to lay me out and use me like cockflesh, like he said he would. Is that even a word?

I pull back, knowing he'll shove my head back onto his cock, and he does, fingers digging into my scalp.

My nipples rub on his legs, heating—from the friction, maybe—and I nearly get off. It's pure madness. Usually I need a lot of help.

But this is Aleksio being Aleksio. He always went too far, and I always loved him for it.

I feel when he's going to come.

"No teeth. Don't you fucking..." He jerks into my throat, forcing me to swallow. The orgasm goes on forever. He holds my head firmly in his grip, panting.

I move my tongue a tiny bit and he clutches my hair. "God! Don't move."

I feel dazed. Heart pounding. This was the wildest and most powerful sexual experience of my life, and I didn't even come.

"Okay," he whispers after a while, gently extracting himself from me. I sit on the coffee table, wiping my mouth and striking the tears from my cheeks.

His eyes shine, and I know he felt the power of what just happened. The mad connection. Deep down, I know that neither of us have been here before. He reaches out and brushes my hair from my forehead.

That's when I see the gun in his other hand, dark and cold and black.

He was holding a gun? Why? Why would he need a gun?

"Don't worry, the safety was on." He puts it aside, eyes averted, and then he swipes his phone off the floor. He presses something. A red light goes off.

My mouth falls open. "What the hell? What did you do?"

"Saved your finger."

Red. A record light.

He tucks himself in, zips himself up.

He recorded us? Why record us like that? With him holding a gun? Why would he want to make it look like he was being a violent asshole, forcing me to do that?

Suddenly everything in the room gets too bright, too real. "No!" I go for the phone.

He grabs my wrist, hauling me up off the couch with him. "Leave it."

"You're going to show that recording to him? No!" I try to twist free. "You can't!"

He can, and he will.

I'm flooded with shame for how much I enjoyed it. And Aleksio made a movie out of it! To frighten Dad!

"Fuck!" I jerk and twist, trying to get at the phone. "You can't! Please."

"Sorry."

"Oh my God!"

That's when Viktor comes in. He regards us calmly, like it's no big deal Aleksio is manhandling me. Aleksio tosses the phone to his brother. "Play it."

"No! Don't!"

Viktor taps the screen.

"Don't watch it!" I go for Viktor now, but Aleksio has me.

"You can't send Dad that clip."

"We're not sending him your bloody finger. Isn't that what you wanted?"

Aleksio. So cool, so smooth. Like it meant nothing to him. And me like an idiot, getting off on his rough treatment. Making myself vulnerable to him. Showing him something I never even showed myself. I want to die.

Viktor pockets the phone. "Her severed finger would be more extreme. More urgency. But this is more pain for the old man."

"You guys are animals!"

Aleksio tightens hold on me. "You need to be done going crazy, or we'll handcuff and gag you."

"You have to erase it!"

"You prefer the finger? That's what you're saying here?"

I trusted Aleksio. I followed him somewhere extreme, and he ripped my heart open. Cutting off my finger seems tame in comparison.

"You're thinking about it? Fuck! No. Fuck that." He turns to Viktor. "Call and see if the sack of shit's awake."

Viktor takes out his own phone.

Aleksio finally has to bear-hug me to keep me still. I try to push him off. I want nothing to do with him. No go.

"Aleksio," I whimper. Imagining Dad seeing that makes me want to vomit. It will quite possibly be the last thing he sees before he dies.

Viktor's speaking in Russian. He sounds upset.

"What's wrong?"

"Aldo is out cold," he says. "He'll be out hours more."

"What the fuck?" Aleksio says.

"They had to give him something. He was making trouble."

"Fuck!" He lets me go. "Don't make me gag and hand-cuff you. I mean it," he warns.

"Has he taken his meds?" I ask Viktor. "He needs them. He keeps them in a plastic thing in his pocket."

Viktor holds up a finger. More Russian. Then he nods at me. "He had his meds. He is fine. Just not awake." He clicks off.

"Fuck!" Aleksio kicks a leather trash can across the room. "He tried to get away?"

Viktor nods.

"You're sure he took his meds?" I ask.

"Yes," Viktor says.

He's out. There's still time, then. "Let's track down the employees. My plan. We'll do my plan. Don't send it."

Aleksio looks at Viktor.

"Six hours he will be out. Minimum," Viktor replies to his unspoken question. "Probably through the night. They fucked up."

Aleksio closes his eyes.

"I'm sorry, *brat*. My guys—"

"No, I know. They responded to the situation in front of them." Aleksio goes to the window and takes a breath. Worried about Kiro.

"You think Lazarus cares about anything besides finding my dad and me?" I ask. "He's not going to be caring about your brother."

"Lazarus's a fucking hyena, Mira. I think he cares about a lot of different things."

"We can't stay the night here," Viktor says.

"Agreed." Aleksio makes a call. I'm wondering whether it's Konstantin. I was always a little frightened of Konstantin—everyone was. He had a scarred face and a military attitude. A retired killer who ran the boys' bodyguard detail.

Aleksio makes another call and gets an investigator on the case. "I want the names and addresses of everyone who worked there—call me as soon as you get them—I don't care if the shit comes in at two in the morning. We get 'em and vet 'em."

He clicks off.

"Merry Christmas. We go at it your way. At least until Daddy wakes up. Not that we have any choice."

I turn and look out at the dark lake, wanting for him not to ever see my face again. Wanting to never give him any bit of truth ever again.

CHAPTER SEVEN

Aleksio

It's just before dawn when we get out to the house we took off a Stockbroker who owes us. It's a place that was owned by one of our loan shark clients up until six months ago. A nice spread in the middle of a lot of trees maybe an hour out of the city.

A good place to lie low.

Best of all, nobody knows about it, which is good, considering the kind of firepower that's out on the streets right about now.

Our investigator checks in soon after. He's tracked down the retired Worland Agency director to a farm in western Illinois, and he's going out there. He feels sure this person has the key. He'll do what it takes. I send one of my guys to help him.

We give Mira the nicest bedroom—the master. It has a sliding door to a patio, and she's allowed to go out there as long as she behaves.

I go out for a run to clear my head. I should be getting new ideas to find Kiro, but all I think about is the feel of her mouth on my cock, and the way her hair felt in my fist.

I fucked her face, but I'm the one who got invaded.

I head back into the kitchen afterwards. Viktor's in there. He tells me Aldo Nikolla is still out cold, and the investigator is still in transit.

The sound of her laughter jolts through my chest.

I look out the kitchen window and see her sitting out on the patio with Yuri and a couple of the other Russians.

She's in jeans that are a size too large and a T-shirt knotted at the waist, thick hair in a ponytail high up on her head, cheerleader style. She and Viktor's Russian guys seem to be joking around. She smiles at one point.

"We should put a stop to that."

"She's under control," Viktor says.

Control isn't the issue.

But I don't have a good explanation for what the hell the issue is, so I turn away. "Did you offer her coffee? In the mug we brought from the mansion? And food?"

"She took coffee—*in her mug*. She says she won't eat."

"She needs to eat."

Viktor shrugs. "A person can go weeks without food and be just fine."

Of course he would say that. Even now, he sees three meals a day as an extravagance. "Not somebody like Mira."

"Yes, somebody like Mira." Viktor turns to me. "What a person can't go without is sleep. You need to sleep." He walks out.

Right. Sleep. A peaceful sleep for me is never going to happen. Not in this life. Every time I close my eyes, I'm right back there with Konstantin's cigar-smelling fingers sealing my mouth like my life depended on it, keeping me quiet. The way my mother screamed when Lazarus caught her. Her terrorized eyes, reflecting in the window. The flash of the blade in Aldo Nikolla's hands.

More laughter. They're teaching her Russian. She repeats a phrase, trying to get it right. Her eyes are so big—they sometimes remind me of those Egyptian drawings from those tombs, except not fucked-up and wrong. Her eyes are perfect.

I decide to make a proper breakfast. I inspect the refrigerator and identify all the ingredients for frittatas.

I dump paprika into the bowl, turning my attention to the meal I'm making, but she's still a ghost on my skin. The gouges she made in my thighs burned while I ran. A good burn. She almost seemed into it. An act, I know. The human animal will do anything to survive, to help its own kind.

I slice a lemon and squeeze it into the mix.

Viktor comes back in, and I know what he's going to say the second he looks at the meal I'm cooking up. "Seriously, *brat*? When I see all this—" He waves his hand around the kitchen. "—I do not think that this is a man who plans to show that video to a girl's father as she cries."

"Have I ever not done what I had to do?" I give him a hard stare. It's simple to do the hard, bad things. You learn to turn something off. Make yourself dense, like cement, and just do it. This is knowledge we share.

One nod. "Okay, then."

I go back to work. "And there'll be frittatas for you, too."

He watches me work. His silence doesn't fool me.

"What?" I ask.

He nods in the direction of the patio. "You can never have her. She's so far out of the game…"

I know he's right, but all I can think of is how she looked up at me while she sucked my cock. The tightness of her lips, the slide of her tongue, the way all that derision cranked the temperature to nine hundred degrees. Pure hot flame.

And then I made it ugly.

"You can never have her," he continues. "If you let yourself think it, it is only pain."

"Are you questioning me here?"

"I am watching you make frittatas."

I made them for him once when one of his top guys was killed. I told him it was my magic meal.

Viktor takes his gun and cleaner out. "Princess in the castle. Her father took our things and gave them to her. She does not deserve anything good. You should tell her what he did. What you saw."

He saw it too, of course, but he was just two. "We're taking enough away from her," I say.

He starts taking apart the action.

"Not near the food," I say, waving at Viktor's gun oil. "I don't want it picking up the smell." I slice the cherry tomatoes into halves. They're easier to eat that way.

"She is the enemy."

"Your guys out there are chummy enough with her."

He snorts. "They're teaching her lines from Russian gangland movies. They think it is funny."

I go near where he works. They're all out there twirling their weapons now, teaching her how to do it. "What the fuck are they giving her a weapon for?"

"Relax. They would not give her something loaded."

Of course not.

"They're teaching her to be Sergei Kazan. In the movies, he twirls his gun like that and says, 'You go ahead and try it, baby, and I'll fill you so full of lead it'll be coming out of your ass.' It's funny if you know Sergei Kazan. Very brutish. Teaching her these lines. Like teaching a cat to talk." He smirks. "What? They're bored. You want to let them fuck her instead? I'm sure they would like to make a movie for her father, too."

In a flash my fists are on his lapels. I drag him out of his chair and push him against the wall.

"You see?" he says, panting. "You let yourself think you can have her."

My blood races. I watch myself being fucked up, putting him against the wall, nose to nose with my brother.

His gaze is steady.

Fuck. I lay off.

He stands, not bothering to straighten himself back up. "Konstantin did some things very wrong, I think. He should not have shown you so very many pictures of that girl. You watched her grow up."

"So?"

"She ate when you starved. Laughed when you cried. Kept safe while you hid. But I think that's not what came through."

"Maybe I was jacking off," I say.

He smiles. "You are good at that."

"What the fuck is that supposed to mean?"

"You are good at answering a question with a question. That's what you did just now. Like a fighter. Slipping the hit."

But he's wrong. His questions were, in fact, a direct hit. I spent long hours watching her, wondering how she was faring. If she'd found other friends. Trying to remember what it was like to feel good. Safe. To have people who care for me. And more, people like her to care about. I owe everything to Konstantin, but we weren't like a family. We were more like weaponsmith and sword.

A call comes in. The investigator has tracked down the old Worland director to a yoga class. "I'll have him within the hour," he says.

Viktor is back at his gun cleaning. I pull out the tomatoes and parmesan. Then I get an idea. I call Tito. "That

accountant old man Nikolla used—Ligne. Go back at him."
I give him instructions—he's to act like we got something
new. Try to shake him that way.

"We decided Ligne knows nothing," Viktor says once I
get off the phone. "That he was kept in the dark."

"I want to look at all the angles again. We have these
few hours."

Viktor holds part of the action to the light. He tends to
channel his passion into weaponry, just like Konstantin.
He fucks women now and then, but he's indifferent at
best. "You really think the old accountant holds something back?"

"I don't know."

"You don't want to show the movie to the old man," he
observes.

I let the chopping fill the silence.

"Don't let the breaking game break you, *brat*."

***

She's lying in a deck chair when I go out there with the
plates. Book in her lap, face to the sun. Even from feet
away you can see her lashes, dark and thick.

The Russians are invisible around the perimeter now,
but she knows they're there. Growing up, Mira and I were
always aware of our bodyguards. Our distaste for them
bonded us. Slipping them was a game. Mira would be
laughing and running, same as me.

I set two plates down on the table and pull out a chair.
"Come on."

"Any word about my dad?"

"Not awake yet. Come on."

She looks out at the forest perimeter. "Any leads on who can give us the key to the code?"

"Our guy's in pursuit. He tracked him to a yoga class."

"Thank goodness."

"It doesn't mean he has the code. We might still go with plan B."

"Dad gave you everything he could. He wouldn't gamble me."

It's on the tip of my tongue to tell her she's wrong, to tell her she's letting her optimism keep her stupid. Such a Mira thing to do, believing in him like that. Her optimism burns like a taunt.

I yank her chair out another noisy inch.

She gets up. Comes over and sits. She eyes the food. "You gonna shove this in my mouth, too?"

She stiffens when I touch her glossy ponytail. Even her hair feels impossibly smooth. All those pictures. The smiling girl in the perfect life. I pull her ponytail aside and touch the spot at the back of her neck. Soft and secret. Sensitive. It's a good spot. A spot I love. "I bet you'd enjoy that."

Red floods her cheeks and the back of her neck.

"Hard and fast and mean. How's that sound? Because you liked it fucked-up."

She gets this thoughtful look. "I did kind of like it fucked-up," she confesses. "I don't know what to think about that."

My heart pounds. Only Mira would repel an insult with an honest confession. Most people put the shields down, but not Mira. She lifts them. She shows you her heart.

You can never have her. I repeat Viktor's words like a mantra. *You can never have her. Never have her.*

"I'll be honest, part of me is just a little horrified I was into it, but I was," she continues. "I mean, what is that, right? At first I didn't know what to think. Then it just took me. I felt like we went somewhere, or just were weirdly connected in this new way and—"

I close my fist around the ponytail and pull—not hard like last night, but just enough to make her look up at me. Her eyes have caramel-colored flecks in the sunshine. Like shards of beer glass. "You think we had a connection? Wake up. I fucked your face and took a movie of it."

Pain in her eyes.

I don't know why I do it. I just think she needs to not have that candor, that vulnerability. It's how people get hurt. It's how people get hurt by me.

She pulls her hair from my grip and puts her napkin in her lap and picks up her fork. She pivots it on the end tine, making a little arc. "Oh, Aleksio."

My pulse races. I don't even know what she means by that. *Oh, Aleksio.* It means everything and nothing, and my fucking pulse races. I swallow down my emotions and take my seat across from her. "Didn't anybody ever tell you not to play with your silverware?"

She stops with the fork and presses it into the side of the frittata.

Tito and Viktor ate theirs with their hands, but she has perfect manners in everything. I remind myself she's Aldo's spoiled daughter, with her smiles and her safe life.

I have this insane impulse to kiss her and promise I'll protect her, but I can't protect her and save Kiro both at the same time. My pulse races with the torment of that. I want to protect her. I want to kiss her. I want to get lost with her.

She takes a small bite.

I should look down, but it's too late. I'm watching her. I'm holding my fucking breath.

Contrary to what you might think, when somebody first tastes something they find delicious, you'll rarely see a blissful look on their face; it's more like stunned horror. I don't know why people go with stunned horror when they taste something delicious, but they always do.

So when I see her getting that stunned-horror look, I'm stupidly gratified. I lower my gaze like I don't care, but I'm a fucking hound panting at her feet.

"Oh my God," she says. "Who made this?"

"Didn't I tell you? We kidnapped Wolfgang Puck, too. Got him back there cooking up a storm. I'm gonna butt-fuck him with a baseball bat later."

She snorts. "Come on, Aleksio, be serious."

I turn my eyes down to my plate. I shouldn't be striving to give her good things. I should be doing the opposite, that's the whole point here.

She takes another bite. This time her eyes drift closed.

"Oh wow. Does this have hazelnuts?"

"What are you, a reporter for *Gourmet Magazine*?"

"It's delicious."

I look down at my plate with my heart soaring because I made her feel good. Stupid. It'll just make hurting her harder.

Don't let the breaking game break you, Viktor said.

CHAPTER EIGHT

Mira

Aleksio has unfairly long, lush eyelashes—giraffe fringes, Mom used to call them—and when he gazes down at his food, those fringes hide his eyes completely. He knows it, of course. He wants to cut me off, shut me out.

He's not that good kid anymore—I know that. He's no longer my friend. But he held me as I cried—that was real. The way he told me about his burn felt like a secret just for me.

And the way I felt with him was real.

And I know something else—he won't cut off my finger. There's still some of that mischievous but good-hearted boy inside him. I wouldn't feel that connection with him if there wasn't.

Which is good, because the shock of seeing my finger could kill Dad—for real. Aleksio doesn't know it, and I can't tell him, but Dad gets violently ill at the sight of blood. And that's the kind of shock that's dangerous to his heart.

Nobody knows about Dad's aversion to blood. It's a secret he guards even from his closest associates. A secret he asked Mom and me never to divulge. An aversion to blood makes him look weak in the world of the Albanian clans, and it's especially bad for the supposedly fierce leader of the vicious Black Lion clan.

My guess is that he's been around blood plenty of times in his life, but that he never looks directly at it—he pretends. That's how he hides it. But if he opens a box with my bloody finger in it? The shock would be too much for his heart. The shock would kill him.

But the film clip could kill him, too.

No—we'll find the key code. It's out there somewhere. Their guy tracked down the director already.

Nobody can see that fucking clip.

Except maybe me. What would it be like to watch us like that?

I flash on the way he looked down at me when I had him in my mouth, like I was the most amazing thing he'd ever seen. Like we were connected in this crazy, wrong way. Aleksio, sitting over me in all his brutal glory, familiar old Aleksio grown into a dangerous man. Fuck, it did something to me.

Moving up Aleksio's legs felt wrong and good. I had no choice. And I was glad I had no choice. I was into it.

How twisted is that? Into it. All my life I've been trying to get out from under the thumb of men like him, and suddenly I'm crawling up his legs, begging to be used. But that's the thing about having no choice—you do it no matter what. You do it if you hate it, and you do it if it's a twisted thing you find out that you enjoy.

It took me by surprise when he grabbed my hair, taking control so violently. My whole body came to attention. His cock tasted of man and secrets and sweat and need. I wanted him to push me harder. And he did.

God, the way he talked to me. The names. The intensity of his breath as the whole thing spun out of control. The roughness of him.

His roughness a forbidden gift. Aleksio always went too far. The roughness felt beautiful. *I know you,* I thought.

And then he turned it into something ugly with the camera and the gun.

I sigh and twirl my fork.

He doesn't have his suit jacket on; just a loose tie over his white button-down shirt. All that white in contrast with his chocolaty hair that's a little too long. He went on a run earlier, and he apparently shaved after; his cheeks are smooth and clear, making him look deceptively innocent. Angelic.

"We're showing it to him as soon as he wakes up."

"It'll kill him."

He stabs his fork into the greens. "You should pray we find the key, then."

"It's just a matter of time."

He cuts a bit of frittata and holds it up, examining it. "How does a spoiled princess who does international shopping as an extreme sport know about anatomization keys or whatever?"

My face burns. But that was the whole goal, wasn't it? Aleksio is the exactly kind of person we don't want knowing about my real life.

I shrug. "Are you telling me you never picked up any useless information in life?"

If he realizes I'm answering a question with a question, he doesn't show it.

I take another bite of the best meal I've eaten all year, not that Aleksio seems to care.

Little Vik comes out. Whatever he has to say, it's bad.

Aleksio sees it, too. "What?"

He shakes his head.

Aleksio stands and pulls his brother away. I sense trouble, chaos. Doors slam inside the house. Guys moving out.

I stare at Aleksio's phone, still on the table. *His phone.*

I look from Aleksio and Viktor to the phone and back to Aleksio. I could grab it and delete the video—this is my chance. He may have backed it up, but I have a feeling he didn't, considering how busy he's been.

He'll be angry. And it's a gamble, but I don't believe Aleksio will take my finger in the end. I snatch the phone and figure out what he used. Fuse. I find the file, hit delete, confirm delete. Just like that it's gone. I set it back down and pick up my fork.

Aleksio comes back and grabs his phone and suit jacket. He swings it on and fixes his shirt cuffs.

Blood whooshes in my ears. I hope I made the right choice. "What's going on?"

"Ligne is dead."

My jaw drops. "Frankie? Frankie Ligne?"

Aleksio nods.

"Are you sure?"

"Most certainly dead, yes," Viktor says.

"He's just a sweet old man. Why would you—"

"We didn't kill him," Viktor spits.

"Who?"

"Bloody Lazarus," he growls.

"Why would Lazarus kill somebody from his own organization? My father's confidante..."

Viktor gives me a jaded look. Like, *really*? Two of the Russians come out, all suited up and holstered.

It can't be true. "Lazarus wouldn't kill Ligne. They're on the same side."

"Take it up with the witnesses Viktor rounded up," Aleksio says. "In other news, we got the key to the code."

"We can read the files now?"

"Yeah," he says. "If we had the right files. The illegal adoptions were hidden in the basement in the fucking *maintenance record files.*"

"That whole raid and you took the wrong files?"

Tito comes out, Glock in hand.

"Wait! What are you doing? You're not going back to the Worland..."

"Until Daddy wakes up, it's what we have."

Of course. He'll do anything to find his brother, and when he does, he'll love him barbarically and unconditionally.

Aleksio's love is the dangerous kind of love that breaks all the rules. It's him killing and kidnapping as he goes after his brother. It's him pulling my hair and shoving his cock in my mouth.

I shouldn't think it's beautiful.

He turns and leaves with his guys, through the patio door, through the house.

The front door slams. Car doors slam. I stand there alone, stupidly wistful.

CHAPTER NINE

Viktor

The area around Worland is quiet on a Sunday afternoon. We find free spaces at meters. We park a few blocks away and split up, moving through the neighborhood like shadows.

The old buildings in Chicago are very blocky. Old Moscow buildings have more imagination. I have argued with Aleksio on this point, of course.

I move alongside him. Tito and Yuri go up opposite. Others will loop around. We are all on edge.

Hitting this place a second time, it's madness. We hide in the dark out of the afternoon sun, looking, listening.

"He may not have heard about yesterday," Aleksio says, hopefully.

Perhaps. But if Bloody Lazarus did hear about our raid yesterday, a raid on the same day as Aldo Nikolla's disappearance, he may very well think of Kiro. We cannot be sure what Lazarus knows. He may have found out from Ligne where Kiro is.

Our attempts to save Kiro may have gotten him killed.

Still, this thing must be done. We go forward. We hide. Listen.

They say a baby of twenty-some months cannot remember things, but I remember violence. I remember fear and death. My memories are more like dark scribbles than photographs. They are memories all the same.

I did not know they were American memories, however.

When Aleksio came to our garage in Moscow, I did not recognize him, but he recognized me.

With his television clothes and scruffy American hair, Aleksio looked very strange, very out of place; I wondered whether I had known him as a boy in the orphanage. And then he began to speak. A brother, he said.

Yuri came up behind me, amazed. *Brat*, he said. Yuri had heard nothing of what Aleksio said, but he looked at our faces and he knew that we were brothers. Yuri clapped his hand onto my shoulder, over and over, so happy. Yuri and I had come up in the orphanage together, always dreaming of family.

This orphanage was a favorite recruiting ground of the Russian mafia. They would adopt the strong boys and raise us like fighting dogs. Vicious to the last.

"Looks clear," Aleksio says, seeing nothing in the alley. Tito makes a hand signal, and he and Yuri flank left with some of Aleksio's men. Our two groups have learned to move together well in the past year. Merging our techniques—his gang, my gang.

There's a dumpster to the left, stacked-up crates from the restaurant on the other side of the alley. We flow around it, avoiding the cameras, keeping to the shadows.

I lock eyes with Yuri across the span of alley. We wait. We let the area speak to us.

Yuri and I rose up quickly within the Bratva. I was to be a Bratva soldier until they noticed my ability to mimic American actors from the television. I could understand what they were saying when nobody else could.

They sent me to classes. I picked up the strange grammar quickly, easily. Because of my good English I was made a hit man. I even spent ten days in New York once, hunting a man who attempted to flee the Bratva. Never did I imagine I was born here, that I spent some twenty months here—not until Aleksio came to our garage and told me about Aldo Nikolla, who killed our parents and stole our lives. We would make him pay, and we would make Lazarus pay, because Lazarus helped him. And we would find our baby brother Kiro and take back the empire.

With the blessing of my superiors, I took five of our best, including Yuri, and went with Aleksio to Chicago. It was not charity, of course, that our mafia bosses let me go. A position at the top of one of the most powerful criminal organizations in Chicago would be a good thing.

Al Capone! That's what Mischa and the guys said when they were told they would accompany me. Each and every one of them said the name of Al Capone.

Chicago was Al Capone to me, too, until I met Aleksio.

Yuri slides up to one of the windows. He gets ears in, pressing a listening device to a small square of safety glass.

I exchange glances with Aleksio. He tips his head. *So far, so good.* Perhaps our enemies do not know.

Yuri steals over. "Is quiet," he says. "Too quiet."

Tito slips in. Tito is Aleksio's Yuri. "What's your feeling?" Aleksio asks Tito.

"Feels like a trap, smells like a trap. Is a trap." Tito likes to make his hair bright blond on the tips of it. He is very formidable.

"A trap," I say.

We have men around the neighborhood, and they text in. Nobody is watching.

Aleksio looks up and down the blocky building. "The files are right inside, and we have the fucking decode key," he says.

No question we'll risk it. Aldo Nikolla may or may not talk. The file is sure.

We discuss what we would do in the place of Bloody Lazarus if he thought we might be back.

"I'd think about torching the place," Tito says. "But then I'd say, how can I go for maximum death? That says explosives to me. And if I didn't have a lot of time? Explosives connected to the door."

"Or to the alarm system," I say. "Sound, vibration."

We narrow it down to the door. Easiest, smartest, fastest.

"Then maybe we should go up the side. Up that old fire escape." Aleksio points. The fire escape is half falling apart, but it's still up. "What happens if we break that window?"

I pick up a brick and hurl it. It sails into the window with a crash. We press against the wall, waiting for an explosion.

Nothing. So we have our entrance.

We argue about who'll go in. "I'm not sending anybody in somewhere where I won't go myself," Aleksio growls. He's like that, a strong leader. But the girl will be trouble. I saw his face in the video clip. I saw the way he looked at her.

Aleksio creeps up the side and leaps to the lowest rung of the fire escape. The apparatus creaks as he begins to climb, balancing on the edges, seasoned criminal that he is. When he is the three stories up top, he throws his jacket over the sill and lifts himself up by his fingers.

He makes it look easy. I know it is not. Aleksio is a strong ally, but a girl like that Mira will weaken him.

I loved a girl once, and then I had to kill her. It was very hard.

An explosion tears out from the second floor below him. The wall buckles—with Aleksio half in the window.

"Fucking hell!" I spring out of the darkness, running toward him as he drops onto the fire escape and grips the rusty pole. The structure separates from the building with Aleksio clinging on. It twists and groans.

Aleksio drops to the alley. He makes himself into a ball and rolls. I grab him, pull him behind the dumpster. He is hurt. His ankle, I think.

"Fucking hell," I say as the assault weapons start.

Our men shoot back.

"Where the fuck did they come from?" he gasps.

"We have it, *brat*." Our men are suppressing. The cops will be here soon. "Can you walk?"

Aleksio wears a grim look. He will.

"I got him," Tito says. "You help cover." Tito wants me shooting because I am the marksman here. I rest my forearms on the metal lip of the dumpster lid and focus my senses on our attackers. I focus and calm myself, breathing, squeezing the trigger, breathing, squeezing. My bullets find their targets as Tito gets Aleksio away.

Soon the guys scream up in an old Cadillac. I dive in the back with the others.

We head out, losing our attackers easily. They thought we'd be inside for the explosion. They were set up to pick off survivors, not for a full firefight.

Aleksio rides in back with me. He concentrates on breathing, pushing back the pain. Yuri throws back the first aid kit. I pat my thigh, and Aleksio heaves his leg there. He grimaces as I begin to untie his shoe.

I instruct Yuri to call his guy—the one holding Aldo Nikolla. It is time to send the clip.

I get his shoe off. The pain on Aleksio's face is not just his ankle. Yes, I know what those frittatas meant.

"Just sprained," he grates out.

"You hope." I touch his anklebone. He winces. I touch another spot.

"Fuck! Stop it. The ankle is fucked up, okay? Is there something we need to know beyond that?"

I rip up an old shirt and begin to wrap it.

It is very bad that we did not get those files. There is only one route to the information now—through the old man. Aleksio does not want to show the cocksucking clip to Aldo. He'll do what it takes to save Kiro, though.

His head is tipped back. He's out of his mind with pain of every kind.

"Aldo Nikolla's awake," Yuri calls from the front.

"Good. We go now," I say. "We show the movie. Tell him how much worse it will get for her next."

Aleksio hisses out a breath.

I grab his phone, unlock it and scroll. He knows it has to be done. Lazarus is hunting now. He killed Ligne, torched the Worland Agency. He wants to get to Kiro before we can.

"Where is the movie?" I ask.

Aleksio takes it and scrolls. Scowls.

"What?"

"Wait," he says, and he taps some more. Then, "Fuck." Then, "*Fuck!*"

"What?"

"Gone."

"How?"

He casts his gaze sideways. "She erased it."

I shut my eyes. Our leverage on the old man is gone. Or at least the video

CHAPTER TEN

Aleksio

Yuri's got us moving at top speed in that old Caddy with its shitty shocks the Russians have been driving around. Every bump sends starbursts of pain through my ankle and jars my vision, because yeah, I hit my head on something in that fall, and focusing isn't that easy.

Viktor wants to stop at an office supply store. He prefers the paper cutter to the cleaver.

"No," I say.

"The paper cutter is cleaner. Better leverage. I have seen it both ways. The butcher knife leaves room for error. It's good in a pinch but—"

"We can't—"

"You would let Kiro die?"

I'm feeling dizzy, having trouble focusing. "We'll cut up the old man—"

"Until he passes out from pain?" Viktor asks.

That's the intel on the old man. Pain doesn't crack him. People have gone at him before.

"She shouldn't have erased it," he says, like she brought it on herself.

"Fuck you," I growl, head spinning to find another way to show the old man we're serious.

The car takes a corner, and my ankle fires like shards of glass.

Suddenly Viktor's in my face, pinning me to the inside of the car door. He has my arms trapped up to my chest, panting with the exertion of it.

He calls up front to Yuri—a stream of Russian.

"What are you doing? What did you say to him?"

Yuri is talking back. The car is slowing. Yuri's pulling over. It's Yuri and Mischa up there. Both of them Viktor's guys.

Fuck.

I lash out at Viktor, going for him with everything I have, going for every blow I can think of, even a head butt. He's ready for them all. The car stops. Mischa's out. I struggle harder, get an elbow into Viktor's jaw.

The door I'm backed up against opens. I freefall against a tanklike chest and feel an arm loop around my neck, muscles like iron. Precise pressure. Mischa.

I kick out.

"This we do for you, *brat*," Viktor says, suppressing my legs as Mischa puts the choke on me. A perfect triangle hitting the veins that feed the blood to my brain. The edges of my vision dim.

Fuck!

I wake up curled on my side, enclosed in darkness. The vibration below me tells me I'm in the Caddy trunk and that we're back on the road. My head is woozy. My ankle screams. I pound like a madman. My good leg and two fists. Nothing.

I check my pockets for my phone, thinking to call Tito and have him put a stop to this. I can't let them hurt Mira. I have to protect her.

No phone.

I go crazy on the trunk top in the darkness.

CHAPTER ELEVEN

Mira

The two guys who stayed back to watch me think it's hilarious to hang around by the pool and help me get my gun spin down while I say the Sergei Kazan phrase. They told me it means, "You go ahead and try it, baby, and I'll fill you so full of lead it'll be coming out of your ass." A really tough movie star apparently says it.

The better I get at it, the more they laugh.

I don't see what's so funny, but then again, American movie lines don't seem like much out of context, either.

I monitor them for signs that they've heard something from the Worland raid. Have they gotten there yet? What if something goes wrong? Will they know? They don't seem worried, but I am. If things get dangerous, Aleksio will be front and center. It's how he is. If there's trouble, he's at the center.

The Russians have their suit jackets off, shirtsleeves rolled up. They're lounging around like disreputable waiters from a thug café, smoking and drinking Beluga vodka like there's no tomorrow. Petitioning me again and again to do the gangster character impression.

It's taken a while to get the double gun spin down. I dropped them a lot at first. Obviously they're not loaded. I keep practicing, though, the amusing trained monkey. I even try to say the line with the intonation they prefer. It's not that I want to amuse them. I have to believe that one of these times, one of the guns they'll give me will be loaded. Or somehow they'll drop their guard.

So I practice the line. I adjust it for maximum shock. I get good. This is about escaping, about getting back to who I really am and away from Aleksio's orbit. He's like a dangerous black hole—he'll pull you in if you're not careful. I can feel his pull working on me with every hour we spend together.

The world I escaped to is a place where laws trump blood vendettas. Where people work together to protect the weak. Where even one death through gun violence means everybody failed. Where kids can still be saved. That's the world I need to get back to.

It's true what I said to Aleksio—I miss Chicago. But I can't be who I am here.

Suddenly the phones are going off. The guns are taken from me. The joke of me being Sergei Kazan is over.

"What's going on?"

The guys are shrugging on their jackets. They're acting like men going to their battle stations. A hit back? Lazarus?

"Are they okay?"

Yuri bursts out onto the porch. He looks intense. He points at the picnic table that's out there. "Sit."

I sit.

Viktor comes out with a bottle of vodka and sets it down on the table, and then he sets down a glass. "This is for you. It's nice. You should drink it."

"Where's Aleksio?"

"Aleksio is not coming."

"Is he okay?"

"He's okay, yes." Viktor pours the vodka into the glass. "It's not even dinnertime."

Viktor sets the glass in front of me. "Was not a request."

"What's going on?"

Viktor pushes it toward me.

Yuri watches Viktor darkly.

"Did something happen to my father?"

"I'll tell you if you drink it."

I take it with shaking hands. "Is he okay?"

Viktor nods at the glass.

I down it and slam it onto the table.

"Your father is not dead." He pours another.

"What, then? Where's Aleksio?"

Again Viktor nods at the glass.

"I don't want another."

"Yet you will have another, *sistra.*"

"And then you'll tell me the rest?"

"I will."

I take the glass and drain it, then slam it on the table, feeling a weird sense of vertigo.

"Your father is awake. We will kill him, of course, but for now he lives."

"You fucker." I go at him but Yuri grabs me and turns me and pushes back down on the rough wooden bench, forces me to sit, using his weight to hold me still, and there's nothing nice about it.

"Another," Viktor says.

"What's going on?"

"Your father needs to tell us more. He needs to get more invested in our cause." He pours another.

"What are you going to do?"

"You know what I am going to do, I think," Viktor says. "Now that we have no movie to show him. It was stupid what you did."

A wave of wooziness washes over me. "No."

"You are right-handed," Yuri says, holding my hands and inspecting the pinky with the birthmark. I try to pull my hands to my belly, but he won't let them go.

Tears come to my eyes. "Get Aleksio."

"Aleksio will not come."

I try to get up from the table, but Yuri won't let me. He seems to know everything I'm about to do before I do it. "You can't. My father can't handle it. His heart can't handle it. You need him alive, don't you?"

"His heart." Viktor sneers. "He does not deserve your care. He does not *deserve shit*."

"You have all this wrong. He and your father were friends and partners! They were like brothers!"

He brings the glass to my lips, but I shake my head violently and it spills all over us.

"You will want that in you, I think." Viktor fills it again.

"Why are you doing this? Think! If he really did send you away, it was to save you."

"You are so stupid." He sounds disgusted. "Aleksio did not want to tell you—out of kindness he did not want to tell you. 'We are taking enough from poor Mira,' he said."

A horrible chill spreads through my chest.

He pours another and pushes the glass toward me. "I told him it was obvious. 'She will work it out,' I said to him, but he did not think that you would work it out." Viktor shrugs. "He was right."

"You don't know shit," I say.

Viktor's eyes go dead. "Drink."

"Fuck you."

"We will make you drink, then." Viktor nods at Yuri. Yuri grabs my hands and holds them behind my back while Viktor brings the glass to my lips. Again I make him spill it.

Viktor fills it again.

"Get Aleksio!"

"This I do for Aleksio. Drink."

I sit there with my lips zipped tight, like if I don't open my mouth I might not be able to drink, and therefore the finger chopping won't go ahead.

"Most do not get to drink vodka," Yuri says, pronouncing it "wodka." "It just happens. *Fwap.*"

"God, you're fucking barbarians."

"Somebody is coming out here with a paper cutter in a few minutes," Viktor says. "You will be drunk or sober."

"A paper cutter?" I try wildly to jerk away, writhing in his arms. I knock him in the head and balls, and he has to put down the glass and help Yuri hold me still.

"It will happen, *zolotse*," he says softly into my hair. "Is sharp. Will be fast." He lets one of my hands free, and that's my chance—I take the bottle by the neck, thinking to hit him, but he's too fast. He snatches it back. I moved too slowly.

"Fuck." I look down at my pinky, a little bent on the tip, with the freckle birthmark. *This is going to happen,* I think, fighting back the tears. The worst thing is thinking of my father seeing it. He'll recognize it. He'll know it's mine. The blood will be too much for him.

"Shhh," Yuri says. "You'll get through."

"Fuck you." I sniffle. I should tell them about his blood thing. Or will they just use it against him? My mind feels hazy.

Viktor pours me another. This time I drink it. "I can't do this."

"It's the adrenaline," Viktor says. "Is still worse if you are sober."

"Aleksio's going to kill you."

"He can kill me after we find Kiro."

I take a drink and look at my pinky against the rough, dark wood of the picnic table, resisting the impulse to sob. Sobbing won't solve anything; it could even make things worse. A door slams from somewhere inside house. I perk up, hoping it's Aleksio. But no, it's one of the Russians coming out with a bag...from an office supply store.

My blood races as the man who was joking with me not fifteen minutes ago pulls out a box. He rips it open and pulls a big heavy paper cutter from its Styrofoam bed. I twist and turn and scream for Aleksio.

Viktor says, "The fact that you are calling for Aleksio is exactly why I made sure he cannot be here. He will not come."

"Fuck," I say, hyperventilating. It's from the shock of what's happening to me. I feel like throwing up. "Oh my God."

I'm feeling woozy. More woozy than I should for just drinking a few shots of vodka. "Did you put something in that vodka?"

"No," Viktor says. "I wouldn't ruin good vodka like that."

"The glass?"

"Maybe."

Things are feeling tilty. Like I'm not really in my body. "Warn my father beforehand. His heart can't handle the shock, but if he's warned..."

"Your worthless father," Viktor spits. "I should open his chest with a machete and fuck his heart as he dies. If it was not for Kiro, this is what I would do."

I swallow past the dryness in my mouth. "The Valcheks are the ones who killed your parents, Viktor. They're the ones you should be angry with. And the Valcheks are dead. Why? Because Dad killed them. He avenged the death of your parents, and this is how you repay him?"

"This is what you tell yourself? That it was the Valcheks?" Viktor wipes the paper cutter. He's careful, deliberate. Lush lashes like Aleksio's, but none of his warmth.

"It's what happened! Everyone knows it."

"Aleksio knows different. He saw."

"What?"

"Aleksio saw your father kill our parents. Your father slit their throats. Bloody Lazarus helped."

My throat feels thick.

"Your father drugged our mother and father and cut their throats. He killed them as they begged for the lives of their babies."

"No," I say. "My father wouldn't..." My heart pounds. "He couldn't!" I'm about to tell him about my dad's secret, that he becomes violently ill at the sight of blood, but I can't form the words.

Viktor draws his face near to mine. "We were all there. Kiro was one. A tiny boy." He straightens. "I was a baby, too, but not so young. I remember the feeling. The blood. Nothing more."

"My father wouldn't do that. Wouldn't and couldn't."

"The man you know now, maybe not. He is old now." He watches me with dark calm. "Your father split those babies up so that they would never find each other. Me he sent to the worst orphanage in Moscow. Kiro he sold. Aleksio got out. But not before he saw all. Old Konstantin pulled him into a cubby and kept him still. Hand over his mouth. They hid in the very room where the killing was."

Viktor wipes the cutting surface with vodka. "There are many cubbies in that playroom, no? Many places to hide. He watched it in the reflection of the window. Your father gave our parents drugs to make them slow. He slit their throats and then he threw up, so disgusted was he with what he did."

"He threw up?"

"He cleaned it up, of course. He is not stupid."

I'm stunned, reeling. *He threw up.*

It's his reaction to blood. The secret he hides, the secret they would have no way of knowing. Could it be true?

I feel like throwing up myself.

Viktor is droning on with the story. When my father could not find Aleksio, he figured out Konstantin must have helped him get away...and my father put out contracts on them both.

I think about the burn. The hiding. That was my father hunting Aleksio. I think about the look on my father's face when he recognized Aleksio. Could it be true? God, to kill a mother and father *in front of their babies!*

"Your father hunted Aleksio unceasingly. You know what the price on Aleksio's head was at the age of nine? Three hundred thousand. It takes only fifty to have somebody killed. But for this young boy, three hundred thousand. Konstantin, too. All the best hitters were out for him. They raised it later. Too little, too late. Isn't that what you say? A baby one year old," Viktor continues. "Our mother begged while her babies screamed."

Tears swim in my eyes. "Why would he hate your family so much?"

"Bad blood between partners. Konstantin saw it coming. He tried to warn our father." Viktor positions the cutter in front of me.

I let the tears fall as the details mesh up into a perfect story. It's got the ring of truth, and not just about the blood aversion. It *feels* right, *feels* like the truth. It echoes with the contours of that dark time.

Is it possible he knows more about Kiro? Is Dad holding back, even knowing I'm in danger? No way.

"We have each other's backs." My tongue feels thick. "He doesn't know more—he can't." The trees are blurry. A three-week-old baby is tiny. Just a little bundle. I'm floaty.

"Bloody Lazarus is hunting Kiro now. He cannot let the brothers unite."

"But Bloody Lazarus would want to find my father first."

"If he has a chance to kill Kiro, he will kill him. He needs that prophecy put to rest."

So many things I don't know. But I know his story is real—I can feel it in my gut. It makes sense with Aleksio's story.

"Was everything a lie?" I mumble, watching the trees sway. Or is that the ground swaying? Or the table? I'm staring at the world from far away.

The slaughter of their parents in front of babies? It would imprint their souls. I can't let it be true. I won't accept it.

Viktor's face floats in front of me. "How do you feel?"

I furrow my brow. "The trees..."

Just then the door slides open. I jerk my head up, but it's not Aleksio. It's an outdoorsy-looking guy with a blond beard. He's carrying a little black bag.

"Currie!" Viktor says.

"What happened to her?"

"Nothing yet."

"What the fuck?" The man called Currie sounds strange and faraway. "You're not going to do what I think you're gonna do with that."

"Hold him," Viktor says. A couple Russians grab on to the man. "You will see to her after."

"Fuck me," the man called Currie says. "What the fuck is wrong with you people?"

"Okay." Viktor comes to me. I gasp as my world spins. He twists my hair and shoves it in the back of my shirt, then he takes my hand and flattens it on the cool, flat surface of the paper cutter.

I'm sweating, flying.

"Don't do it, man!" Currie shouts. He sounds like he's on another planet.

Viktor pulls my pinky out to the side so that it hangs partly over the edge.

"Get away!" I try to jerk away. Another guy comes to press my wrist into place. I can barely move—they're too strong, too determined, too expert. It's like a dream. A nightmare.

"Breathe," Viktor says.

Little Vik. A baby can't understand that kind of violence, but it goes into its psyche all the same.

"Look at Yuri's eyes," Viktor says. "And breathe."

Yuri's face is blurry. I can't tell if it's the drugs or the tears. There's a crisp metal-on-metal sound as the blade is lifted. It's happening. Everything is too bright.

And then a crash.

Not my finger—it's from somewhere else. A yell rips through the air.

Aleksio.

"Fucking hell." Viktor lets my pinky go and straightens.

Aleksio's limping, half-running across the patio past Currie to get to us. Our eyes lock. He's the one steady thing in my seasick world. His white shirt is bloody, half tucked in.

Yuri mutters something in Russian, but all I see is Aleksio. He came for me.

Aleksio practically falls to the picnic table, next to me on the bench. He takes my hands in his, checking my fingers. His knuckles look pink and raw. "Are you okay, Mira?"

"Yes," I say. He seems slightly unreal. Like he's part here and part not. "It's okay now."

He stares into my eyes.

"Intact," I say, proud I found that word. He claps a hand onto the side of my head and presses his thumb onto my eyebrow, forcing one eye open wide.

I laugh. "Stop it, 'Leksio."

He turns a feral gaze to Viktor. "What the fuck did you do to her?"

"What you will not," Viktor says from somewhere far away.

Aleksio's gone just like that. Everything's cold and I'm alone again. Where is he? I look up and spot him flying at Viktor. He tackles him onto the green grass, a sea of lime soda.

He's on top, pounding Little Vik in the face. *Whap.*

That straightens me up. "Stop it!"

Another crack.

Tito tries to pull him off. "Don't do it, man!"

Yuri's in there. It's a whirlwind of fists. White shirts, black jackets, blood all over.

I stand, gripping the table. Everyone's fighting!

Aleksio hits Tito, and then Viktor's on top, pounding Aleksio. They're fighting wildly, rolling around, grabbing at each other's arms. A blur of motion. Black and white and blood all over.

I sway on my feet.

They fight like animals, these brothers. Separated so long ago.

The world comes in and out of focus, blurred with tears. Need to do something.

And then I spy the gun. Sitting out on the table. Waiting for me.

It's cool and heavy in my hand. I fit my palm around the grip. Trigger on my finger like half a ring.

CHAPTER TWELVE

Aleksio

We stop fighting when she shoots the gun.

In a flash we're off the ground, hands up. There she is, staggering, waving that gun. We're all freaking.

"Put it down," Viktor says.

"Stop fighting!" Tears stream down her cheeks in streaks.

"We stopped! We're okay now," I say.

Except we're not. Mira is staggering around with a loaded Glock, finger on the fucking trigger. She could shoot without even intending it.

She's going to shoot us, that's my thought, and I wouldn't blame her. I blew up her house. Abducted her. Degraded her. Made that movie. Viktor nearly chopped her finger off.

I keep my hands up, showing her I'm no threat. "Baby—"

"Don't call me that! Or 'Kitten'!"

"Mimi," I say. "Put it down." Ten guys are out here—Dr. Currie and the Russians and my guys, looming around, hands half-up. Shit, a pack of guys won't improve this situation. I flick my fingers, signaling everyone to back away.

They pull back fast. All except Viktor. I growl—I can't look at him.

He, too, backs off. In a soft voice I say, "Give me the gun."

She gazes into my eyes, lip quivering. "Did he really do it?"

"What, Mira? Your finger?" *Fuck.* Is she asking me whether Viktor cut off her finger? How bad did he drug her? I'm so fucking angry I can't think.

"My father! Did he really kill your parents while you and your baby brothers watched? And he hunted you?"

I grit my teeth. No wonder she's so fucked up. She had to know her dad was a killer, but I can only imagine the picture Viktor painted for her. The young parents. The babies crying. The way the killed my father, then lunged for my mother as she darted away. I remember that so vividly. And then Lazarus held her for the blade. Her eyes. The blood.

"Is it true?"

"Yeah," I say.

"He just..." She stares off at the trees, swaying. "He just killed them? In front of their babies?"

"He killed them in front of the babies."

Her voice is small. "You're sure?"

I swallow. "He drugged their drinks, and then he chased them up to the top floor of our home and slit their throats. Him and Lazarus."

"In front of the babies."

"Yeah, that's what he did. They went up there to protect their babies."

"Why didn't you tell me?"

This, I think.

She's frowning, focusing intently on me. The moment seems to slow, and I feel her like I always have.

"And he wanted to kill you, too? Is that true, too?"

"Yeah. He needed to take me out because he knew I'd be a threat to him. I was old enough to know what happened. To want vengeance. Konstantin hid me while it happened. He kept me quiet."

The tears are coming again. "And you heard Dad throw up after?"

"Yeah." It kills me, seeing her like this, hurting and fucked-up.

"And that was my dad and Lazarus chasing you? When you got burned?"

My pulse whooshes. "And now I'm back good as new. Let's have the gun. You don't really want it, right? We're going to work it all out."

"Lazarus is trying to kill baby Kiro. You're worried about baby Kiro."

If he's not already dead.

She walks unsteadily toward me, finger still on that fucking trigger. *Nobody move,* I think. *Nobody spook her.* I blank out the pain in my ankle, my head.

Her dark hair is wild and wavy around her shoulders, as if morphed with her mood. "You need to find baby Kiro."

"We'll find him. You remember him?" I say, willing her to lower the piece. "Remember his little hat? His little fingers?"

"So tiny."

"Yeah, we need to find Kiro. He's running out of time. I promised I'd protect him."

"You keep your promises."

"I do. How about giving me that gun, Mira."

She's right in front of me now. I consider grabbing the gun, but any fast movement could make her twitch. Suddenly she's doing something with her hands, pulling a ring off her finger, still holding that damn gun.

"Be careful where you point that," I say calmly. "Real careful."

She keeps working at the ring, the gun pointing this way and that. It seems like it's stuck on her middle finger, and she's pulling and pulling.

"You need help?"

"No." Finally she gets it off and presses it into my palm. "This was stuck on my finger for years. Dad and I even went to a doctor to ask about cutting it off. But I lost weight recently...I never told him when I finally was able to get it off and on and off and..."

"Uh-huh," I say.

"Don't you see?" She's swaying. "If he sees the ring…" She forms her words with difficulty, hopped up on whatever Viktor fed her. "If he sees the ring, he won't look at the finger. We'll fool him. Pretend it's my finger. But without showing him blood."

"What are you talking about, Mira?"

"He can't look at blood. It's why he threw up. He won't look at it. We'll give him a fake finger. He won't ever look at it."

"He's not stupid. He'd look."

"No. He'll pretend. He won't look at it. He gets sick."

"Wait." I straighten, remembering the smell of his puke after he killed my parents. "Blood makes him sick?"

"So sick, Aleksio. He keeps it secret." She sucks in her lips, focusing on nothing, fighting through whatever haze she's in. "He'll pretend to look, but he won't. Get an already dead finger. Wrap it in something bloody. When he sees the ring…" She swallows, swaying. "…When he gets the ring he'll accept the finger. No question. Won't look. He'll accept it." She looks up. "Do you get it?"

"I get it." *Could it work?*

"Give him warning. Don't just unveil it. You don't have to kill him." Tears in her eyes. "Promise."

"Promise what, baby?" I whisper, held in a trance by her cinnamon gaze…and, admittedly, the waving gun.

"Don't kill him. You can't kill him. Not ever."

Fuck.

"Promise," she says, swinging it up to chest level.

"Okay. I won't kill your dad."

"Promise. Not Viktor, either. Not any of your guys. You don't have any of your guys kill Dad."

Viktor growls.

I glare at him, choking down the rage. "Promise her, Viktor."

"I promise," he says.

Yeah, he'll settle for making him wish he was dead.

She lowers the weapon. As usual, she's forgotten herself. Viktor told the old man we'd kill her if we didn't get Kiro back. She didn't try to get that promise from us. Because that's what's inside her. She blows my mind—raised in a nest of vipers and she turns out strong and good. This is the real Mira. Not the Mira Mira shopping shit or the mafia princess at the party. This.

I hold out my hands. "Come here."

She comes to me.

I slide an arm around her and gently grab the cool barrel, keeping it downward. I whisper in her ear, "Let go of the piece." She loosens her grip, and I take it from her and hand the thing behind me to Tito.

I press my face in her hair. "You're okay, baby."

Her chest begins to shake. I realize she's crying. My ankle is screaming, but all I hear is Mira.

I stroke her hair. "It's okay. We'll make it okay."

She pulls away, eyes swollen, still gorgeous. "He killed a mother in front of her babies! Promise me...promise you'll help him if he needs it. Promise you'll get him medical attention if the blood fucks him up."

"But he probably won't even look, right?"

"Yeah, but *if*—"

"Sure." I brush back her hair. "What kind of criminal gang would we be if we didn't have a doctor or two on our payroll?"

"Hold on, what?" Currie says. "Me? Are we talking about Aldo Nikolla?"

I give him a look. We handled some deep loan-shark trouble for him. He owes us his life.

"I'm wearing a mask," he says.

"Wear a fucking mask, then." I nod at Viktor. "The morgue. We need a finger and some blood in an hour. Tito knows a guy." Viktor and Tito start working it out. We need to get this together fast.

"Wait, I might have a source," Currie says.

"Work it out," I say. It'll cost us, knowing Currie. Like I give a shit.

"We need to save baby Kiro," Mira says.

My heart hammers out of my chest. "Thank you."

"I'm sorry," she says.

"There's nothing to be sorry about. We're sorry. *Viktor's* sorry."

She narrows her eyes at him, trying to focus. "But you love him."

I twist her hair around my hand, feeling crazy.

She tries to focus on my face. "He's your brother," she says, words thick and strange, as if in a trance. "He's trying to save his baby brother. You love him."

I push my face into her hair and breathe in the scent. I let myself be half-insane.

Mine.

Dr. Currie's coordinating with Viktor. They've got Tito and Yuri hitting a medical school. Currie knows about an insecure entrance. Bodies donated to science.

He leads the others into the house. He wants us in the kitchen. I'm having trouble walking. Fucking ankle.

Currie slaps the kitchen table. "Up here, Aleksio."

"Mira needs you more. Take her pulse and shit. She's been drugged up and traumatized." I clench my fists, resisting the impulse to fly at Viktor.

Currie sits her down on a kitchen chair and checks her pupils with a small light. Now that the adrenalin is ratcheted down, Mira's being silly, saying that stupid Russian action-star thing at one point.

Viktor leans in the doorway. His face looks like shit. Eye swelling up. Lip a fat, bloody mess. He's fucked up and sparkling and defiant, military haircut sleek and smooth. "What about Kiro?"

"Watch me burn the world for him."

"We lost time." His gaze goes to Mira.

I stalk over to him and throw him against the wall.

Viktor's nostrils flare. "You will kill me, *brat*?"

Mira whimpers.

"Take it the fuck outside," Currie barks.

I squeeze my eyes shut tight. I hate that I'm distressing her. I have to stop, I have to…

Viktor grabs my wrists. "I am frightened for him."

Kiro. He's talking about Kiro.

"Do I need to give Mira the gun again?" Currie says.

"I don't remember him," Viktor says softly. "You knew him. You got to hold him."

Fuck. I let Viktor down. "We'll get him."

We watch Currie listen to her heart. We talk in low tones about how to present the finger to her father. What would make the most impact? In a napkin, in a box. We know now if we smear it up with blood and give him the ring separately, he won't look at the finger. He'll tell us what we want to know if there's more to tell.

It's then that the call comes in from the chop shop. Our guys holding Nikolla. I answer. "Talk."

"The fucker's in the wind."

"What? He's gone?"

"Old man got out. He turned Driscoll, we think."

My heart pounds. "Driscoll?" Driscoll's one of my guys, who I sent to help Viktor's Russians. I've always had his utter loyalty.

Viktor's face goes white. He's heard enough to get the picture.

My man drones on. "That's what we think. Dima's dead. We think the old man turned Driscoll, and then Driscoll shot him and got out."

Dima. Viktor's youngest guy. A great guy. Viktor slams a fist through the wall.

I close my eyes. "I will destroy that fucker."

Viktor lost a guy. Because of one of mine.

"I'm sorry. So sorry."

Viktor stares bleakly at the crater he made.

"What?" It's Mira's voice. "What? What's going on?"

She's sitting up, looking worried again. Currie's glowering. "Take it outside."

I suck in a deep breath. "Your dad got away."

Mira's eyes widen.

I feel sick. Kiro is out there, undefended. The old man was our only way to find him.

She squints at the clock, trying to focus. "Um...he'll be at his restaurant in two hours. You can find him there."

I straighten. "You really think he'll show up there after he got taken? After all that's happened?"

"Eggs...zactly." She folds her arms on the table and lays down her head. "He has to," she says dreamily. "He has to show he's in control. Nobody's bitch. He will definitely, absolutely, positively be there."

"What restaurant?" Yuri asks.

"Agronika," I say. "On Fourteenth. Old-school Albanian joint. Kind of his office meeting room." The heart of enemy territory.

Tito grunts. "Going in there is suicide."

Even with Mira as a hostage, it's risky. "He'd never expect it."

"Hmmm," Viktor says.

I decide to walk Mira to her room. Currie doesn't like it. "I need to look at that ankle," he says. "You're going to have permanent damage. You're looking at a life of hell with that."

"After we find Kiro."

He nods. I know the nod. Placating. He doesn't think Kiro is alive, but I know he is. I feel Kiro alive out there— I always have.

I get her to her room and into bed. She smiles, then she seems to remember something and frowns. "I have to get away from you," she says.

"I know, baby." I tuck the covers around her.

"I don't want to sleep."

"Close your eyes and count to twenty. Then you'll wake up fresh with energy to get away from me."

"Can I just close my eyes?" she asks. "And not count?"

"Yes," I whisper, wanting nothing more than to get under the covers with her.

She closes her eyes. "It's nicer," she says. "To not count."

"I agree." I tuck the blanket all around her arms. She's dozing off.

When I limp back out, Viktor's making coffee. "I spoke with my network. We picked up one of Lazarus's guys. Lazarus has been running down information on Kiro, scouring for leads on him, but you know what he hasn't been doing?"

"What?" I ask.

"He has not been searching for the old man." Viktor looks at me significantly.

I frown. "Find the king, rescue the king. That should be his priority."

"Unless Lazarus is making a move on the king," Viktor says. "Nikolla is old. In boxing, you deliver the body blows before you try for the knockout. You soften your foe. Perhaps we softened the old man up for Lazarus to knock out."

I nod. Viktor would have seen this kind of thing a lot—the Russian gangs are famously cutthroat. Leaders don't tend to last. "Whatever Lazarus has planned, Kiro's in danger. We're hard to kill, but not Kiro. Lazarus will want that prophecy off the table."

"Why?" Yuri asks. "Why concern himself over superstition? Lazarus, he is not one of the old ones from the mountains, is he? Tito said he grew up here, no older than forty. Maybe he does not believe—"

"It doesn't matter if he believes," I say. "He knows other people do. The Dragusha brothers rising together is as embedded into the community as a fable."

"Like the tortoise and the hare or some shit," Tito says. "Trust me. The clans are all about the fucking stories. The sleeping Dragusha king. The three brothers prevailing. I knew about that shit when I was ten."

"Psychological edge," I say.

Yuri nods. He gets that. Crime is more about psychological edge than any other business.

The three brothers together will rule. Fucking Miss Ipa with her weathered brown skin and nails like red arrows. *Apart they are weak, together they are strong. They will take everything.*

The bitch has been dead for years now, but the damage was done with that prophecy of hers. It could be why Aldo Nikolla split apart my family in the first place. He wanted it to be him, and not me and my brothers.

"The brothers together," Viktor grumbles. "We brothers might be together today if not for her."

"If Lazarus could kill a Dragusha brother and take out the old man in the same week, that would give him much credibility. He will more easily unite the clan."

I look at the clock. Ninety minutes before the old man arrives at the restaurant. "They'll never expect me to show up there," I say.

Tito groans. "To strike twice at the heart of his territory—"

I hold up my hand to silence him. I don't want him to say not to go. I don't want him to say it's too dangerous. "We have his daughter as insurance," I say.

"But if Lazarus's there, us having Mira won't matter. Lazarus doesn't give a shit about Mira. He'll just kill you instead. Killing you is even better than killing Kiro."

Too true.

"If we courier the finger..."

"I need to be there. I need to press him. I know his weaknesses. I know his people."

"I'll back you," Viktor says.

I give him a look. If the worst happens, he needs to stay alive to find Kiro. "I'm the one who was studying him all these years."

"How will we know if Lazarus's people are in there?" Viktor asks. "We don't know Lazarus's people anymore."

Viktor has a point. Konstantin and I focused on Aldo, not Lazarus.

Viktor continues, "We need to know who's with him. I will not let you walk into a nest of Lazarus's guys. I'll put you in the trunk if I have to."

"No, you're right," I say. "We need to know what people are Lazarus's. We need insight that's more recent than those old photos."

Viktor tips his head, waits for me to say it.

"Right. Mira." I turn and limp toward her room.

"Are you fucking kidding me?" Currie's up and blocking my way. "She needs to sleep."

I take his shirt in my fist. "And now I'm going to wake her up."

He sees I'm serious. He growls and moves aside.

I head down the hall, hand on the wall. I open the door and go into the darkened bedroom. She's lying there pretty much how I left her, perfectly tucked in. I sit next to her on the bed and rest my hand on her shoulder. "Mira," I whisper. Nothing. I shake her. "Mira."

"Huh," she says.

"Wake up." I shake her again.

She resists, but I shake her and call her name a few more times, and that does it. She rubs her eyes and regards me woozily. Her sleepy eyes widen in horror the moment she remembers. "My finger!"

"Shhh. Nothing happened—you're okay." I tighten my grasp on her arm.

She begins to shake. She's all fucked up and crying now. Fucking drugged out of her mind.

"You're okay. I'm here." Which is the laughable phrase of the century when you think about it. I nudge her. "Move over." She doesn't comply, so I really shove her, and finally there's room. I get in and wrap my arm around her. "Shh."

She begins to sob. Fuck. I just hold her tight, wishing I could swallow up all that sadness for her. Eventually she quiets down.

"I need to ask you some questions. About Lazarus."

"Huh?"

"Who does he like? Who does he trust these days?"

"I dongeddit."

"Who is a friend to Lazarus?" I have an idea, but I need it from her. "Who does he like best? Of all the Black Lion clan guys. Who did he show up to dinner with on Friday?"

"His brother," she says. "Ioannis."

We know that, of course. Lazarus loves his brother. "Who else?"

"Ferit. Best buds." The way she says it, it sounds like *best buzz.*

"Okay," I say. "That's good."

She seems to drift off a bit. "Hey." I shake her. "You were telling me about Lazarus's buddies."

"Right," she whispers.

"Who does he ride with places? Besides Ioannis? Who did he hang around with at the ribbon-cutting ceremony?"

"Engjell. Like the four musketeers."

"Good," I say. "That's good. Who else? Who owes him?"

"Why?"

"The bastard wants to know, baby."

She laughs softly and suddenly gives me a stream of names. It's like she's hypnotized or something and the names are just falling out of her. Her names are helpful. I grab my phone from my pocket and text to Konstantin. He needs to know what's happening. He'll have photos of the guys. I'm thinking Viktor can send a team of advance people in to the restaurant as off-the-street diners. They'll be on the lookout. A layer of protection for when I go in, and they can warn me if Lazarus has filled the place with his people.

I could see Bloody Lazarus going after me and letting Aldo get caught in the crossfire. That would be a brilliant plan. Two birds with one firefight.

"Aleksio?" She turns to me. I touch her nose with the phone. She tries to grab it, but her reflexes are fucked from the drugs.

"You should sleep," I say.

"Aleksio," she whispers. I know what's going to come now—it's in the air between us. It's in her eyes. She splays her hand against my chest.

"No, baby."

"I liked it like that."

My blood races. "Mira—" I've never wanted a woman so much. But no. Not like this.

She reaches down between us; I grab her hand before she can make contact with my cock. "No, baby."

"Please," she begs. "Let's do it that way again."

"You're going to sleep." I pull her tight. "That's an order."

"Let's be messed up," she whispers into my ear.

Lust whooshes through me. It's not like we don't have the time. An hour or more before dear old Dad shows up at Agronika. But I won't do it.

She turns back around in my arms, facing away. I move to keep my straining erection away from her perfect ass.

"What was the question? Did you have a question?"

"You already answered the question. We're good."

Her breath gets even, and I think she's sleeping. But then she sighs peacefully. I stroke her hair, wondering what it's like to feel that peace. All those years watching her from afar, wondering what it was like.

Konstantin made me into a killer, yeah, blowing guys' heads off while they begged, while they cried, while they went about their days. He made me into a merciless weapon sharpened for battle with old man Nikolla, but he never succeeded in making me hate her.

Mira was the untouchable goddess. In a way, it seemed right that she was in the world. Like it's right that there are stars or the sun or something. When you're a killer, ugly and bloody and beaten to shit, you don't hate the stars for shining. You're glad there's something good out there.

I pull her closer. "Help me remember what it was like to feel safe," I whisper before I can think better of it. "Just an endless green lawn. Soldiers under command to die for you. What was it like?"

"I don't know," she says. "You were there. Don't you remember?"

"I remember the fact of it, but I can't remember that feeling. It got covered over."

She doesn't move. After a long silence, she says, "I don't know."

"You have to know. Try, baby."

"It's a hard question."

"Try."

"What?"

"What it was like to feel safe?" I ask, frustrated. I picture her at birthday parties, picnics on the grounds. The boating outings. Plush, wall-to-wall safety.

I know I can't have that feeling, that goodness, but I had it once.

It took Konstantin quite a few years to figure out I looked at the photos she appeared in way more than the others. When he figured that out, he hit me so hard he nearly knocked my teeth out. That was back when he was bigger than me, of course. Back when he was in charge of things.

I think she's gone to sleep, but then she speaks again. "It's a hard question. Like if I asked you, what does it feel like to be alive? How can you answer if you've never been anything else? Safety…" She drifts off. "I don't know."

She doesn't know.

Her answer is a fist slammed into my gut—safety is not knowing what safety is.

It's the one answer I never imagined, but it's obvious now. You can't describe what safety is when it's all you've known. When you've never been moved in the middle of the night because of a crackle on the phone or a light in the alley. You never had an itchy fake mole put on your chin or got whacked upside the head for trying to pick it off. Or getting dropped in the middle of unfriendly street gang territory and made to fight your way out.

Safety is going to the same school every year with the same name. Safety is looking forward to going to sleep. Safety is walking down the street without having to worry that someone back there knows who you are. Safety is never thinking about safety or knowing what it is.

You'd think with all that safety she'd be weak, but she's strong.

I pull her closer. Is that where her optimism comes from? If she lost her safety, would the optimism go with it? I don't know whether I had optimism back then, but I definitely don't have it anymore.

"Do you feel safe now?" I ask.

"Yes," she whispers. Her breathing evens out, but then it changes, gets ragged. "Except he killed your parents." She's getting agitated. "He killed them. And the babies..."

"It's okay now," I whisper.

"We're supposed to have each other's backs," she says.

I hold her more tightly. Even in her fucked-up state, she cares about rules. She wants people to be good. She wants to think we're all not animals.

She says, "My mom had my back, but she died."

"I know," I whisper.

"Got cancer." She's doing that uneven breathing again. Stupid of me to not think about that. Like I'm the only person who lost something.

"I bet she loved you a lot," I say. "I bet she loved you so much."

"Yeah." I can feel her calming.

"Remind me what she was like." I remember, but that's not the point.

"She liked old things."

"And?" I shouldn't be getting her to talk right now. I should be getting her to sleep.

"She was beautiful," she whispers. "She laughed a lot. Picnics. She liked ABBA. Scrabble. Badminton down by the lake."

"A prissy sport."

I can see from the shape of her cheek that she's smiling. "*You* played it."

"Maybe once."

"The birdie in the air and Mom laughing. And Sundays..." She trails off. "Umbrellas in the sun Sundays. Tea party. With cubes of sugar. Flowers on them. What was the question?" she says after a while.

She's drifting off, but I don't want her to go.

I put my face to her sweet-smelling hair. "Up in the playroom. The happy baby animals? Are they still painted on the wall?"

Her chest moves. I suppose it's a sort of laugh.

"Are the baby animals still up there? In that secret cubby?"

"You know?"

"I lived there, remember?"

Another jerk of her chest. Laughing, crying. It sort of doesn't matter. She won't remember any of this tomorrow, that's the idea I'm getting. "The happy baby animals," she says. "Yeah. Their faces are lit by the sun. But only in the winter."

The shock of the memory goes through me—the sun illuminating those stupid painted faces in the dead of winter. I'd forgotten about that.

"Sunny faces. But then you ruined happy baby animals for me," she says. "Aleksio—I feel like I'm spinning."

"I've got you." I hold her tighter. It's bad what I'm doing—I might as well be fucking her now, because I'm violating her emotionally, yanking out her memories. "And the Chris-Craft? That big old boat. Remember?"

"Picnics in the Chris-Craft," she mumbles.

"What did the engine sound like? Do you remember?"

She's gone quiet. I shake her. "Tell me, Mira. The Chris-Craft."

"Gargly. Gargles." She lowers her voice, sounding drunk. "Burgh-burgh-burgh."

"That's pretty good." I fucking loved that big, powerful Chris-Craft engine. I loved those baby animal paintings too.

Until the end.

Until Konstantin held me inside that little cubby with his cigar-scented vice-grip of a hand clapped over my mouth to keep me from screaming, holding me tight as Nikolla slaughtered my parents while my baby brothers screamed. I saw it all in the window reflection. The fast way Nikolla moved against my parents, made sluggish with drugs. Darting for my mom. A dog going for a throat.

The baby animals are where I kept my gaze in the hour after the screams died out.

It was in the wine, Konstantin told me later. Konstantin had been drugged, too. An unarmed hit man past his prime, veteran of the Kosovo war, too drugged up to fight a killer like Nikolla and a twenty-year-old Lazarus. Konstantin did the only thing he could—he grabbed me and hid me in a child-sized cubby Nikolla wouldn't know about, a nook in the wall, an accident of architecture made functional for kids.

Looking back, I sometimes marvel that Konstantin was able to keep hold of me for so many hours with the way I squirmed. I wanted to get to them. My mom and dad were right out there. They'd taken my brothers away in a sack, but Mom and Dad were right there. Motionless. I couldn't see them any longer in the window reflection, but I knew they were there.

It was the dead of night when we finally stole out of there. The first day of my new life of being shaped into a machine of pure revenge and violence.

She begins to sob, silently now.

"Shhh," I say, stroking her hair, but she's inconsolable. My questions dredged up some essential kernel of sadness. "Stop it," I say.

She won't.

It rips something out of me to hear her crying. It's my fault, bringing her into this hell with me. Making her almost lose her finger. "It's okay, baby," I whisper. "You're okay now."

I never cried for them. Much. Old Konstantin would hit me when I did. It wasn't malicious, really, he just wanted me to channel all of that emotion into training and revenge. He was doing the best he could, and I learned to bottle up my feelings. Now, lying here with Mira half-unconscious, the girl from my opposite world, I feel like that bottle's cracking and shattering.

When I'm sure she's sleeping, I untangle myself from her and get off the bed, disgusted by myself.

Fucking happy baby animals. Fuck them.

I text Konstantin to send over pictures of Lazarus's people, then I get myself a vodka in the kitchen. Viktor and I have been rubbing off on each other in the past year since we hooked back up. Or more like corrupting each other.

He's at the table with Currie. "You get the intel?"

"Yup. Konstantin is sending pictures." I slam it back. "I'm glad I blew up that fucking house."

"We leave in ten minutes," he says. "Tito drops you. Currie stays with Mira. I'm out there circulating with my team. The minute you get a lead, you send word and we're on it. Okay?"

"You see what she did?" I tip my head toward the lawn.

"Yeah, I saw what she did, *brat*."

"Fuck. With that gun?" I limp over to the table.

"For fuck's sake, Aleksio," Currie says. "You need X-rays."

"Just wrap it."

"You need real attention. Don't blow it off—you're screwed for life if it doesn't heal right."

I start pulling off my sock. The thing is so swollen, it looks like something from outer space. "All I need is for you to get it stabilized."

"You really want to let your ankle heal wrong?" Currie demands. "Is that what you want? Because keeping yourself fucked-up is a bullshit way to atone for your survivor's guilt."

I push him against the wall. "Are you suddenly a psychoanalyst? Because here all this time I thought you were a fucking EMT who has a Mustang and a second house instead of being six feet under." Which is where he'd be without our help on his gambling bills.

He's looking at me scared. I'm dimly aware of Viktor trying to talk me down.

"Answer! Are you our EMT or what?"

"I'm your EMT."

"Then don't you be fucking psychoanalyzing me. I'm fucked up enough to rip your face off if it starts annoying me. Will that atone?"

"Chill the fuck out," Viktor says, pulling me off.

I get in Viktor's face, put him against the wall instead. Mira being fucked up is fucking me up.

"Save the anger," Viktor says.

I sit. "Wrap it enough to get me through, then I'll think about the X-ray." Currie starts on the wrap, being his professional, diligent self.

"Sorry," I say.

"I get it," he says. "I understand."

The guys come with the finger and the blood. It's from an older woman, and it's frozen. It doesn't look right until Currie puts it in the microwave with a bowl of water to hydrate it. I make a mental note never to use that microwave again. We'll sell the house eventually.

I watch the clock while Viktor and his guys seal the finger in a plastic baggie with some blood they got from fuck knows where. They nestle it in an eyeglass case with the ring on top.

Konstantin comes through with instructions for Viktor's men. They're to go into the restaurant ahead of me and take pictures, and he'll vet the patrons himself. I get on the phone with him and thank him. He's not happy about any of this.

"We're gonna bring Kiro home safe, and then we'll take what's ours in a tornado of fucking bullets—you watch." I'm channeling Mira's optimism now, not that she'd approve. "The brothers together will take the whole thing back."

Five minutes until we leave. Hit Aldo and his men at the heart—exactly what Konstantin didn't want us to do until we were all three together. In spite of what I said to him, I know perfectly well this thing is going downhill fast.

I wince as Currie wraps my taped ankle with a soft, stretchy bandage. Viktor's texting, marshaling the troops.

Konstantin's health isn't so good, but he's set up in a posh assisted-living apartment with a part-time nurse to help him out. I'm talking very posh, out in the western suburbs. Don't let anyone tell you crime doesn't pay.

I have this fucked-up idea of us all together at Christmas, the three of us and Konstantin. To give Konstantin a Christmas with all of us there.

***

Ten on a Sunday night, and Agronika is pretty packed.

It's a dark place, and not for any lack of lights—there are plenty of them around, but they glow instead of actually lighting the place up. Same with the candles on the white-cloth-covered tables. More glowing. Lots of dark wood paneling. Classic Albanian mob. Like an old ship.

I stroll past the soft-talking diners and steaming plates of roasted lamb and stuffed peppers, air rich with the aroma of warm bread with an edge of pickled cabbage.

I straighten my cuffs and move through, smooth and strong like my ankle isn't crunching in on itself. I feel enemy eyes on me.

It's laid out in an L with the front being mostly public, but once you turn the corner, you're in Aldo Nikolla territory.

Walking in here goes against every survival instinct I have. All those years of running from these faces. The target on my back feels like it's lit in neon.

Viktor's guys are at the elbow of the L. They've been in contact with Konstantin, letting him see the place through the eyes of their iPhones. So far none of Lazarus's guys have shown. I don't make eye contact as I go past; I just tip my head in acknowledgement.

The buzz in the air fades as soon as his soldiers see. I can feel the fucking hands reaching under the tables, guns coming out of holsters. Fingers on triggers.

The temperature seems to drop ten degrees.

Going in there is suicide, Tito said.

I'm completely vulnerable. Not even a vest, not that it would help. These guys shoot for the head.

Still I go, heart thundering.

All these men know about the million bucks on my head. It'll just take one guy who doesn't know I have Mira under wraps to go for it. One guy who doesn't know I have that leverage.

Something inside me twists when I see him at a rounded booth in the corner with a few of his minor guys. My fingers stretch and curl with the deep need to tear him apart, muscle from tendon, tendon from bone, sinew by sinew.

That need is so much at the surface right now, it scares me a little bit.

I can still hear the way my mom screamed just before he killed her. My dad made no sound—he was fighting Nikolla and Lazarus to the end, but my mom screamed until Aldo cut off her scream with a hunting blade, turned it into a guttural sound I'll never forget. And then that thump on the floor. And then the sound of Nikolla puking. My brothers' cries getting faint as they were taken off.

My skin feels clammy. It's these soldiers around me. I can feel their fear and loathing. I get that tickle on my back that tells me I'm being sighted.

I shove the feeling back and smile when he catches sight of me. The old man looks stunned. Yeah, it really is insane that I'm walking in here, strides long and lazy. I reach down and adjust my cock, taunting him.

He rises up out of that booth like somebody yanked a string on the top of his head.

I sneer, like I have nothing to fear.

Nikolla grabs me and pushes me to a wooden post between booths. I allow it, laughing. The laugh is for him, but a little bit for Viktor's guys, who are keeping watch. "What're you gonna do, old man?" I say.

His eyes bulge a little, the way old man eyes sometimes do. His cheeks are red, and his breath smells like scotch.

"Got something for you," I say. "It's from Mira."

"You didn't—"

"You want it or not?"

He's trying to hide the dread, but it's not so easy because he doesn't know what I'm made of. He's wondering right about now how bad a motherfucker I am. Would Aleksio Dragusha chop up his little girl? Worse?

A lot of guys say shit like that, but they don't follow through. And their stock goes down because of it. You need to follow through on your threats in this business. It's a matter of loyalty, dignity, the honor of your word.

"Well, do you want it?"

He studies my face.

I smile. I want him to hurt so bad it makes me crazy. It's a minor miracle my hands aren't around his throat.

A few of his guys have closed around us, waiting for his orders. It's unnerving, being alone, surrounded by so many guys itching to kill me, face to face with Nikolla.

"Little privacy," I say, cool as I can manage it.

He nods, and the guys ease off.

He lets go of my shirt and backs off, motioning me to a booth off to the side. I go, and he follows. We sit across from each other in the booth.

I reach in my jacket pocket, pull out the eyeglass case, and slide it across the table. "Hint," I say. "It's not eyeglasses."

He creaks open the lid. The ring is on top, the finger in a baggie wrapped in a cloth underneath. He takes out the ring and studies it. I wait, curious what he'll do with the finger, how he'll hide his blood aversion. He tips the case toward himself, rustling the cloth, pretending to look at it, just like Mira said he would. Then he snaps it shut, clearly shaken. The ring sold it like Mira said it would.

He holds the ring in the tips of two fat fingers. "I won't kill you fast," he manages. "I will hunt you. I will find you. I will kill you slow."

"Yeah, well, until then you need to be thinking how bad you don't want another gift like this."

He studies my eyes.

I sit back. "Service is slow here."

"What do you want?"

"I'd take a vodka," I say. "Up."

It's not what he meant, but I could use a drink. He motions over a waiter and orders.

"Let me talk to her."

"She's sleeping," I say. "It's been a busy day."

Silence. "You did it."

"Now you need to give us everything on Kiro. If you love your daughter, you want me to get to him first."

He waits a bit. Then, "Fine."

I'm instantly suspicious. It's too easy.

"Ligne has a drinking buddy, Archie Vega," Nikolla continues. "He offloads some of his work to Vega, but he doesn't want me to know. He confides in Vega. And Vega is the type...let's just say he likes to know things. He collects secrets and blackmails people. I've been thinking about taking him out. I don't know that he knows, but I could see him getting it in his pocket. I've always thought if I needed to find your brother, it would be Archie Vega who could point me."

"Address."

He takes out his phone.

"Easy. Show me."

He looks it up and lets me read it. Archie Vega. Contact info. I pocket his phone and text Viktor the details. Viktor will be on him in ten minutes.

The waitress brings raki for him, and a vodka for me.

"You couldn't have told me that in the first place? What's wrong with you?"

The old man sips his drink. All the old generation, they drink raki—a licorice-y cross between grappa and ouzo.

"I'll sit here for a while and make sure you don't warn Vega." I down the rest of my drink, then I turn the glass around and around on the table.

Something feels wrong. This is all going too easy.

CHAPTER THIRTEEN

Viktor

Here is a secret about the orphanage that nobody will ever tell you: When you're in one, you always hope that you were not wanted. An accidental pregnancy.

Because the alternative is that you are a product of violence, torture, horror. That you are ugly and hated from birth. That's what you always believe, though.

When the families pass you over, you think they see your ugly heart. It's worse when they take you home only to return you. Moving into the Bratva, I became an overachiever in violence. It was a way to get at least somebody to want me.

Now with that talent I help my brothers.

We find Archie Vega is alone in his house, on his Exercycle watching the eleven o'clock news. The TV and the Exercycle keep him from hearing us, and when he sees us, it keeps him from running. He nearly falls off it, trying to get away. I pull him off.

Yuri and Mischa hold him at gunpoint while I ask about Kiro. He tells us he knows nothing. I see in his eyes that this is a lie.

"You want to tell us," I say simply.

He shakes his head. *Ta quift bota nanen.*

Tito translates: "May the world fuck your mother."

"Okay then." We tie him to a weightlifting bench. It's metal. Good and strong. "I will fuck you up then." I cut his clothes off him. He needs to feel vulnerable. I need the information fast. To get Aleksio out of that restaurant.

The day Aleksio arrived changed my world. A blood brother.

I belonged. I wanted to drop to my knees and weep there in the garage when Aleksio told me I had a family that actually wanted me. He was so angry with for what I did to Mira. I didn't think he'd be so angry. It fucked me up, as Aleksio would say. But I will earn back his love.

I wish I could have walked in there with him. Of course it would be madness for us both to go in there. If it gets bloody, the other must remain for Kiro. Still, I hate it. If Aleksio dies, I want to be by his side, dying with him. It would be a privilege to die with Aleksio.

I press the knife to Vega's belly. I feel the clock ticking, but I smile and laugh. You never let them know you're in a hurry. It gives them power.

Easy things first. What he ate for dinner. Make him visualize the inside of his belly, and what I will do. Pirogi, he tells me. With white fefferoni. I send Mischa to check his dinner dishes.

Now he begins to freak. Why is this so important? Why do we want to check his dinner dishes? I wait, as though bored. Scaring a man is in the crazy fucking details.

Mischa comes back and confirms it all—in Russian—and I smile. "Okay, then."

Just like that he calls his maid. An old woman with a head scarf. She was hiding. She leads Mischa to a box of paper files. She says Lazarus got jpeg images of these files. These are the originals.

I find the file about Kiro. A Worland file, like the ones we stole, except nothing is blacked out. An address.

I text Aleksio. I have the address. But so does Lazarus. Yuri drives like hell back while I go through the box. There are other files, too. Lots of secrets here.

CHAPTER FOURTEEN

Aleksio

Aldo Nikolla has finished his raki, and a new one arrives without his having to ask for it. He lowers his head, voice gravelly. "You want to kill me so bad it hurts," he says. "You could, you know. You have everything I have on Kiro. You might get out alive. I'm guessing you have guys in here, right?" he looks around and then back at me with curiosity. "Why don't you go ahead and try it?"

Because I promised Mira. Not like I'll say that. I turn my tumbler of vodka on the napkin. Something feels wrong. This is all going too easy.

"Is it Lazarus? You don't want Lazarus in charge?" He picks up his newly arrived raki, cloudy liquid in a slim glass. "A lot of men are scared of Lazarus running the show. But you're not scared, are you? You don't scare. Konstantin would've beat that right out of you."

"Say his name again and I'll take one of *your* fingers."

"There it is. Loyalty. Sentimentality. Just like your father."

179

I know what he's doing—trying to unbalance me. We're in a standoff, here in this booth. Neither of us can move on the other. I give him a cool stare. "You don't know shit about me, old man."

A kid comes by with a tray of cigarettes, and Nikolla takes one. Chicago has laws about smoking indoors, but Agronika is another world.

"You have a CEO strategy, but inside you're volatile and emotional, just like him. He played the hard guy, but emotions made him a puppet. Emotions made him *my* puppet." He lights up.

My face burns. "You're calling my father sentimental for trusting his supposed best friend and partner? You are *I pa besa,* old man." Without loyalty, without honor.

It's the worst thing you can say to a man like Aldo. And in his case, it's true.

He gives no sign of caring. He barely seems to have heard. Suspicious movement to my side. I don't like it.

"Your father never saw me coming. Never imagined. That's how I got the drop on him. He didn't think strategy; he ruled by his heart. He let his emotions cloud his mind."

Stay cool, don't take the bait, I think through the surge of heat that moves through me. I could make him mad, too. I could tell him how Mira's lips felt, wrapped around my cock. But, sentimental fucker that I am, I don't. I protect her. The motherfucker's right.

He looks up, cold dark eyes under bushy brows. "You really think you will find Kiro alive?"

My heart pounds. I feel him. I know he's still alive.

"The foolishness of you moving on me before you have Kiro. The three brothers together would have given you credibility. I have a little saying: 'You only have to shoot when your threats don't work.' With Kiro, your threats would have been enough. But you couldn't wait. Had to ride out to find your brother. Konstantin wouldn't have allowed it, but he's old now, isn't he? You're running the show now."

"I will be."

"*Pah*. You Dragushas. You're easy. Your father was easy. Your mom was even easier."

I power through the surge of rage.

"She lay there after with her mouth open. Eyes open. Nobody to close them—that's what she was worth."

"I closed them," I say.

This surprises him.

"You didn't know? I was there the whole time. Konstantin pulled me into a nook by the window. We saw what you and Lazarus did. We waited until the house was clear. You were searching the grounds for us. So stupid of you not to take a little extra time. I went to her, and I closed her eyes and her mouth. And my father's. And I vowed to destroy you. You're already gone, old man."

I say it calmly, and I make it sound as if the vow was the huge thing, and not creeping around the blood and touching their eyelids like that. I trembled when I closed my mother's eyes, wanting to throw myself down next to her. And then pushing their lips back together, as is the custom. Konstantin made me do it. My father's lips wouldn't stay together, and I nearly lost it—it's always the little things that put you over. Maybe Konstantin sensed it. He forced my father's jaw closed for me and we got out.

"Why not kill me? You're so white hot, you can't even think straight right now, can you, Aleksio? Why not go for me?"

"You think I won't?"

He tips his head like he's just getting something. "Did she make you promise not to off me?"

Shit.

He smiles. "And you fucking went for it? You can't let her take advantage like that."

"Advantage? Jesus, you're her father, and you let us cut her finger off. Why not just tell me about Vega on the lawn? You wait until we start with body parts? Don't you give a fuck about your daughter?"

"What do I have right now?"

"What?"

"What do I have?" he asks. "Look where I am in this game we're playing. Let's compare ledgers, shall we? I bought the time I needed, time to find Kiro myself. Lazarus'll beat you to your brother and put this prophecy to rest. What's more, I'm free. I'm safe from you, aren't I? And what do you have? You took Mira's finger. Oh, I very much give a fuck about her. I wasn't playacting out on the lawn, and I *will* make you pay."

"Your daughter's finger—"

"I didn't think you'd do it." He shrugs.

"We threatened to kill her if Kiro died."

"Please," he says smugly. "You won't kill her. When Viktor said that, I knew instantly you hadn't discussed it. More than that, I remember you and Mira together as children—probably more than you remember. You two had a rare kind of bond. I knew the more time you spent time together, the safer she would be. Anyway, you're like your father—I see him in you. Ruled by emotions. Soft when it comes to innocents. Mira's finger. I'm impressed—"

"How the fuck do you look yourself in the mirror?"

"I'm not the fuckup here, Aleksio. You moved on me without the psychological advantage of the three brothers united. You put sentiment above strategy, and it told me how to play you. And you're going to walk out of here leaving me alive because you still think you have a chance to rescue Kiro and you won't leave Viktor to decide Mira's fate. Lazarus is going to kill Kiro if he hasn't already, then we'll take you and Viktor and all his worthless Bratva orphans, and Mira will go back to her life. You'll just be a sad and hated memory."

My heart pounds. The text comes in. Viktor. He has the address. I am full of rage—he's right. I feel Kiro in my heart. I love him. I know he's still alive—he has to be. And I'll protect him, and I'll protect Mira, too.

The old man's eyes sparkle. "You can't win this war. You'll go down just like your daddy."

I stand and slip my phone in my pocket. "What do I have?"

Aldo narrows his eyes. He doesn't get the question.

"You asked me what you have. Your fucking ledger comparison and all that. Well, I'll tell you what I have. I have love, and I have honor. I have a family I'll die for right on this fucking spot."

He looks up at me with his poker face, and I don't give a fuck what he's hiding. Because for the first time since that bloody night, he seems small.

I turn and walk out.

***

Viktor drives like a maniac back out to the Stonybrook place.

"You got out alive, *brat*," he says. It's really all there is to say. We're both freaked about Kiro.

We have a name and an address for Kiro's adoptive family. The Knutson family in Glenpines Grove, a couple of hours northwest. Soybean and river country, that's where the family that got Kiro lives. Being that Kiro is twenty, it's unlikely he's living there, but you never know.

If he's there, he could be dead.

Because of me. My fucking sentimentality. Wanting my family.

The plan is to grab every piece of weaponry we have and get the hell out there and hope Bloody Lazarus doesn't have too much of a head start.

We argue about whether to bring Mira along. Viktor wants her stowed in the house, but it's too dangerous there.

"She is trouble, *brat*."

"She comes." I try to ignore old Nikolla's words ringing in my head—*you put sentiment above strategy.*

"You think because she called out for you, that she loves you? That she's yours? That there is something between you?"

I watch the strip malls blur by.

"She was on drugs," Viktor says. "Drugged out of her mind. She would've called for the devil himself if she thought it would keep her finger attached."

"How about you concentrate on getting us there."

"You kidnapped her and fucked her face. You think she would go anywhere with you willingly?"

I have nothing to say to that. She has every reason to hate me, but she's mine. The thought doesn't even surprise me. She's mine. She always was. And I'll probably do some more things she hates today, but she'll still be mine.

"We found something else interesting. Look in the back seat. Look at this file that I got from Vega."

I twist around and grab the manila file folder. Official seal. State of Illinois Medical Examiner's office. The tab says "Nikolla, Vanessa." Mira's mother. "What the hell?" I open it up, and I see. It's from the coroner.

"Mira's mother. What does this have to do with Kiro?"

"It has nothing to do with Kiro," Viktor says. "Look inside. They say her mother died of cancer, don't they?"

"Yeah, they say that. Mira was there." I page through. It's medical stuff. "Cause of death...what is this?" It says homicide.

"Pharmaceutical toxin. Untraceable. Interesting, no? That was the original report. She didn't die of cancer—she was murdered. Aldo Nikolla must've paid a small fortune to get her illness reported as cancer. To make this the official story. The original coroner, you see his report there. Archie Vega was holding it for blackmail. His box full of secrets. Konstantin will enjoy this box."

"Aldo Nikolla killed his wife? Mira's mother?"

Viktor takes a corner without slowing down. "Mira will not like it, I think."

I close the folder. "We can't show her. It's too much. We'll hold onto it."

"Why not show her? Think how this hurts the old man."

"Showing her hurts her more than him." I say. "And it won't get us Kiro."

He eyes me darkly. I eye him back.

"Do you still feel him alive, *brat*?" he asks. There's so much vulnerability in his voice, it kills me.

"I still feel him alive."

CHAPTER FIFTEEN

Mira

I'm lying there in the darkness in the middle of the night, trying to deal with this new information about Dad. I can't fit this information into my heart any more than I can fit a square peg into a round hole.

He slaughtered his closest friends! His mentor and Mrs. Dragusha, an innocent mother. Sent away the boys, hunted Aleksio. A little kid!

And Aleksio went to the restaurant, walking right into the middle of his stronghold. It's crazy, even with me as a hostage.

I slide my palm up the side of the bed where he was, up and down. It feels like he was just here, holding me, talking to me. I felt safe and good in his arms. Like coming home.

Which is crazy, because this shit is everything I've ever tried to escape. It's like I'm being sucked into some sort of enchanted looking glass, but this is not my real life. And things are going to get bloody.

Aleksio and Viktor are good for their promises—I know it in my bones. Aleksio said he wouldn't kill Dad, and I know they'll uphold that promise. But what will Dad do?

And what will Viktor do? He promised to kill me if Kiro doesn't turn up alive. If Kiro is dead, Viktor will need to uphold that promise. He'll need to. And Aleksio will stop him.

Either way, I have to get out of here.

I can't go back to the Advocacy Center. It will be too easy to poke holes in the fake international shopping Mira persona. That persona works only if nobody's kicking the tires. As long as Dad has the kind of power that he has, I'll always be in danger. The only weak link he has.

I've decided to flee to an old high school friend's family cabin near the Mississippi. We used to sneak out there for the weekend. I know where the key is hidden. Nobody would find me. Not Aleksio, not Viktor, not Dad's people.

I go back to the door and put my ear to the wood. I find myself hoping that the brothers unite and fulfill the prophecy. Take back the Black Lion clan. Aleksio on the throne.

My mind goes to Aleksio on the couch in the hotel room and the way he focused down at me. The way he handled me. The hot brutality of it.

Stop it! I rub my aching head. I can't let myself be sucked into this mafia drama. I have to save myself.

They come back in a frenzy a while later. It's the sound of trouble. Relief whooshes out of me when Aleksio walks back in.

He reaches out, as if to touch my cheek. "Don't worry, dear old Dad's still breathing. We have a lead on Kiro."

My belly turns. "Dad was holding back? No…"

"We didn't get the address from your dad directly," he says. "He had an idea where we could look."

"In other words, he withheld information."

"Don't take it…"

"*Personally*? That Dad played chicken with me? Tell me that's not what you were about to say. I mean, don't take it personally that Viktor almost sawed off my finger, and that was a gamble Dad was willing to take?" I wrap my arms around myself. "We're supposed to have each other's backs."

"He didn't think we'd really do it."

"Is that supposed to be consolation?"

"It's a shitty consolation." Aleksio goes to the dresser and throws me a white shirt and an orange skirt with pink flowers. Bright and summery, the opposite of him. There's nothing more to say. He knows it. I know it.

Tito comes in and tosses him a holster. "Saddle up, *brat*," he says, using the name for him that Viktor often uses. Pronouncing it all Russian-sounding.

Five minutes later, we're in the car. It's around two in the morning, judging from the dashboard clock.

I'm in the dark back seat with Aleksio. Tito's riding shotgun, and Viktor drives. His face is really beaten up, one eye so swollen I'm sure he can't see through it. He pulls out his flask and takes a swig of vodka.

I make sure my seatbelt is snug. There's only the waist kind, unfortunately. It's an old Jaguar, and you can tell it's been modified. Probably bulletproof. We're in a convoy of guys, a Hummer up ahead, a van behind.

Aleksio's focused on his phone. In his own world. Looking for his brother all this time and now we're nearing the moment of truth. He's doing a lot of mindless scrolling. Now and then he looks out the window. He's worried. They seem to think Lazarus might be ahead of them.

Eventually we're out of the city on a two-lane road. The terrain is darker. Signs less frequent. He clicks off his phone, but he still looks at it. A blank, black screen. "I know he's still alive."

I say, "He's lucky to have you."

Aleksio turns away, staring out at where our headlights flash on the edge of rows of crops. He presents such a good front, but there's so much underneath with him. "Unless Lazarus got there first. Because of us. Because of me."

"No, even then he's lucky to have you."

More phone staring. Viktor and Tito converse softly in the front. It's as if Aleksio and I are in another world. Even when we were kids, we managed to make our own world.

"You think he's lucky to have us even if us looking for him is what gets him killed? Because I'm not so sure about that."

"You're risking your life to find him," I say. "Don't you think he'd risk his to find you?"

"It's a choice that should be his."

"I would risk my life to see my mother again," I say.

He nods solemnly, eyes averted.

"And you're risking your life to find Kiro," I continue. "Why wouldn't he want the same?"

He takes my hand, touches the finger Viktor wanted to chop off. "I'm so sorry for what Viktor did. And your ring."

"Who cares?" I say.

He keeps my hand, there in the dark back seat. I slide nearer to him. He pulls in a breath as I lay my head on his shoulder.

"I think you might be getting Stockholm syndrome."

"Oh, Aleksio." I enjoy his nearness. I found him again, and I'll lose him again. "What do you think Kiro will be like?"

"I have no clue. Maybe like Viktor and me, but maybe not. He's twenty. He could be in college with a chance at a nice life. He may be going to school to be a cop, who knows. I don't need him to join Viktor and me. I don't care. I'll love him no matter what."

"You and Viktor hit it off right away, I bet."

"Yeah."

"You look alike," I prod.

"Yeah," Aleksio says. "The guys at the place he was working in Moscow, they all knew the minute I walked in that I was his brother. We have the same sense of humor, too. We were both of us in gangs a world apart. Separated at birth, but still like we share a brain."

"A year ago? That's when you found him?"

"Yeah. It was magic, how we linked right up. We were instantly stronger together. I found my *brother*, you know?"

A passing car strobes our cocoon of a backseat. "I can't even imagine that," I say.

"It blew my mind. Especially because I always thought Kiro and Viktor were dead. I think I felt every emotion in the world." He lowers his voice, speaking only to me. "Kiro has to be alive."

"He was a sweet little baby."

After a span of silence, he says, "Tell me what you remember." His tone breaks my heart.

"Just snapshots. Kiro with his little lick of brown hair. Kiro waving his fists all around. Always so alert. Smiling."

Aleksio's trying not to grin, but I can tell he likes that I remember. "He was...active."

"A crazy bundle of energy."

Aleksio's love for a brother he hasn't seen for two decades is beautiful. "Yeah. Flying fists. Just like his big brother, huh?" His smile fades then, and he stares darkly into the distance. "I promised my mother I'd protect him. I'll give anything to see him safe."

"Why do you have to give up anything? Maybe you'll find him, and he'll be thrilled to meet you and you guys...I don't know, go out for a beer or something."

He looks at me like I'm an alien.

"What? That could happen. You think everything has to be hard. You think you have to give a pound of flesh to get one good thing. What if it's easy? Why not trust that things can be okay for once? Why can't the universe be good to you? Why can't people surprise you?"

"Is that the way the world looks from a penthouse apartment in Rome?"

"Aleksio." I lift my head from his shoulder, not wanting any more secrets between us. "I don't really have those apartments. It's fake."

"What?"

"I live in the Bronx. With *two* roommates. I'm a lawyer at an advocacy center."

He just stares at me.

"What?" I tease. "Is there a bluebird on my shoulder?"

"What the fuck?"

"Lawyer. The Bronx. As in New York. And not the nice part."

I catch sight of his smile in the glow of passing headlights. "Tell me you didn't write that fucking blog, either."

"God, no. And if I don't come out of this, you need to let the world know it."

"Don't joke like that." He shifts beside me, strong and solid. "A fucking lawyer?"

I breathe in his scent like I'm breathing in his raw passion, his loyalty, as if I can store it up inside me for when I escape. "Yeah."

"But not the kind in a tall glass building. No, that's too much like your dad. That would be robbing people with a briefcase."

"A tall glass building is not on my vision board, no."

"Advocacy for what?"

"Families in crisis. It's mostly just poverty. You can't imagine the spiral people get into just from losing their home. A little bit of immigration work. I'm more of a generalist on that, though."

He touches my collar in the dark. "I'm thinking of this one time down at the marina beach—you remember that place?"

"Oh, yeah," I say.

"Some kids had made a sandcastle. They were gone, and it was just there. I went over and kicked it down."

"I couldn't believe you did that."

"It was just there and so fucking kickable," he says. "You remember what you did?"

I bite my lip, imagining the twinkle in his eyes, feeling just fucking happy. "No."

"You spent the whole fucking day putting it back. Rebuilding it."

I laugh. "I did?"

"You got some other kids to help. I even helped. That's who you are. Rebuild, repair. You made it better. I should've known the shopping thing was bullshit. You'd be gunning for justice. Wait—"

I bite my lip, imagining the twinkle in his eyes, feeling just fucking happy.

"To help people. To help kids," he finishes.

Aleksio. People were so quick to buy shopaholic Mira. But not Aleksio. Nobody has ever focused on me so intensely or seen me so clearly from every angle. He even guessed my candy bar. Or maybe remembered it.

"A lawyer for kids? Am I right?"

"Juvenile and family law. Keeping kids out of the system before it's too late. Before they end up—you know…"

In the darkness, he says, "Like me."

"That's not what this is."

"Then why not finish that sentence? Before those poor kids end up like what? What were you going to say?"

My throat feels thick. "They lowered your fucking coffin into the ground in front of me. They put you in the ground."

Aleksio seems so cool, even detached, but when you come to know him even a little bit. you know he feels deeply, endlessly. Then he says, "Now you fight to uphold the law, and I break it." And I hear the emotion in the statement. It's like the statement scrapes everything out of him. Outlining our differences.

"Do you still have that photo of you three that you showed Dad? I want to look. I want to see."

He leans up and gets Viktor to hand it back. Aleksio lights it with his phone flashlight. I hold it by the corners.

It's one of those staged photography studio photos. Aleksio is a boy in a suit, same dark eyes and dark hair, sitting on a velvety backdrop with his two tiny brothers. Viktor caught midcrawl, and baby Kiro on his back in front of them, so tiny. Mr. and Mrs. Dragusha in back.

"Look at his sweet little face. Happy."

"I remember him happy like that," Aleksio says. "Part of me hopes he turned out different. Viktor and I remember that day in the nursery. The violence of it. But maybe Kiro doesn't."

I look at the scrap of paper, a moment in time, and my heart breaks for the three of them, and for their parents. To be ripped from those little sons, not knowing what would become of them. My *father* did that. I look up at Aleksio, and I can see the knowledge in his eyes. "I want so fucking bad for you to find him."

He takes the picture from me and turns off the light. We ride there in the back seat flying through the night.

***

It's five in the morning, nearly dawn, when we reach Glenpines Grove. The guys pull off at a townie gas station, talking between cars about how to approach the house, studying satellite images from Google Maps. The town is tiny, and our cars—a shiny Hummer, a slick SUV and a vintage souped-up Jaguar—are way too obvious here, not to mention how they'll stick out in the driveway of Kiro's adoptive family.

Aleksio decides to have the two backup vehicles orbit on the main road while he, Tito, Viktor, Yuri, and I take the Jaguar and scope out the scene at the home.

We start back up and head off the main drag onto a small road that runs alongside the river, lined with run-down homes on either side and lots of huge trees. This is an old neighborhood. River neighborhoods usually are.

It's hard to make out the addresses, but we don't need to—the red lights flashing in the treetops tell us where the Knutsons' home is.

Emergency vehicles. It's a bad sign.

Aleksio slams a sideways fist into the door. Viktor slows the car.

The blue and cherry lights intensify as we near; there's a fire truck, an ambulance, and three marked police cars in the Knutsons' long driveway. Two empty stretchers are lined up near the door. Personnel all around.

"Bloody Lazarus." Viktor pulls the flask from his pocket and drinks, angrily wiping his mouth with his sleeve.

Aleksio's face is bathed in red from the lights, steely gaze fixed on the house. "Fuck that. Kiro is not dead."

I'm blown away by Aleksio's faith in his own gut, his own heart, whatever you want to call it. Aleksio sees himself as such a twisted person, but he's not. He has heart like I've never seen, and he has no idea how beautiful this quality of his is.

We pass by. A cop eyes us from afar, but we probably aren't the first to have driven by. There's a light on at the next-door neighbor's place.

"Pull in here," Aleksio says. "Into this drive, and right into the garage."

"Seriously?"

Aleksio texts, face lit underneath by the garish phone light. Probably telling the guys up on the road what's up. "Small-town neighbors, they know each other's business. Konstantin and I learned that pretty fast when we were on the run. Pull it in. Now."

Viktor shuts off the headlights and heads into the yawning mouth of a garage.

We get out quietly. It smells like lawnmower and turpentine. A door on the side leads into the main house. Viktor strolls up, shoves something into it, and pulls it open. Aleksio signals the rest of us to wait in the cool, dank garage. Moments later there's a scream.

"Damn," Tito says, heading in after him.

Aleksio tightens his grip on my arm.

Tito comes to the door. "Mira. You keep these oldsters feeling calm, okay?"

"They better not be hurt." I wrench my arm from Aleksio's. And I'm thinking I could find my chance to escape soon.

We enter a cozy little kitchen. Viktor leans on a counter holding a revolver on a couple sitting at the kitchen table. The man wears a dark blue Atari T-shirt; he's bald on top, with strands of longish gray hair in a ponytail. You can tell from his skin he used to be a redhead. The woman is slim, with bright white hair—very short, very beautiful—contrasting with her turquoise robe.

A mug lies broken on the floor in a puddle of coffee. A tray of muffins is cooling on the electric burners of the goldenrod-toned oven.

"They don't know what happened," Viktor says.

Aleksio and Tito go upstairs, probably to see what kind of a view they can get of the Knutsons'.

"We're not going to hurt you," I say, eyeing Viktor.

Aleksio comes down. "Can't see shit. Who was home over there?"

"Donald and Shauna Knutson."

"How old is Donald?"

The woman holds a napkin in her trembling hands. "Maybe sixty-five?"

Aleksio and Viktor exchange glances. Aleksio sends Tito and Yuri upstairs to monitor the scene.

"We're not here to hurt you," I say. "We think some-body attacked your neighbors and that they're really after one of their kids. We need you to help us find him first. What's your name?"

"Ronson," he says. "This is Lila. You're not the ones—" He nods at the Knutsons' home.

"No, no, I swear," I say.

"Which kid are they after?" Ronson asks.

"An adopted son. He'd be around twenty now."

"No son like that," Ronson says. "Mike's twenty-eight, and Glenda is nineteen."

"Kids are grown and gone," Lila says.

"No. That doesn't work." Aleksio's on edge. Desperate. "You're lying."

I give Aleksio a hard look. He takes a seat at the far side of the table and sets his gun in front of him, right out where they can see it but not close enough for them to take it. I take the chair between Aleksio and Ronson.

"You close to them?" I ask.

"Our dearest family friends," Lila says. "A good family."

Aleksio scrubs his face. I put my hand on his arm and give him a meaningful look. Then I stand up. "Where're you going?" he asks.

I head to the bookshelf lined with floral photo albums, each with a date on the spine. I pick out a selection—the year the Knutsons would've gotten Kiro, and some of the years after. It's possible they're lying. Lazarus could've gotten here first. But if they're dearest family friends, there will be photos. River photos, picnic photos. I bring the stack to the table over the protests of Ronson and Lila.

"You can't go through our things," Lila says.

"Shut up," Aleksio says, grabbing one of the albums.

I take another and page through. There are lots of shots of Lila and Ronson's family, but eventually I get to the multifamily photo. I spot a baby that looks like Kiro.

"That's him," Aleksio says, pulling it toward himself greedily. "That's him." Aleksio slides the photo out of the sleeve and pushes it across the table. "You fucking lied!"

"No, we didn't," Ronson says.

"A name," Aleksio growls. "Now."

"Keith Knutson," Lila says. "But that boy died."

Everything seems to still.

I press my hand to my mouth.

Aleksio's eyes glaze over. Refusing to believe it. "No," he says.

Lila takes a deep, ragged breath.

"That boy, he died camping up in the Boundary Waters. He drowned in a spring torrent up there, camping with his father and his brothers. Age eight or..." He turns to Lila.

Lila's napkin is pretty much shreds. So frightened. "Eight," she says.

"It's okay," I say to her. I feel like I'm connecting with her, like she gets I'm okay. "You're okay," I say aloud.

"He drowned..." Ronson says.

Lila grabs one of the albums and takes a folded newspaper article from a pocket in the back. My heart is breaking for Aleksio and Viktor. I look around at exits. My heart is breaking, but I can't be stupid now.

Aleksio takes it, reads. "It says they never found the body." His voice sounds so far away. "Maybe he survived. You can't be sure—"

"It's sure," Ronson said. "It was the dead of night. Donald heard the shouts. They think Keith stole a blowup floating toy, a sort of inner tube, while the rest of the group slept. He was like that."

"He *was* like that," Lila says.

"They searched for him for days. Cops, volunteers. You think they wouldn't have found him if he'd survived? They even had the copters out. But the spring torrents up there, with the snowmelt out of Canada, it's dangerous on those rivers," Ronson said. "The inner tube was found downstream caught in some roots, but Keith was never found."

Aleksio sucks a breath in through his nose.

"Half of the camping area was impassible that spring."

"Then why the fuck bring the kids up there?" Aleksio says.

I squeeze his arm.

Ronson defends the Knutsons, telling us how they'd adopted three special-needs children over the years. "They were good parents, upstanding." He tells us how Donald Knutson owned the hardware store and some properties in town. The kids would build everything with him, but Keith was wild. They had a lot of trouble with him. He'd fight with the neighborhood kids. He hurt some of them badly.

I go to Aleksio and rest my hands on his shoulders. My heart is breaking for him.

"He had a lot of...spirit," Lila says. "He was protective of his sister."

"Keith always went too far."

"His name is not fucking *Keith*," Aleksio says softly. "Fuck. They named him *Keith*?"

Aleksio was so sure Kiro was alive.

He turns back to the album, tearing through for more shots, like he might find them in there. He does—Kiro at age seven or so, looking a lot like Aleksio. The big eyes, the dark lashes, the lush, dark curls.

Tito comes down. "What?"

I shake my head.

Tito stills.

"What'd you see?" Aleksio barks.

"What you'd expect," Tito says. "It's not ketchup."

Viktor comes down. The second he sees Aleksio's expression, his tough-guy beaten-up face softens with pain.

"Gone," Aleksio stands. "They say he died. Eight years old. But he still feels alive..." He presses his hand to his heart.

"*Brat.*" Viktor's eyes shine as he covers the distance between them.

Viktor pulls Aleksio into a bear hug. Aleksio slams his face into his brother's shoulder.

"I still feel him," Aleksio whispers.

Viktor clutches Aleksio, speaking in Russian. It sounds almost prayerlike.

They stand there, holding each other, these dangerous, lost men who love each other with every fiber. I feel like I'm on the outside looking in at something beautiful and tragic.

I catch Lila's eye. "Brothers," I whisper. "These are Keith's older brothers."

She has a strange expression. At first I think she doesn't comprehend, but then I think it's something else. Like there's something more she has to say.

"What is it, Lila?" I ask.

Ronson shoots her a look.

"Sad, that's all," Lila says.

Aleksio pulls away from Viktor's hug.

Viktor grabs his brother's shoulders. There's this long silence between them. I'm getting nervous.

"Let's get bloody, brother," Viktor says.

"No!" I say. "Think!"

Aleksio takes a ragged breath. His pain feels like cut glass in my throat. I want desperately to go to him, to hold him, to press my beating heart to his, to say, *I'm here.*

But he's beyond my reach now.

"The old man took our *brat*," Viktor hisses. "I say we start a trail of destruction that does not end until we hit him."

"You guys!" I say.

"We have soldiers, weapons. We go to war this minute."

"No. Wait." Aleksio places his hands on top of his brother's hands, trapping them there on his shoulders. "We do this smart. We're not fucking puppets. We don't let emotions make us into puppets."

"You sound like Konstantin."

He pulls away. "I say, we don't let Kiro's death make us stupid. Let's let his death make us smart. Let's let his death make us dangerous. We don't just take blood, brother. We take everything, now."

"How about if Kiro's death makes you want a better world?" I say.

Aleksio isn't hearing that. He lets Viktor go and flips through the photo album to one of the pictures of Kiro. I try to catch his eye, but he won't look at me. I know the one he wants to take—Kiro on a tricycle. Ronson tries to stop him from taking it, but you can imagine how that goes.

While Ronson's distracted, I write Aleksio's number on a tiny shred of napkin for Lila. I put it back in her napkin shred pile. "If anything comes to mind," I whisper. Because it really seems like there was something she wanted to say. I'm thinking she might have something. Mementos, maybe? Something she doesn't want Ronson to know about. I have to get away while I can. But maybe Aleksio will hear from her.

"Thank you for your answers," Aleksio says, voice calm, but inside he's wild. I can feel it like we're one person. Maybe I never stopped knowing him, somehow. "And if I see any police sketches out there looking like us? If you breathe a word of any of this to anyone? Life as you know it is over. Repeat it after me, Ronson."

"Life is over," Ronson says.

"Do not doubt our fury," Viktor adds with a snarl, turning and heading for the mudroom with Tito and Yuri. I hear the door to the garage door open. Out in the garage, a car door slams.

Aleksio hasn't moved. He stares out at the river. Kiro would've played out there. Explored out there. Aleksio is wired up with a raw energy that scares me.

"Ready?" I say, pulling his hand. I say goodbye to Lila and Ronson, like good manners might make up for anything, and pull him out of the kitchen and into the mudroom, past the line of coat hooks and mitten and boot cubbies. Just before we reach the door to the garage, he stops, nearly pulling my arm from the socket.

"What?"

He stumbles toward me, seeming out of his mind, and pushes me to the doorframe. He presses his forehead against mine, his breathing heavy.

He grabs my hair, like he can't bear for our foreheads to stop touching. It's a good hurt, a raw hurt from a violent man in pain. "I do want to let loose," he whispers. "I want to kill everyone."

I grab hold of his hair. "You're better than that."

"I don't think I am."

"You are."

"Fucking fantasyland."

"Fuck you," I say. He looks up, expression torn. Everything is going full blast, and he won't hear anything else over the storm except for "fuck you."

So I say it again. "Fuck you, and fuck that. Your humanity is what's beautiful about you."

"He's dead."

"But Viktor's not. Tito's not. Konstantin's not. I'm not."

His intensity ratchets up. His grip on me tightens. He presses me hard to the wall. "I need you, baby."

I should say *you have me*, but I can't, because I'm leaving.

The way he looks at me now, it's like he hears my thoughts, and he smashes into me with a savage kiss, flattening me, claiming me. He shoves his tongue into my mouth. He shoves his pelvis into mine.

I grab onto him. I hold on to him for now, letting him take me, taking him back. All his emotion goes into that kiss.

He pulls away, panting. "You're mine," he says suddenly. A feral man's way of saying *I love you.*

My heart pounds. I begin to speak, but he kisses me again. Stops me from talking. Footsteps at the door. Viktor. "Fucking hell, come on."

We return to the car and roll out. Aleksio slides in the back with me. I can feel the rage and grief washing over him. I feel it as sure as I taste the blood in my mouth from a savage kiss that was pure Aleksio. A savage kiss I loved too much.

I'm his.

Sometimes it feels like we've never been apart. As if some dreamer far, far away has been dreaming us in a life together, and we're only now discovering it.

I'm his. Just another one of the reasons I have to get away.

CHAPTER SIXTEEN

Viktor

I stare out at the endless farmland as Yuri drives. It's morning. Aleksio and Mira ride in back.

So much farmland. It's no wonder Americans have so much food. I think of poor Kiro. *Keith*, they called him. I don't have the bad associations with the name like Aleksio does. But if Aleksio says it's a shit name, it's a shit name.

I want to kill old man Nikolla and Bloody Lazarus and all of the crew. I want to cut a bloody path through Chicago. Finish off every one of them with my bare hands. I want my face to be covered in their blood.

Killing does not dull the pain, but it *changes* the pain.

When you are in pain, any change is good. Even a change to the worse seems like relief.

This pain I feel for Kiro. My *brat*. I would change it to anything else.

But, yes, Aleksio is right. Be smart, be deliberate. Be dangerous.

But really I want to get bloody. If Aleksio were not here, I would get bloody. It is my way.

You would think, after Tanechka, that I would know better.

The pain of Tanechka's betrayal was unbearable. Like battery acid in my heart.

Then I killed her. And that was worse.

Tanechka was the only woman I loved. I would be dead if not for Yuri.

I should be dead, but Yuri needed me. And Aleksio needs me. I stay alive for them.

Aleksio remembers Kiro as a baby. I have only the old photo, and now this boy on a tricycle, looking very much like Aleksio. On the back, it says *Keith Knutson, 5 years.*

"He is very big for a boy of five," I say, fingering the stiff rectangle of paper. "Our brother would have grown to be big. Strong. A good fighter."

Aleksio stares bleakly out the window. "We have to tell Konstantin ASAP."

I nod.

This news will devastate Konstantin.

I look back down at the photograph.

I never had a tricycle, or any kind of bike. I do not know how to ride one. If not for Mira's father, I would have known how, and maybe I would have helped this little boy ride one, too. We would have ridden together.

CHAPTER SEVENTEEN

Mira

"Really?" I say as Aleksio pushes me into the windowless bedroom at the Stonybrook house. "After all this? You can't lock me up like a fucking dog in a kennel."

He and Viktor are about to head out to Konstantin's to break the news. "You have to stay. It's how it is," he says.

"You can't keep me."

He shuts the door and locks it. I fly to it and jiggle it.

Crap.

I listen for the car roaring out. I put my ear to the door. Loud music comes from somewhere—the kind of metal that Viktor and his Russian friends like to listen to. I listen for a long time. The last time I was trapped in here and listened at the door, I could hear the clicks of a phone and the sound of a man clearing his throat once in a while. There's nothing here. Just the music. Probably the kitchen—that's where they like to hang out.

I'm still in the clothes I went up north in—a drapey embroidered white shirt and the short summery skirt. Sandals. Not the best for running, but I'll take them with me. I'll go in bare feet across the lawn and then put them on for the woods.

I listen at the door. No sounds. "Hello?" I call softly.

Nothing. Nobody out there.

Dad once had one of his best guys tutor me on how to get out of places—handcuffs, trunks, locks. Picking a lock won't help here, but he made the point that you go for the weakest link where you can.

The weak link here isn't the bolt, it's the door itself. It's an interior door, a bedroom door. It's not hollow like some of them are, but it's soft. I'm not under any illusions I can muscle through it like the Kool-Aid man, but the place where the screws grab the wood—that's the weak link.

I scour the bedroom and the bathroom for something to use. I settle on the hinges from the cabinet under the bathroom sink—they're flat metal triangles. I could slide the wide end into the door crack and then whack it. It's the same principle as a chisel, except I'm not trying to pry something apart so much as pop it out the other end.

I use a barrette from my hair as a makeshift screwdriver and pull one of the bathroom cabinet hinges off. I try to fit it into the crack. It's tight, but I shove hard, and it works—it slides in and stops when it hits the metal of the bolt on the other side.

Then I evaluate mallets. The wood base of the bedside lamp seems best. Really solid. I unplug it and do a few practice swings, but not connecting. There will be a loud sound. I'm hoping the music is loud enough to cover it.

I put my ear to the door. Nobody there. As the song gets fat and loud, I do it—I smash it once, twice. Listen at the door. Nothing—except a lot of noise.

I whale on it then, just slamming it, and finally the metal plate goes through and pops the hinge.

I ease the door open and push it back into place. I sneak down the hall away from the direction of the music. I slip into another room. It's an empty bedroom, and the window is open—just a screen. I punch the fucker through, climb out, and find myself in the dizzying sunshine, bare feet on the warm grass.

I run across the expanse of grass, legs shaking. Free.

I don't look back until I'm in the woods.

Nobody coming. Just the sound of distant music.

I keep on, feet getting torn on branches and sharp things. I stop only to put on the sandals. I've committed to going west, following the afternoon sun. It's important to commit to one direction in a situation like this, because you hear so often of people going in circles.

The woods get thick and brambly. My legs are getting torn up. There's no path here, but I can hear a highway in the distance. I need to get to that highway. I'll hitch a ride and hide at my friend's cabin.

I think about Aleksio with me in the dark back seat of the car. The way he felt as I held him. So much violence in him. So much pain.

Aleksio will be shocked that I'm gone. Angry. But it's best for everyone. We belong in different worlds.

CHAPTER EIGHTEEN

Aleksio

We head over to Konstantin's place, west of the city. We're wild with grief and vengeance. Dreading the news we have to tell.

"You don't touch Mira," I say. "You understand?"

He says nothing.

"You understand?"

"I understand what you're saying," he says.

I give him a hard look. He gets it.

Konstantin lives in a beautiful old red brick building on the edge of a park. He has his own place, and a nurse lives in a place next door, there to care for him. I support them both. My gang isn't huge like the Nikolla army, but we're smart and lucrative.

"Old man is more interested in ducks than in people. If he was in the city it would be the pigeons," Viktor observes as we pull up. "It's the same in Moscow, with the old people. It is suddenly the little things."

But Konstantin still sees the big things, too.

He's in his wheelchair in front of a fireplace when we arrive.

He's made a nest of comfortable furniture and photos of old buildings, mostly from Albania, Greece, and Turkey, mostly that he shot himself.

"Boys!" he says. "My boys!" I bend down to kiss his cheek, and he pats mine, then turns to Viktor and clips his chin. "Who fucked up your face?"

"It's nothing."

The nurse puts out a plate of cookies and kafe turke, then leaves, back to her flat. Konstantin notices I'm limping. "You need that looked at."

"Konstantin," I say. One word.

The old man's face falls. He knows me that well.

I think about Mira in the car, the way she reached out to me. I find myself wishing she were here beside me. In the past few hours, she's begun to feel more like an ally than a hostage.

Viktor takes a sugar cookie and chews it angrily.

I tell Konstantin about Kiro. For a brief moment we thought we'd get our baby brother back. Telling Konstantin makes it worse. Makes it more real.

His wrinkled hands tremble as he examines the newspaper article we took from Lila and Ronson. He clutches the photograph of Kiro.

"I still feel him in my heart, though," I say. "They never found the body, but..."

"Things are typically as they seem," Konstantin says curtly.

I know he's right.

"He was such a happy baby," Konstantin says. "Beautiful, happy, good. A gift. Strangers would stop on the street to admire him. He was loved."

Viktor takes another cookie. He was too young to remember Kiro, but I know he tries. Like grabbing onto clouds.

"Viktor," Konstantin says, looking at him sadly, as though he can read his thoughts. Viktor shrugs.

I can't stop thinking about Nikolla. Wishing I could kill him.

"You were loved," Konstantin says to the photo.

I have to do something—anything—so I go out to the car to get a bottle of vodka and bring it back.

Viktor looks over with his usual darkness as he takes his glass. Just us now. Two brothers instead of three.

We make a toast to Kiro, the three of us.

"We want to get dead fucking serious here, Konstantin," I say. "You always said to be smart. Kiro is gone, but we can still go after them the right way. The way you wanted. We weaken them. We take our empire back. I know we don't have the element of surprise, but..." I almost say we have nothing to lose. It feels like that, a little. "You always said I was rash. I get it. Going after Kiro that way?"

"You wanted your brother," Konstantin says. "In the end, you were right not to wait. We would've had to wait forever."

"I'm ready to do some real damage. And I don't give a shit about the old bat's prophecy, because we *are* together—Viktor and me."

"And Kiro is with us here." Viktor slams a fist into his chest. "The brothers are together." I wonder whether he really believes it, or whether he's just saying that for Konstantin.

I grab my glass, drain it, pour some more. "Keith," I spit. "No wonder he ran away at the age of eight."

"You are the sleeping king, Aleksio. And you, Viktor, the prince." Old Konstantin straightens in his chair and speaks slowly. "Best you didn't kill Aldo Nikolla. Bloody Lazarus would rise up, and he is violent and unpredictable—too hard to fight. We do this the right way. It's time."

Konstantin commands Viktor to go to his desk and bring out his laptop. He has something important to show us.

I push up his TV table that fits over the armrests of his wheelchair.

Konstantin turns on the computer and shows us spreadsheets, flow charts, graphs. "I have made something for you boys. Years ago I began the long game, filling in names and places." He goes on to detail what he has been doing. As he speaks, I realize that he has been slowly putting the puzzle of businesses together using a network of private investigators and administrative assistants.

He has been working in the dark, working in the quiet, to prepare the way for us to weaken the Nikolla empire and take it back.

An old criminal at his jigsaw puzzle.

"We choke off their cash, their protection, then we strike…"

"Jesus," I say, amazed. "You had this all this time, and you didn't tell me?"

"I was saving it for after we found Kiro," Konstantin says.

I hit the keys, flipping through. The spreadsheet is madness. It's everything we need.

His plan is to infiltrate their flesh trade, their most profitable business, especially their underground brothel, Valhalla.

"The nerve center of their billion-dollar operation," Konstantin says. "The jugular. No one understands this as I do."

He has more—blueprints to the money laundering, the chop shops, people in and out of the clan who can be bribed or blackmailed. "I helped stack that empire," he growls. "I know how to make it fall. Then the true sons step up."

Konstantin wants Viktor to infiltrate the brothel. Viktor grumbles like a kid who got the bad Cracker Jack prize. Infiltrating a brothel isn't bloody enough for Viktor.

Konstantin shakes his head. "It needs somebody who can speak Russian but pass as an American. A lot of the pipeline is Russian."

Viktor avoids my eyes as he grabs the paper with the URLs Konstantin has written. "Writing websites on a piece of paper like an old man."

"I am an old man."

While other old men do crossword puzzles, Konstantin has been up to this.

Viktor is darkly focused on his flesh-trade flowchart, looking at the names. A lot of Russians. The names of the victims are mostly Russian, too. I see why Konstantin put him there.

"I would like to kill them," he says. "All of these on the chart."

"But you won't," Konstantin says. "Because you know others will replace them. We will destroy the structure itself. Like termites. Your father would never have run such a place as Valhalla."

Viktor frowns. "I will be a termite for a little while. Then we will kill the shit out of them."

"Good boy."

We discuss how to get the American side of the Russian mafia involved.

He closes the laptop. He reaches out to grip my arm, tightening and loosening as if in extreme emotion. "You two brothers together take your vengeance." Konstantin lets go of me and beckons Viktor over. He adjusts Viktor's tie. "Some of Aldo Nikolla's people may come over to you. Some you will be able to trust, some not. Use your gut. As you weaken Aldo, there will come a tipping point where you can finally pull everything to yourself." He looks up, so full of emotion. "Your father built his empire to pass on to you, his sons. He would be proud."

CHAPTER NINETEEN

Mira

I crash on. I think I hear people behind me, but it could be my imagination, like footsteps in the dark.

The way up ahead gets lighter, as though there are fewer trees up there. It's a good sign—it could mean I'm coming out the other side. My legs are bleeding, but I don't even care. I burst out from the trees, and there it is, a two-lane highway. Not much traffic, but all I need is one person, one driver willing to help.

And coming, in the distance, is a black car. I slide down the steep, grassy slope and wave and jump, right in the middle of the road, thankful I'm wearing bright colors.

The vehicle slows. Coming.

I move to the side, waving more frantically. "Help!" I call out.

And then I recognize Yuri. Eyes boring into mine. Angry.

I turn and scramble back up the side.

The vehicle pulls off. I run into the woods. My feet are getting torn on roots and branches. I trip, and suddenly he's on me.

He pushes me down and presses a knee to my back. I'm squirming, trying to get free, as he makes a call.

A voice on the other end. Viktor. They speak in Russian.

I feel something cold and hard on my arm. I jerk away too late. The Taser shock jolts through my body.

And then the darkness closes in.

***

Familiar arms around my shoulders, under my knees. "Mira. Baby."

Aleksio.

An angry voice nearby. "She would run to her father. Tell him everything."

Viktor.

I open my eyes, blink in the sunshine.

Aleksio's looking down at me, gaze dark with worry. "Are you okay?" Trees above. Dizzying sky. Part of the roof. We're out in the driveway of that Stonybrook house.

I force my lips to form his name. "Aleksio."

He's holding me like I weigh nothing. "Fuck, Mira."

"She was going to run to Daddy," Viktor says again from somewhere nearby. "She would tell him where we are. Show the *patsani* we are weak."

"I wouldn't," I mumble. "Wouldn't...tell..." I try to speak but I can't. Yuri Tasered the hell out of me.

I can feel the rage pulse through Aleksio. He must have pulled me from the truck. "She would never do that," he says. "She would never betray us."

"She's a Nikolla."

"This conversation is over."

"She's hurting us, *brat*."

For once I agree with Viktor. I'm hurting them, tearing them apart.

I feel the growl in his chest, deep and possessive. "You don't touch her."

"Kiro is dead, and she lives," Viktor says. "They would see that she even has her fingers. She weakens us. She shows them we don't keep our promises."

"This shit between us right here is the only thing weakening us." He carries me into the house, through the foyer, limping.

"Your ankle," I say. "Put me down."

He tightens his arms around me.

Viktor's drunken voice follows behind, talking half in Russian.

Aleksio pulls me more tightly to his chest. It reminds me of the first day in the yard when they shot up Dad's boat.

We pass Yuri, standing in the kitchen holding a blue ice pack to his eye.

Viktor keeps coming. "Aleksio—"

"Lay off! And if you or any of your men touch her again, I'll kill you."

"Don't say that," I say. "Never."

Aleksio doesn't seem to hear me, as though he's far away in rage. He slams the study door with his good foot and settles me down on a leather couch, putting pillows around me.

"Stop it—I'm not made of glass." I sit up. "And you can't fight with your brother like this."

He goes to get me a glass of water from the wood-paneled bar in the corner. He hands it down to me. He seems wild.

I clutch the glass. "I'm sorry."

"Don't be fucking sorry. But you can't do that again."

"Think, Aleksio. How does this even work with me here?"

He loosens his tie and undoes a button, baring his neck. Raw power pulses around him. "Drink. Now."

I drink. He watches me as if from on high, a dark god with unruly curls, chest rising and falling. I think about that night in the hotel with a rush of lust. But this is not the time for lust.

I hand him up the empty.

"Good girl." He sets it on the desk and pauses there, with his back to me. He stacks up some files and puts them aside.

It seems strange he's suddenly focused on files.

"I can't stay."

"You have to stay."

"I wasn't going to Dad, I swear. I would never betray you."

"I know."

"I was just going to disappear. You have to let me do that."

He kneels in front of me. My skin heats under his gaze.

"You have to let me go."

He takes my hand and turns it over, exposing my palm. He just holds it, staring at it like a trembling fortuneteller, trembling at the story that he sees in the lines. "I can't let you go. It was only you. It was always only you."

"You know I can't stay."

He kisses my palm. It feels intimate—forbidden—like he's kissing the very secret part of me. I try to pull my hand away, but he won't let go. He pulls back my fingers, and he kisses my palm again, feverish breath on my wrist.

Heat blooms through me. He's invading me, taking me, and it's just my palm. "You can't keep me prisoner."

He lifts his wild gaze to me, chocolaty hair half in his eyes. And fuck if that's not a *yes I can.*

I want him so badly I can't breathe, but he's not thinking right. If he had his head on straight, he'd understand how destructive it is for me to be here. "It was the perfect solution. I was going to go somewhere where you'd never find me."

"I would tear apart the world looking for you." He kisses the inside of my forearm. I have the crazy sense of him as a large animal, consuming me from the edges in.

I gasp as he rips my sleeve, then he kisses the tender skin on the inside of my upper arm.

"I would tear apart the fucking world," he says.

"The longer I stay, the harder it will be to let me go."

"I'm not letting you go." He kisses my neck, melting my resolve.

"You're grieving," I say.

He brings his mouth near mine, hovering there. Electricity builds in the blank space between our lips. "I need you."

I could close the space between us. I could push my face to his and be lost in him. It starts with just this kiss. I would care for him and love him. Be his.

I want that kiss more than anything. But I push him away and stand.

He sways. His pain is rough and raw. He's all heart, and right now that heart is wounded in a thousand ways.

"If I stay and drive out Viktor, you'll come to hate me. And I'll hate myself because this shit? All of this? It's everything I ever wanted to be away from. I won't give up my autonomy, and I won't be with somebody in a life of violence and vendettas. This can never be for me. You know it."

He comes to me. "We're never over. We weren't over when Konstantin took me away. We weren't over when they lowered my coffin into the ground. We're sure as fuck not over now."

I back up and hit the wall. "What are you going to do, lock me up my whole life? Shoot me?"

He grabs my wrists and slams them above my head, pinning them there.

My heart stutters as he runs his fingers down my neck. He unbuttons the top button. The next button. "Don't."

His breath comes in gusts on my forehead. "Don't what?" The next button. "Don't use you like a dirty whore?"

His words are dark magic. His words set my skin on fire. "Don't talk to me like that."

"Why? Because you don't want to like it?"

Exactly. This is the wrong time to be turned on. I twist, but he has me, muscles like steel under the fine white shirt.

"We're never over." He kisses my neck. He kisses my ear, warm and tingly. "I always watched you. Always saw you. You were always mine."

I hiss out a breath I didn't know I was holding.

"You need me just like I need you. Say it. 'I won't leave you, Aleksio.'" He shoves his tongue in my ear, and I start to melt. "It makes me fucking crazy to think of you leaving."

"You need your brother—"

"I need you." His fingers dance against my bare skin as he rips apart my shirt. "We belong together, that's all we need to know."

All of my protests fall out of my mind under his touch. I feel like a trapped animal, half needing to get away, half needing to follow him anywhere.

He rips open my shirt the rest of the way. He pulls aside the right cup of my bra and plants a kiss on the fleshy inside of my breast. "Deep down you're an animal who wants to be used by a twisted, bloodthirsty killer like me, aren't you? Say it."

I shake my head. Things are starting to feel dangerous.

He slides a hand between my legs, cupping me through my skirt. "If I touch you here, how wet will I find you? How hot are you to let me take you however I want you?"

I twist in his grip.

"How hot? Tell me. Say it."

"Aleksio..."

He pushes up my skirt and kicks my feet apart, then he presses his fingers between my legs, making contact with my soaked panties. His fingers graze over my pussy. I tremble with his every move.

"Aleksio..."

"What do you want, baby?"

I want him to call me a whore again. The word has a sharp point that I want to feel.

He strokes a finger between my legs, up and down, hitting nerves. His fingers graze over my pussy.

I tremble with his every move. I'm becoming more and more his with every stroke.

"No matter where you run I'll always find you." His strokes are strong and steady. He's found the spot that's sending me partway into the stratosphere. "Because you're my dirty fucking whore and this is mine." It feels like he's sliding all four fingers through my pussy. "This is mine to use how I want, got it?"

"Yes," I breathe.

He keeps going, stoking the energy higher. "And right now I want you relaxed and dripping so I can do you hard." He slides two fingers into me, invading me, pushing me into oblivion. Shapes pulse and build whenever I close my eyes. He's not holding me anymore, but I'm not going anywhere.

He picks me up and carries me to the desk. He shoves everything off it—the files he so carefully stacked, the mugs, the laptop. "Lie back for me, baby."

I lie back. I want him so bad I can't think. I'm flying. Trembling. I'm completely his.

He pushes open my legs and stands above me, then he yanks his belt open with a hard jerk and starts unbuttoning his dress slacks, regarding me hungrily. The heat of his gaze is too much, and I press my knees together.

He shakes his head. "No, this is mine, remember?" He pushes my legs apart again. "Touch yourself."

"Wh-what?"

He pulls out his log of a cock, dark and veiny and fiercely beautiful. I get hot remembering the way he shoved it down my throat. "You have to touch yourself right now." It's part plea and part decree.

I touch myself. He watches me with that invasive gaze of his. Everything between us feels impossible. Like everything is lost and all we have is this impossible madness, and it feels good.

Our impossible madness feels like the only true thing in the world.

I touch myself for him.

He climbs up on the desk with his pants half down. He kneels over me, his pants like a band around my chest. "Open, whore. This mouth is mine, too."

I open my mouth and he arches into me, shoving his cock between my lips. I'm spinning, stroking myself, bending to his will, taking him.

"That's it," he says. "Suck it. Feel me moving in your mouth. I want you to feel every throbbing vein. That's what you do to me."

I whimper.

"Shhhh, baby." He hovers over me and grabs something from somewhere beyond my head. He places it in my hand. It's round and smooth. "That's a paperweight. You can crack my skull when you get tired of what I do to you. That's your safe word."

I grunt. It's all I can do.

"Kill me, fuck me, love me," he gasps, invading my throat.

I move under him, panting through my nose. I'm about to come.

"Oh no, you don't." He pulls out and gets off of me, pulling my hand away from my crotch. "Wider. Open up for me, give me everything, baby." He grabs my knees, spreading me wider himself. He holds me there, holds me open.

The air on my throbbing pussy is wickedly cool.

I groan as he penetrates me with his fingers, pushing in deep and merciless. He nips the side of my thigh, and I gasp. He's doing something with his fingers, curling them as he slides them inside me, like he means to pull an orgasm right out of me.

I'm panting, needing him to never stop. He kisses down my belly. Down, down, he goes until he touches his tongue to my clit. I let out a cry. He licks once. It's not a dainty lick, it's a hard, mad, rough lick. A lick and a suck while he moves his fingers inside me.

He does it again, and I drop the paperweight. It shatters below. He licks me again and again, and I shatter, too, into a zillion pieces.

My cries are throaty and low and like an animal and I don't even care. I've lost touch with everything normal.

"I like you like this. Like an animal broken for me. Touch yourself some more. Keep yourself swollen and ready for me."

I feel shy and exposed now that I've come down from coming, but I touch myself like he says. I think I'd do almost anything for him.

"What are you?"

"Your fucking whore to use."

His hands tremble as he rolls on a condom, panting. "God, Mira," he whispers. "I can't...I can't..."

He's not making any sense. Not that it matters.

Roughly, he shoves away my hand, like it was too much for him to watch me touch myself for even for a second more. He's over me, so gorgeous. I feel his fat, hard head between my legs. He's pushing into me, shoving into me, looming over me.

He presses my arms over my head and slides in.

I look into his eyes as he fills me. He's impossibly thick inside me. Us together feels real and forever. The most honesty there can ever be in this world of lies.

"You feel better than I ever dreamed." He moves in and out of me, harder and harder.

"You do, too."

I'm on the knife edge of another orgasm, trying to make it last, but the way he's panting, just gone, gone, gone, sends me over the edge, screaming his name

And then he comes with a shout, clutching me, crushing me. I love the way he feels, the way he hurts.

After he comes, he stills, fully sheathed in me. It's a long time before he pulls out.

I lie there boneless while he limps over to the wet bar. He grabs a bright blue towel and limps back.

"Your ankle."

His lips quirk. "My *ankle*." Like it's so funny. "Lie the fuck still. This pussy is mine, and I plan to take perfect care of it." He wipes between my legs—gently, thoroughly, gazing into my eyes.

I can feel myself getting addicted to his edge, to his possessiveness. Part of me wants to lie there and be his thing forever, like the rest of the world doesn't exist.

Except it does exist.

When he decides my pussy is back to its perfect, pristine condition, he tosses the towel and lies down next to me on the desk, clothes half-off. He pushes my hair off my shoulder. "You look sad."

I am sad. I'm sad for him. For us. "Our worlds are so different. You see darkness everywhere. Happy baby animals make you think of death and blood."

"I guess I ruined happy baby animals for you."

"You didn't ruin them for me. You showed me your heart."

He traces the line of my cheekbone.

"Be better than him, Aleksio."

"It's too late."

"Fuck you," I say. "You think I don't know what you are, what you can be? I remember you as a kid. Maybe you don't remember, but I do. I remember when you were good. I knew your heart, and yeah, you kicked down a few sandcastles in your time, but you had a good heart. I remember."

"Are we back to this again?"

"You have a good heart. And if you would just let yourself feel anything, feel just one thing, you would feel your good heart, and you would know you were better than him. Better than all of this animal shit."

"Do you I need to fuck you senseless again?"

"Aleksio. You can make me want to fuck dirty and be talked to...dirty. But you won't make me forget your beautiful heart. Why not leave all this? You could come back with me."

"I can't."

"Why not? You're alive. Fuck the crime empire. Your father left you and your brothers huge amounts of money. You can do what you want."

"It's not that simple. I can't just turn and run."

"You won't, you mean."

He slides a knuckle over my lower lip.

"I need to go back to my life," I say. "In the Bronx. You can't stop me."

His phone rings. He watches my eyes.

"Your fucking crime empire awaits."

"Ignore it," he says.

It rings again.

I slide off the desk and hand it to him. I need space. He takes it, not moving his gaze from mine. "Yeah." Then he looks away. His brows furrow. "Who is this?"

I hear a woman's voice.

"Hold on." He passes it to me. "Lila."

I take it and sit up. "Lila?"

"Mira," she says.

He jerks the phone out of my hand and puts it on speaker so that he can listen, too.

"Is everything okay?" I ask.

"Fine," she said. "Donald and Shauna Knutson are in the hospital—they're badly beaten, but they're going to live."

"I'm glad," I say. "Will they let you see them?"

"Soon." She pauses. "Ronson's out there pulling in their boat." I get the feeling this is why she called—she can finally speak now that Ronson's not there. Even with Ronson gone, she sounds furtive, like she's imagining she might be overheard if she's not careful. "I wanted to tell you something about Keith. But I want your word...I don't want the Knutsons to get in trouble. But if Keith has brothers..."

I shoot a look at Aleksio. I'm ready to give my word, but is he? He understands. He gives me a nod. "I give you my word," I say. "Whatever you have to say, the Knutsons will not be hurt by this."

"That little boy, Keith, he was wild, like we said," she says. "The Knutsons adopted a number of children. They opened their home. They were good people. But not with Keith. He would fight, and it was bad between him and Donald. It wasn't a legal adoption, you see. Things weren't right."

Aleksio's face has gone stony. I can practically read his mind: *What the fuck did they do?* I give him a warning look.

He twirls his finger in a circle, eager to get the story.

"What happened?" I say. "You can trust me."

"It's true, the story Ronson told. Donald Knutson and the boys went up to the Boundary Waters Canoe Area, but the story always felt a bit off to me, in terms of how deep they went. They went so deep in—you don't bring kids that deep in for that length of trip." She pauses.

"So it sounded odd, something not right," I coax.

"Don Knutson always did say Keith belonged with the animals. He liked to wander off. He was smart, curious, and constantly wandering off. And Donald Knutson would go through periods of impulsive behavior. Poor judgment. They completed these illegal adoptions, you see. They had money."

I look at Aleksio. This is sounding bad.

"The place they camped that year, they went far up into a remote area. This area, it's wilderness as vast as the Sahara. Do you know it?"

"No."

"There are places inside that wilderness area nobody goes. It's not easy to search."

"Very remote," I say.

"I always wondered about the drowning story. Could he have wandered off? Or been left? There was so much trouble with him. And because they believed him drowned, they didn't search for him as thoroughly as they would have, had he been lost."

Aleksio looks like he wants to kill somebody. I put my finger to my lips as she goes on.

"I put it out of my mind, having nothing but speculation, but then two years ago, a private investigator came to visit the Knutsons. The Knutsons were on a cruise at the time, so he came to our house to ask about Keith. Keith had been gone ten years by then. He told me that a wild boy had been found by campers—"

"Wait. What?" I widen my eyes at Aleksio.

"A savage boy, maybe eighteen years old, a boy who seemed to have grown up in the woods. Found by campers, half-dead from a wounded leg. The years lined up. If Keith was lost at eight, and this was ten years later, he would be eighteen."

"Ten years in the woods?"

"I don't know how the investigator got involved," she continues. "This wild boy, he was big news up north. He made a stir on the social media. They had a name for him. I don't remember. The investigator described him, asked if it could be Keith." Her voice reduces to a whisper. "But I lied and I told him no. I made up a story about a birthmark. It was wrong of me to lie, but no good could have come from reuniting Don Knutson and Keith. It seemed the most harmful thing in the world for them both. God help me, that is the decision that I made. But blood brothers, that's different. I could see how your friends grieved for their brother. Ronson was against me getting involved, you see."

"I'm so glad you called. So glad, so grateful. Do you remember the name of the investigator?"

"He gave me a card. Quickly. Do you have a pen?"

"Yes." I motion to Aleksio. He grabs a pen and looks around for a piece of paper. My eyes fall to the folders he'd shoved off the desk. I'm thinking he could write on one of those. That's when I catch sight of a familiar name on one of the tabs. Vanessa Nikolla.

I stiffen.

What's he doing with a file on my mother? He moved it when we came in...and it seemed strange. What is he hiding from me?

"Okay," he says, pen poised over a notepad.

I study the file discreetly while Aleksio takes down the information Lila gives. The folder looks old. Official. There's a routing grid on the outside of it with initials.

Lila is going on about what she knows. "The investigator was older. Very sickly," she says. "I hope that those boys find their brother. That they can heal. I could see the resemblance."

I thank her and click off. Aleksio kisses me. "Thank you!" Then he yells for Viktor.

"You should thank Lila."

Viktor bounds in with two of his guys. "What's wrong?"

Aleksio goes to him, full of emotion. "Kiro might be alive.

CHAPTER TWENTY

Aleksio

I leave Mira at the house with Tito watching her. She seems willing to stay, at least long enough to see this Kiro lead through—I think she's as interested in seeing him alive as I am. Still, I tell Tito he can't let her leave.

Viktor and Yuri and I drive through the night, racing to reach the investigator. Karl Hawthorne. He's in some sort of nursing facility in northern Wisconsin.

I drive. Viktor is unusually silent in the passenger seat, consumed by whatever is on his phone. He's not doing anything on it, just staring at it. Not even scrolling. His lip where I hit him seems to have gotten fatter overnight, but his eye looks better.

"What the fuck are you watching? Are you finding something new?"

"Nothing new," he says.

We found the story about the wild boy Lila was talking about pretty easily. He did make a stir on social media around two years ago. Nobody ever got a photo of him, but crews were camped out. They even gave him a name—Savage Adonis. There was a lot of media hunger for a handsome wild boy until it was determined to be a hoax. But what if it wasn't?

Nobody got a picture, but this investigator—this Karl Hawthorne—maybe he saw him.

"Then what's so interesting on there?"

"Nothing," he says. It's what he said the last time I asked.

"It's obviously something," I say.

"Valhalla feed," he says.

"Is something happening at Valhalla?"

"Nah," he says.

I frown. I don't know why he should be so interested in that feed. It's just cameras trained on captive girls in rooms. Men bid on them. Basically, they sit there for long stretches of time looking unhappy. We checked it out at Konstantin's place.

"Is the bidding heating up? Is somebody trying to out-bid you?"

"No."

It's weird. He resisted this Valhalla gig. He didn't want anything to do with it. Now he can't tear himself away from it. "Are they revealing the secrets of the universe through interpretive dance?"

He just grunts. Fine. I suppose it's good that he's invested.

We pull up to the senior complex at around ten in the morning. It's beige-and-white concrete block. It smells of coffee, sausage, and Lysol, and the nurse at the desk tells us that Hawthorne's daughter needs to okay all visits.

I lean on the desk and smile. "His daughter okays this one, trust me."

"I sincerely doubt it. She hasn't okayed a visit in over a year," the nurse says.

I look over at Viktor, and Viktor looks at Yuri, and Yuri pulls aside his jacket, revealing his .357. "She okays it," I say softly.

A look of fear comes over her, but she still doesn't do anything.

An orderly appears now, sensing a problem. He's young and thick and pale, and when he sees Yuri's gun he goes for his phone, but I pull out my own piece, letting it hang down by my side. "We just have a few questions." Gently I take the orderly's phone. "Nobody gets hurt. Let's get a room number."

The nurse straightens. She doesn't want to give it. Looking to be a hero.

Viktor goes around the desk and picks up a photo of the nurse with two dogs. "Nice dogs," he says. "Are they at your house right now—" He reads off her nametag. "—Donna Fleishcher?"

Threatening dogs. Only Viktor.

"We just have questions," I say. "We need information he has on a missing-person case, and then we'll leave. We'd go through the daughter if we had time, but this is an urgent matter."

"Are you the cops?" she asks.

I get where this is going. Afterwards, if something goes wrong or if we actually kill Hawthorne, she can say that we told her we were police officers. "We're law enforcement," I tell her. Because in a way, we are.

Yuri stays up there with her, and we go with the orderly down the long hallway, through the dining room, and into a large sunroom. He points at an old man in a wheelchair. A rack above the chair holds bags of fluids that trail down to him. "That's Karl."

"What's wrong with him?" I ask.

"A lot," the orderly says.

I nod my head at a chair next to the door. "You're going to sit there and not talk to anybody while we have a private conversation."

Karl has a bald head and bushy eyebrows; he's dressed in a black sweatsuit, and he's watching us, or specifically, watching my gun. Viktor and I leave the orderly sitting there and go over.

"Sig P229R," he says, nodding down at my side. I'm surprised he can see it, no less get the make. But then, he was a P.I. "If I'da known it was that kind of party, huh?"

I look at Viktor. Is this guy not sane?

"Joke," Karl says. "Coming in here loaded for bear like that? Suits and ties? What hornet's nest did I hit?" He sends a mischievous glance toward the orderly.

"We have questions," Viktor says.

Karl smiles. "You're Russian. This the Russian mob?"

"It's not your concern," Viktor says.

Karl glances again at the orderly. "I only ask because, you got any booze?"

Viktor pulls his flask from his pocket and hands it over.

"Got any cigars?"

"Just questions," I say. "We're here about the savage boy. The wild boy. You went asking around about him two years back."

"Savage Adonis? Yup." He takes a swig from the flask. The orderly sits up with a jerk. Karl sniggers and hands it back to Viktor.

"Tell us about this boy and you can have it all," Viktor says.

"Don't mind if I do." Karl sucks down a bit more. "You probably saw what was online about him. That boy caused quite a stir up in Rhone Rapids. Campers found him half-dead and portaged him out of there. Dressed like the fucking Nanook of the North, this kid."

He wipes the back of his mouth. "They gave him something to cut the infection, the fever, bandaged him up. Cut his hair and fingernails. But once he came to, he went crazy and wrecked the place. I'm talking, a wild animal. Had to call the cops to subdue him. Lotta property damage. It was clear pretty fast that he wasn't a normal teen. He was one of these kids they find existing in the wild every once in a while, bottom of their feet thick as leather. Killing with their bare hands. Eating raw meat and roots. Impervious to cold."

"You saw him. Could this be him?" Viktor hands over some of the photographs we took from Lila and Ronson.

Karl studies them, one after another. "Yeah, that could be him. Probably. A lot older, but this is the look of him. He a relation of yours?"

"Brother," I say.

"I could see it. He had the look of you two."

"Where'd he go?" I ask.

"After the clinic, he was brought to the psychiatric unit in East Webster. Lockup in the psych ward. You had social services trying to find his origin, you had the media pounding down the door, because, let's face it, a photogenic wild boy—and we're talking raised by wolves here—that business sells papers. They gave him that ridiculous name."

"Wolves?" Viktor says.

"That's what the professor believed," Karl says. "He's the one who hired me. Louis Jourdan, PhD. He was petitioning hard to get custody of the boy. Professor Louis Jourdan, PhD, wanted me to exhaust all possible leads. He wanted custody pretty bad."

I kneel down. "Did he get it?"

Karl fixes me with a sharp gaze. "Here's the thing, I felt like Professor Jourdan... I didn't like him toward the end, let's just say."

A sense of alarm rises up through me.

"Didn't trust him. Instincts, you know? I felt like he was having me on the case to make sure nobody would ask after the boy once he took him or maybe he was involved in something off color." He wipes his mouth with his sleeve.

I glance over at Viktor. He's not loving this, either.

"I don't know what his PhD was in—psychology, maybe," Karl continues. "Behaviorism. Some such shit. He always struck me as one of those fellows who might raise a kid in a wooden box just to test out a theory. So I didn't like him having that kid, though I didn't like the media or the system having at him any more. And there were fights over his age. He could understand English perfectly, but he couldn't much speak it. Or he didn't *want* to speak. And then one day he was gone from his room, and that was the last anyone heard of him."

"Gone?"

He nods. "An attendant was knocked unconscious. Boy was gone."

Viktor swears.

"They said it was a hoax. Covering their asses. In truth, the wild kid disappeared." Karl sighs. "If you were to accept that he was eighteen, could take care of himself, and wasn't a danger to himself or others, he had every right to take off, so they dropped it. A lot of people covering their asses at the end is what it was."

"They said it was a scam to get the media off their ass."

"Yeah." He looks us over, back and forth. "Definite family resemblance," he says.

My heart swells.

"The question in my mind was always, how did he get out to knock out that attendant? The attendant said he was knocked from behind outside in the hallway, so who unlocked the kid's padded cell?"

"You think he had help?"

Karl takes another drink. "Kid was a real looker, once he was cleaned up. The nurses were fascinated with him. He could get them to give him things. He had that kind of charisma. But in my gut, it's the professor. The professor was obsessed with this kid. How he had lived, how he'd gotten through the winters. Wolf society shit."

"Where does this professor teach?" Viktor asks.

Karl shakes his head. "Here's the problem. Jourdan is a real professor in Madison, a specialist, but this guy wasn't him."

"You're a P.I., and a man fooled you like that?" I ask.

Karl fixes me with a hard stare. He would've been a badass in his day. "Man paid me big money to identify a savage kid. That's who I was looking at. Not my employer. You like your private eyes looking into you?"

I frown. "What else? We need to find him."

"I'd start with the man posing as Professor Jourdan. The psychiatric hospital up there has an image of the fake professor—I know they do, and you could try and get ahold of it and run facial recognition. They have logs of who visited, too. They're going to be very cagey about letting that information out, considering there were some major fuckups made."

He points at my piece. "Going in like this—no. There's a better way. There's an LSW—a social worker—there who you could lean on. Noel Tucker. He would sell that information to you. It would take a bit for him to bird-dog it because he has to get into other people's computers, but I used him a few times. He's where I'd start." He looks up, shaking the flask gently back and forth as if to evaluate how much might be left.

"How did the wild kid seem to you? Your impressions. Was he...okay? Or..." I barely know what I'm asking. How does a kid spend ten years in the wild?

Karl shifts in his chair. "He seemed powerful. Pretty fucking angry. Well, a straitjacket doesn't make a man feel so cooperative, you know?"

A straitjacket. I grit my teeth.

"The kid made people nervous because he could get loose so easy and they'd have to be on him with five or-derlies armed with needles full of tranquilizer. Smart, too. More than smart—brilliant, really, in how he'd get out of restraints, or get people into his thrall. Your brother was beautiful, brilliant, and completely violent."

"*Brat,*" Viktor says softly.

Karl eyes Viktor's gun. He seems drunk. "Yeah, I imagine you'll all get along just fine."

I pull out a card and write my private number on the back. "Don't repeat this information to anybody else. If anybody else comes asking after him, call us." I hand him the card. "We'll make it worth your while."

"And it will be not worth your while," Viktor says, "to repeat these things."

"I hear you." Karl puts the card in his pocket.

We get out of there and into the daylight, stunned.

"Beautiful, brilliant, and completely violent," Viktor says proudly.

We get back in the car and head up north to find the social worker. We're halfway there already, and this is the kind of thing you want to do in person. Nothing like dealing with a man in person for showing what good friends we can be...or what dangerous enemies.

I make a call to Tito. Things are good at the house. He's psyched to hear about Kiro. I ask him how Mira seems. He tells me she's good.

"Don't crowd her," I say. He gets my meaning—I want him watching her, but not obviously.

Tito tells me she's about to take a nap. I get him to put her on.

"Aleksio," she says.

I feel like I left a part of myself back there with her unfinished. Like there are so many things still to say to her. I tell her what Karl said about the professor, and that it's definitely Kiro out there. She laughs at his description of Kiro. "Not in cop school then," she says.

Something's off.

"Is everything okay?" I ask.

"I just want you to find him."

"We need to get to this social worker snitch first." It'll take a little doing. He's in northern Minnesota. More fucking driving.

And the person driving will be me. I look over at Viktor, back on the Valhalla feed. What does he see there that has him so riveted?

I hold the phone tight, feeling a rush of affection for her. And hope like I've never felt. It feels good to talk to her, like this strange surge of happiness in my heart. It's stupid, because things are so twisted between us.

"We're going to make everything right," I say.

CHAPTER TWENTY-ONE

Mira

Tito is trying to make it seem like we're just hanging out, like he's just around, but he doesn't get who he's dealing with.

Men watching me and controlling me and keeping secrets from me is old news. And guys trying to not seem like they were watching me? I've slipped away from the best of them. And I'll slip away from Tito.

And grab that file on my mom.

We make pizza. We all watch a movie. I'm the sleepy, compliant girl. I wait until Tito is snuggled in under a blanket with a nice, hot, buttery bowl of popcorn to announce I'm going to grab a sweater and then I just do it. Guards are most likely to ease up when they have fresh food—that's the voice of experience. Instead of heading to my room, I slip into the study and grab the folder and a Taser I spotted in Aleksio's drawer. I put it in my room and grab a sweater and come back out.

It's a fuck of a thing to sit there and watch the rest of the movie, but this is about keeping things looking right. Again, experience. When the movie ends I go back into my room. They've fixed the door, of course. Tito locks me in there, and I dive into the file.

The file is the coroner's report from 11 years ago—it's clearly genuine. It even smells genuine. Like an old library book.

I go through the sheets. It's an autopsy report. That doesn't make sense—there was never an autopsy of my mother. You don't autopsy a cancer victim. But according to this document, there was an autopsy. The cause of death is listed as poisoning by a substance I can't pronounce.

Poisoned.

I stare at it, trying to make sense of it. The doctors said she died of a rare form of cancer. The doctors *told* me that. But somebody ordered an autopsy the day she died.

Little things from that time flow together. Doctors arguing. The speed with which she was whisked off to that hospice. My father's strange reluctance for me to raise money for the research for the rare cancer. But I wanted to do it. I needed to do something.

This file says she didn't have cancer at all.

This file says my mother was murdered.

I sit there, shaken to the core.

Why does Aleksio have this? And why keep it from me? Was Dad covering for somebody? Was Dad involved? Were Aleksio's people involved?

I try the door and find it locked. When they fixed the door, they reinforced it. My face heats. I'm so done being a prisoner. I need to get out and find the truth. I'm not so stupid as to think Dad'll give me the answers. There's a name on the report. I need a phone and a vehicle.

I sleep fitfully. There's a soft knock at the door around seven in the morning.

"Yeah?" I say.

"You awake?" It's Tito.

"I'm awake," I say. "You guys have coffee out there? What'll it take to get some brought in here?"

"No problem," Tito says. The footsteps recede.

I have on shoes this time, and the stun gun. I've ripped up the sheets into strips, braided them into ropes and hidden them.

Some fifteen minutes later there's another knock. "Coffee delivery."

"Please," I say. "Come in."

The door opens, and Tito appears. He smiles. He has a tray with kafe turke and a warm scone. "Aleksio and Viktor should be back in a few."

"Thank you." I motion to the dresser where I want him to put it. I feel bad for what I'm going to do.

As soon as he sets it down, I jab the stun gun right into his flank. He falls heavily, much as I try to prevent it. I grab my makeshift ropes and bind his hands and ankles. When he rouses I jab him again. I gag him and then tie him to the radiator.

"I'm so sorry, " I say, taking his phone, his revolver, and his money. He looks mad. Aleksio will have a fit.

I slip out and steal through the house. I avoid the back where they're all smoking; instead I go out the side door. I run up the driveway and hit the fob. The lights on a BMW flash on.

I start it up and drive like hell. When I get a few miles away, I pull over, heart pounding, and call the medical examiner's office. I ask for Fazli Jashari—that's the name at the upper right-hand corner of the file. Albanian. The man who signed off. They tell me he's not in until the afternoon. No, I won't leave a message.

I Google and get a home address.

Jashari lives in a low flat rambler in a near suburb. Nobody answers at the door, but the car is there. I go around to the back, a sliding door by the kitchen, and I see an older man with thick silver hair and a thick beard. "Hey!" I pound on the glass with my piece, nearly breaking it.

He rushes over and opens it. Every molecule in him seems to freeze. "Mira Nikolla."

"You're Fazli Jashari?"

"You know how many people are looking for you? There are rumors...about Aleksio Dragusha..." He search-es my face like a man who really wants to know whether it's true.

"We need to talk. Inside."

"Does your father know you're free?"

"Don't worry about my father. I'm here to talk about my mother."

He swallows, looks confused.

I raise the revolver, and he backs in.

"Just tell me if Aleksio is back," he says.

"He's back." I set the file on the counter. "Look familiar?"

He just turns and heads through his home.

Don't I have the gun? I follow him across his place and into his bedroom. He pulls a suitcase from his closet. "I'm glad to see you alive, Mira," he says.

"You going somewhere?"

"If Aleksio Dragusha's still alive? Yeah, I'll be going somewhere, and you should get the fuck out too. You're the best way for him to hurt your father." He pulls out a small carry-on. Already packed. A go bag.

"Tell me about this report."

"Can I ask you one thing first? Are any brothers with him?"

Like hell I'm going to tell him that—especially not that Kiro is alive. If anybody is innocent in all of this, it's Kiro.

He pulls socks out of a drawer and tosses them onto the bed. "I'm just asking because, if the brothers are together, the fire will rain down from the skies. You know that, right?"

"You're talking about that prophecy? Why does everybody believe that thing?"

"Because everybody *else* believes it," he says. "Why do stock markets collapse? Because everybody thinks everybody else is freaking. Why does everybody believe the Kardashians are somebody? Because everybody else believes it. Are the brothers united?"

"I have the gun here. I'm the one who gets the answers."

He's throwing clothes into the suitcase. "You're a Nikolla. Get out of town. Get out of this thing." He stops and looks up. "Everyone knows you hate guns."

"Maybe I hate lies more."

He goes back to his packing. It's like he doesn't even care that I have a gun. "You need to give me a head start."

"Tell me what happened with my mother."

He slows in his packing, but he doesn't turn.

"Talk to me or I'll shoot something. I swear it. I won't shoot you, but I'll shoot something, and then the police will come."

He turns, finally. "What do you want to know?"

"Was she killed? Poisoned? Is that report accurate?"

"I felt it was."

"You were paid to change it."

He frowns. "Shit."

"By who?"

"Who do you think?"

"My father?" I try for a steady voice. "Did he kill her?"

He stuffs a balled pair of socks into his case. "That wasn't for me to know. I changed the findings. That was my part."

"Paid by my father."

"Yes."

"Tell me about what they found in her. Tell me what killed her."

"Designer pharma."

"He made you cover it up. He was either responsible or complicit."

Jashari keeps packing.

My heart feels like it's cracking apart. Us against the world. Dad and me. A family. Even learning about what he did to Aleksio's family, there was this tiny part of me that held on to Dad being a good guy. Even when he withheld that last lead until he thought my finger was gone, I held on.

"So you just let them get away with it." My own rage sounds weird to my ears.

"Yes," he says. "They paid me to let them get away with it. The DA who ordered the autopsy was found in pieces. So yeah, they paid me, but I probably would have helped if he simply asked me. And I think you know why—I have children, grandchildren. You know what your father is. This isn't a good time to be in denial."

"I'm not in denial. Excuse me if—" *Excuse me if I just found out my father probably killed my mother.* I think of the way they used to fight. The secrecy. The whispers. I know from my job that the child needs to believe in the goodness of the parent. The love of the parent. Even in the worst cases of abuse, they create fictions. Somehow the parent loves them.

I wipe angry tears from my cheeks. "Did you help him fake the deaths of the Dragusha boys?"

"I'm done talking. Shoot me if you need to."

Of course he did. He asked whether the brothers are together; it means he knows they're all alive. "I guess I should be happy my dad didn't have the balls to kill infants."

"He does love you," Jashari says.

I feel as hollow as his words.

"You're upset. Just get out of town." He goes to a closet and yanks out a tennis racket. "Go far. That's the best and last advice I give you. If Aleksio had you, I don't know how you got away. But you did. Take this chance and go." He shoves it into his case. "Aleksio wouldn't come back around if he wasn't here for blood. This is where you save yourself."

"Like you."

"My name's on their death certificates. They'll see that sooner or later and figure it was me who put the sand in their caskets. They're going to want to bring down everyone who was connected with taking their family and their birthright." He leaves the room and comes back with a steaming mug of coffee. "You take cream?"

I barely understand the question.

He puts the mug in my hand and zips up his bag. "I'm out of here. You need to clear your head and make your move. You can stay here a while, but I wouldn't recommend it." He glances at his phone.

I stare at the folder. "I thought he loved her."

"He loved you," the man says. "You were a beautiful girl. Such a good girl. They both loved you."

"*She* loved me."

***

Jashari leaves me standing in his kitchen. Just walks out the back door.

They say you only become truly adult when you've lost both of your parents.

I'm not so sure. Maybe it's more like you become truly adult when you've lost your illusions about your parents.

There's nothing I want to do more than confront my father. To rage at him and make him face me and tell me the truth. I always thought Bloody Lazarus was the psycho, but Dad covered up the truth of Mom's death. Somebody killed my mother, and my own father helped them get away with it. Or worse—he killed her. Could he have done it? The question turns me inside out.

And deep down I know the answer is yes. He probably did.

I find an unopened box of corn flakes on the counter and pretty much suck them down. I'm in a state of shock.

Confronting him would be reckless. I can't be reckless now.

Tito's phone vibrates at one point—it comes up as A. I'm sure that means Aleksio. Aleksio calling Tito. I don't answer. Are they back yet?

I get back in the BMW around lunchtime and drive. I don't know where I'm going until I find myself at the graveyard. I buy daisies at the little stand outside the cemetary, and I go and tuck them into the side of Mom's grave and settle in on my usual spot right in front of the stone, right up close. I pick up a fallen maple leaf, brilliant orange, and set it next to the daisies.

"Mom." I put my palm to the gravestone. I feel so raw, like I've lost her all over again, and so full of rage for Dad it makes me queasy. Could he have had a hand in it? Even going near the question in my mind makes me feel physically ill.

I think how scared she was at the end—more for me than herself, I think. The supposed illness took her like wildfire, but she cared for me to the end. And he stood by and watched. Did he know it was poison and not cancer? How could he not?

Everything is too bright. Feels too surreal. I try to shut him out of my mind. I slide my hand along the cold stone, trying to feel her. "I just miss you so much."

There's a chill in the air. Mom always loved autumn.

"Aleksio's back. He's the same. Beautiful and wild and loyal. Always getting into something. Such a big, fierce heart. You always liked him. You still would." I pick up another leaf and twirl it. "Things are good at the center." I go on about New York. How Chicago is so much better, but I'm making new friends. It's hard not to keep focusing on Dad, though. Instead of feeling love for Mom, I'm feeling rage for Dad.

I wander out of there and sit in the BMW in the nearly empty cemetery parking lot. Tito's phone is vibrating. A again.

Suddenly a car pulls up in the space next to me, which I don't like at all, being that the lot is mostly vacant. I lock the doors and start up the car. I catch sight of the driver.

One of Dad's men. No way.

With shaking hands I get the thing into drive. Another car pulls up—right in front of me.

I reverse and smash into something behind me—another car. There's a knock on the passenger window. It's Rondo, one of Dad's enforcers.

I shake my head.

He shoves a slim piece of metal into the door and in a flash, it's open. "Mira!" He slides in. "Your father has been worried sick about you!"

"Get out."

"You need to come with us. We're getting you to safety."

"I don't need to go to safety."

"Your dad's at the Beverly Inn. Come on."

"I have one errand… I'll drive there on my own. I hardly need an escort."

Rondo shakes his head.

How did they find me? Did Jashari do one last favor for Dad? Fuck! Can I be any more naïve?

The passenger door opens and Lazarus's brother Ioannis slides in and slips the gun from my pocket, like taking candy from a baby. Then he reaches for the keys in the ignition. I snatch them out and he grabs my fist.

"Give the keys to Ioannis," Rondo says.

"No! Leave me! I said I'd come—"

"Orders," Rondo says as Ioannis pries the keys from my fist. "You can't know how upset and worried he is."

My heart pounds. "I'm not going."

Rondo closes a hand around my wrist. "I'd prefer to bring you uninjured."

Another car rolls up, blocking mine from behind. I look around wildly, knowing this isn't going to be voluntary. I yank my hand away. "Fine."

I'm ushered into the back of the town car. "Dad is not going to be happy when he hears how you treated me," I say.

Nothing.

Ioannis gets in back with me.

I look away from him, staring out the window. We're heading downtown. Afternoon rush hour slows the traffic to a crawl. It's nearly four by the time we make it into the hushed, dark lobby with the twin stallion statues and small fountain. The desk clerks key the elevator for the top floor.

Dad has a penthouse suite at this place that he sometimes uses. The elevator lurches upward. The ride seems fast. Something's not right.

The doors slide open to a small hallway with a few sets of double doors. Rondo guides me into the living room area, and there's Bloody Lazarus with a big smile on his hard, angular face. He's surrounded by a handful of his soldiers and lieutenants.

My heart pounds. People are looking at me funny. The guys I know well aren't saying anything. As if they're holding their breath. I don't see Dad.

Lazarus clasps his hands over his suit jacket, beaming like the psycho that he is. People who don't know Lazarus think he has a nice smile, but when you know him, you know his smile is never nice.

"Mira. Always a breath of fresh air. Look who's here, Aldo."

I hear a wheezing sound from the corner of the room. "Mira."

Dad is slumped in the corner of the room, pale, wheezing. He's in a bed of curtains below a tilted curtain rod, as if he pulled them down.

I rush to his side. "Dad!"

"Kitten."

All my anger evaporates, seeing him in danger. "Is it your heart?"

Stupid question. Of course.

I pull away the curtains and loosen his tie. "Did anybody call 911? He needs medical attention!" I look around at the dozen guys just standing there. "What the fuck?" I take out Tito's phone. I don't know the code but you can always dial 911.

Lazarus comes over and snatches it from my hand. "I don't think so, Kitten." He slips it in his pocket. "Say your goodbyes."

They won't help him? My blood goes cold, and I see this for what it is: a takeover. All these men are loyal to Bloody Lazarus now.

Why did they even keep him alive? In case they needed persuasion to get me here? Of course.

I look into Dad's eyes. He's in pain. "Do you have your pills?"

He moves his hand then and I see the blood he's been stopping up with his hand, blood all over the white shirt under his jacket. Gut shot. "I tried to stop him—I'd hoped you'd be safe. But Jashari—the ME—he called me to tell me you'd been there, and Lazarus..."

Lazarus was in control and sent people to get me. And predictably, I went to the cemetery.

"Daddy." Tears blur my vision. "Oh, Dad." I take his other hand. He feels cold. I should hate him. Why can't I make myself hate him?

"I know what I did," he whispers. "I know what Jashari told you."

"Why?"

"She was going to take you away from me...never let me see you again. I couldn't bear that."

"So you *killed* her?"

"I was weak. I was wrong. I'm so sorry—I never meant to..."

I'm sobbing. My voice sounds gravelly. "She was my mother!"

"I won't ask for your forgiveness—it was unforgivable, what I did." His breathing is fucked up. I squeeze his hand.

"Every day I died a little, to see you sad. But you bounced back. Always so fierce and optimistic, my Mira. And the way you knew your own mind—you were a gift to me I never deserved."

Images tumble through my memory like bits in a kaleidoscope. Him swinging me around on the playground. The time we won the three-legged race. When he taught me how to sail out on Lake Geneva. Setting up that stupid blog as cover so I could be my own person. His crimes don't erase that love, much as I wish they would. I wish it could be simple like that.

"God, Dad," I whisper.

The guys are on the other side of the room, talking and laughing and smoking. Like it's a party.

"I had your back sometimes, didn't I?"

"You did." This seems to hearten him. "You have to hang on," I say. "I'm going to think of something. I'm getting you out of here."

A strange look comes over Dad's face. "He didn't do it." He's looking at my hand. My finger that's supposedly gone. "Pull your sleeve over your hand. Don't let Lazarus see."

I pull down my sleeve. His breathing is wrong. "Hang on, Dad."

"I wanted too much."

"Shhh. You're okay."

"Lazarus is dangerous. I made him into a powerful monster. It's right my monster should bite me, that you should hate me."

"Oh, Dad—"

"I was so proud of you." His voice is barely a whisper. "Listen, they're mounting an attack on Aleksio and Little Vik. They figured out where they are from the GPS on the car you stole." My eyes widen. "Shhh. Once they're successful, they'll kill you. You have to get away."

"He's sending men to Aleksio's now? How many?"

Dad looks at me warily. "Everything. Those boys won't survive it. It's already too late."

My heart pounds.

"You can survive it, though, Kitten. You will have one opening. Take your opening. This is the last thing I give you."

"Dad!"

He squeezes my hand and fumbles with his lapel, pulls out a blade. I stare out in horror. He's going out. He's going to try to take Lazarus with him. "Call him over."

"No." They're arguing and laughing. Fuck! They're going to surprise Aleksio. Kill him. Maybe he's not back yet. But I'm sure he is. Tito said he'd be back in "a few." It's been more than a few.

"Mira," Dad says. "I won't survive this. Let me choose this."

It can work for sure—it'll take the focus off of me long enough for me to get out. Especially if he kills Lazarus. But it's suicide.

"Call him over."

"No!"

He does it himself. "Lazarus! A word," he calls. "A deal. A deal for my daughter's life. A secret." He nudges me away.

I stand, wrapping my arms around myself. I meet Dad's eyes. He mouths the words, *Got your back.*

Lazarus strolls over, stands towering over my father, there on the floor. "What?" He reaches an arm around my neck and pulls me to him before I can move any farther away. "Why kill her when she's so pretty? Is that what you're wondering? Maybe I'll put her in Valhalla."

My heart thunders. Whatever Valhalla is, I know it's can't be good. My father mumbles something. All I hear is "Barbados accounts."

Lazarus eases off, but he's suspicious. I twist away. "He needs medical attention!"

"Shut up," Lazarus says. "What was that, old man?"

My father mumbles something more about Barbados accounts. My heart pounds. I back away as Lazarus kneels in front of my father. My father grabs Lazarus's tie. He's going for his neck with the blade. Men close in.

I head for the door, pull it open, and run like hell for the stairway down the hall.

Lazarus's voice—"Get her!"

I yank open the door, tears in my eyes. If Lazarus survived, it means that Dad didn't.

Footsteps behind me. Strong hands close onto my shoulders just as I hit the first landing. I kick and twist as Rondo drags me back into the suite, back to a smiling

Lazarus. Dad's lying in the corner at the foot of the drapes, eyes open, blood everywhere.

I fall to my knees.

Lazarus just smiles. "Sucks when things don't work out how you plan."

CHAPTER TWENTY-TWO

Viktor

Mira is gone when we return—gone with Tito's car, his phone, his gun. Tito tells us what happened.

I thought Aleksio would be enraged, but he seems more hurt. He can't believe she's escaped—again. "I thought she...I thought we..." He doesn't finish. He doesn't have to. He thought she was with him, that she would wait to see us together with Kiro. He was wrong.

"You kidnapped her, *brat*," I say. "You filmed her sucking your cock. Threatened her. She tried to get away once already."

"But—"

"But what? But you saved her from getting her finger cut off?"

"We were together." He calls everywhere. He sends two men out to look for her. Our tech guy tries to activate Tito's GPS remotely. They find it disabled. Of course. Aleksio looks like he wants to crush the phone. "She won't even answer." He storms into the study.

I go to my bedroom and check my laptop to the Valhalla feed. There are webcams to all the girls' rooms, including the one we chose for me to bid on. The one we chose for me is not the one I watch.

There's only woman I watch in Valhalla.

I haven't slept at all since I saw her on the webcam.

I place the laptop on my bed and sit in front of it.

Turn, I think. She will not.

She's dressed as a nun, and she prays at the side of her small bed to a small icon. Her blonde hair peeks out from the bottom of her head scarf. I would know that hair anywhere. I know that cheekbone, that way of sitting. I know that walk as she steps out of the room—to use the toilet, or maybe she's called from the room. Even the casual way she avoids the camera, never showing her face…this, too, I know.

I don't need her to show her face. I know it's her. I know.

I'm not the only one who wants her to show her face. Men type things to her. Some of the girls answer when men type things to them, but she never does. She sees the notes—there's a monitor there for her, always on, always lit. What the other men type come across the screen. Sometimes lewd, sometimes not. Some speculate that she doesn't know English.

She knows English. She's quite fluent. Not so much as me, but close.

There's a dollar number below her, as there is with all the girls. For the nun, the bidding is highest. A night with her is well into six figures now.

This is Valhalla, the brothel, the nerve center of Aldo Nikolla's billion-dollar flesh trade. We don't know where Valhalla is located; nobody does. This will soon change.

We've set up a bulletproof identity and an account for me with a credit card to match. I'm bidding on the cheapest girl, a young scrawny one named Nikki. Nikki's virginity auction closes soonest. The plan is for me to get in there and hook up surveillance. It's the scrawny girl I should be watching, but it's the nun I can't take my eyes from.

A knock. Yuri.

I grumble and shut the lid. I can't let Yuri know.

He comes in. His gaze goes to the closed laptop. "What?"

"Valhalla feed. Disgusting. So many of our women in there being auctioned off to the highest-paying..." I attempt to channel my emotion into it. My emotion needs somewhere to go. "Virgins, girls. A nun, even."

Though I happen to know she is not a nun.

I force myself to ask about the search for Mira.

I pull up the Valhalla feed on my phone as Yuri speaks. I felt sure she would turn just a moment ago, but no. Tanechka and I used to be able to sense each other. Why can't she sense me now?

I want to tell Yuri what I've discovered, but he'd say I am crazy. I threw her off the side of a cliff into Dariali

Gorge. She could not have survived. Yet there she is. Alive. It has to be her.

I fall back into the picture.

Turn, dammit.

CHAPTER TWENTY-THREE

Mira

I watch two of Bloody Lazarus's men roll a massive plastic bag up around my father's legs and over his bloody body. Body bag, I think dimly as they close it with a zip tie and haul him away. I mouth the words "I love you" only to look over and catch Lazarus's cruel smile.

"Touching," he says. "But it's nothing compared to what I'll do to your boyfriend."

My heart thunders, but I manage to plaster on a smile. You never tell your enemies what's important to you—Aleksio was right about that. "You mean the boyfriend I ran away from? Stole a car from and Tasered a guy to get away from? Maybe that's how your girlfriends act toward you, but—"

Lazarus shoves me to the wall, hand on my throat.

"He's not my boyfriend," I rasp.

"Show me your hands, then."

I curl my hands into fists deep under my sleeves.

Lazarus laughs and tightens his grip around my throat. I cough and sputter. I start to claw at his massive hand.

He lets me go. "I already saw. You think I wouldn't notice? Maybe you ran, but it wasn't about getting away from him. Don't lie to me again."

My mouth goes dry.

He watches my eyes. "The sleeping king. Well, he'll be asleep when we're through with him, won't he? And you'll be our plan B. It's good to have a backup plan, don't you think?"

I sit there miserably and listen to their scheming. Lazarus has fifty men assembling near the day trader's Stonybrook place. Killers. Hitters. They're staging a mile down. Aleksio will be focused on finding me; he won't see it coming.

At one point Lazarus looks over at me and smiles. I'm not just alive as plan B, whatever that is. He wants to see me suffer.

It's then that Tito's phone vibrates. Probably Aleksio again. *Shit.*

"They know she has the phone," Ioannis says. "Has to be him."

Lazarus hands it to me and presses a gun to my head. "Tell him you're alone in the car," he says. "You're driving around to think. You're coming back. Ask him to wait for you there. If you tip him off, you will die slowly." With that he hits speaker.

"Hello?" I say before he can call me "baby" or anything like that. "Aleksio?" I say in as weird a voice as I can manage.

"Mira, where are you?"

"I'm driving around. To think." I consider blurting it all out—they're coming! But the men are already near. They'll just rush him.

"Mira, what are you doing?"

"Aleksio—" I can't focus. Lazarus is pushing the barrel of the gun harder into my temple, and it's all I can see.

"Kiro really could be alive. We got an amazing lead on this social worker who'll help us find him—"

I can feel the shock waves roll through the room. They didn't think he was alive. Now they know.

"I found the folder on my mom—" I blurt.

"Mira. Baby—that's why you left? I'm sorry—shit. I know you're probably reeling—"

"Aleksio—" I suck in a breath. "Stay there. I'll come back."

"Of course I'll stay."

"It'll be happy baby animals," I say. "Okay?"

There's a silence where I think I've shown my hand. Surely he'll understand that by "happy baby animals," I mean "blood and death."

"I'll wait for you," Aleksio says. "Hurry, baby." He cuts the connection.

"What's happy baby animals?" Lazarus demands.

"That house is in the middle of a forest," I say. "Baby animals frolicking around."

"It's fall," Lazarus says. "Baby animals are born in spring."

"Squirrels have two litters," Ioannis says. "One in spring and one in fall."

"Ioannis, you are such a fucking nerdboy." Lazarus takes a bit of my hair and rolls it around his fingers, expression unreadable.

CHAPTER TWENTY-FOUR

Aleksio

I set down the phone, heart thundering in my fucking ears. "They're coming," I say to Tito. I storm into Viktor's room. "Nikolla's on his way."

He stands. "She told? She told where we are?"

"She *warned* us," I growl. She sounded so scared. *Her father wouldn't scare her like that, would he?* Shivers crawl up my spine. "It could be her father, but I think it's Lazarus. He's making his move, and he has Mira."

"She told you this?"

"More or less."

"What is more or less?"

"More or less means I know her. They're coming, got it? They made her answer my call. She endangered herself warning us. They could be out there now." And if they know she warned us? I can't think about that.

"You trust her? One word and you trust her?"

"Yeah. I trust her."

"Just like that."

"We're connected, Viktor. I need you to trust me on this. I just know."

He seems to contemplate this. What is he thinking? Then just like that, he accepts it and shuts his laptop. "I understand, *brat*. We have that C-4. We rig the house to take them all down if they come. If not…" He shrugs.

"If we move on them like that, they'll know Mira warned us." "Happy baby animals" wasn't the most natural comment.

"They'll know either way. If we run or if we kill them, they'll know."

I scrub my hand over my face. "I need to get her out."

A text. My tech guy comes through with a location— the Beverly Inn. Her dad keeps a suite there. I stand. "I'll go in there and get her out before they realize what she did."

"*Brat*," Viktor says. "You can't—"

"I love her."

He looks surprised. Hell, I'm surprised.

"Just like that."

"Always."

"Aleksio," he says darkly. Leave it to Viktor to see love and trust in a dark and tragic light. "Go, then. Take Tito. Brewer. Take all of my men."

"Leave you?"

"Yuri and I will rig it. Then we'll wait in the woods and pick them off. It'll be bloody as hell."

"Viktor—"

"We've done this many times. We could do this drunk."

Mira would want to prevent more killing, to be neutral like Switzerland or something. Too late for that.

Yuri and Mischa get to work rigging the place, just like Lazarus did with the adoption agency. They're like an Indy 500 pit crew, laying down cascading triggers. A lot of people will die. The three of them will snipe the survivors from the trees around. This won't end the war—it'll make it worse.

The remaining seven of us sneak out the side in case we're being watched. We head into the forest, cram into one of the vehicles we have stashed over the ridge, and crash out the side road.

It takes forever. Viktor has agreed to text me when the action starts. We have to reach Mira before they arrive. Once they suspect her of warning us, she's done. Does she realize what she did?

The traffic is shit. I go up on the shoulder at one point. Let the cops try to stop us. Tito argues with me, tells me to be smart.

I'm not thinking straight, I know. I just need to get to her.

CHAPTER TWENTY-FIVE

Mira

Lazarus holds the phone, knuckles white, wild eyes turned to me. "You little bitch!"

I back up. "What?"

"'Happy baby animals' was a code, wasn't it?" He throws the phone at the door. "The place blew as soon as they entered."

I hit the wall.

He's in my face, digging his fingers into my shoulders.

"You're h-hurting me." *He's going to kill me.*

"You tipped him off."

"You think we have codes?" I rip out of Lazarus's grip and move along the wall toward the window. I'm scared out of my mind. I feel like he can see right through me.

Lazarus advances on me with murder in his eyes. He grabs me again.

It's then that the door bursts open. I gasp when I see Aleksio shoved in...his lip is bloody, and two of Lazarus's guys are right behind him, guns at his head.

"Grabbed him out in the hall," one of them says, setting Aleksio's weapons on the table. *Clack. clack. Clack.*

Lazarus wraps an arm around my shoulders. Aleksio's eyes shine with hatred.

"I get not taking the finger. But showing up like this?" He smiles. "Why, this is just too delicious. And I'm in such a mood."

Aleksio's watching us, steady on his feet...barely.

"Ioannis, how many men did I lose out there?" Lazarus asks.

"Twenty-one we know of," Ioannis says.

"That's going to be twenty-one hours I'll need to hear her beg to die. Or should I split it up between the two of you?" He grabs my hair. "Maybe I'll play it by ear. And I'll make Mira tell all about this social worker of yours so that we find Little Kiro, too. Just so that you die knowing that's handled. It's good to have closure, don't you think?"

The blank look on Aleksio's face is killing me because of what it conceals. This is all my fault for leaving.

"We'll have to get Konstantin involved, too," Lazarus continues. "We don't want to leave him out."

Ioannis smiles.

Aleksio jerks away from the guys holding him, but they take him back easily. It's not enough that he's fucked up with a bloody lip and face and his ankle and who knows how many injuries—no, two guys have guns on him. Like he's this huge threat. Like he's a nuclear bomb, liable to go off.

"You had to come for Mira," Lazarus says. "I can't imagine she was that good. Guess we'll see about that."

Aleksio goes at him then. He actually manages to rip out of one guy's hold. All the attention is on him.

All off me.

Suddenly it's like I'm animated from some other planet—I see myself reaching for nearby weapons, taking one from Lazarus's back belt and one from another guy's holster. I take off the safeties before they can even react, and I put one to Lazarus's head and one to Ioannis's head. "Let him go."

CHAPTER TWENTY-SIX

Aleksio

It's sheer and utter madness. Mira, taking their guns. She hates guns.

One second I'm utterly fucked in a hotel suite with some of the biggest hitters on the planet, all with pieces trained on me, and then Mira moves like a fucking goddess of lightning and wrath.

Two cannons in her hand, one pointed at Lazarus, the other at his brother Ioannis. The two people in the room who matter.

But I'm freaking. What if they call her bluff? Everyone knows she hates guns. I know it most of all. Mira would never shoot a guy in cold blood. It's not in her.

Lazarus smirks. "Mira, Mira. You don't do firearms. I bet you don't even know if the safety is on or off."

He's trying to shake her. My heart thunders.

"On or off," he says sweetly. "You don't have the balls." Lazarus's about to make a move.

Then she speaks. Or more like, she growls, "You go ahead and try me, motherfucker."

That voice—it's like she's possessed by a demon or something. Everybody freezes.

"You try me." Oh, God, it's *not* the voice of a demon—it's the voice of Sergei Kazan, Russian action star. And then she starts spinning the fucking pieces like a hoodlum.

It's a total mindfuck—Mira, talking like that and spinning guns, Wild West style. Like the sun rising at night. Like the moon crashing into the stars.

"I'll fill you so full of lead it'll be coming out of your ass," she says.

I don't know whether to laugh or cry. Mira's holding a room. With guns.

This is what Yuri and the guys taught her, the gift they didn't realize they were giving her. In a flash the guns stop spinning and come to rest in her hands like she was born with them there. Like she's itching to shoot up the room.

Again she trains them on Lazarus and Ioannis. Right on their heads like she's Jesse fucking James. Like she was born to it.

The atmosphere in the room shifts completely. A minute ago I was the biggest problem in the room. Now it's Mira, and like magic all of the guns come off me and go onto her. The men do this instinctively. She's a wild card. Something they don't understand.

But I understand. This is the woman I love. She makes everything possible.

She's given me a window, and I'm not wasting it. I take the distraction to grab a guy and use him as a shield while I grab another guy's weapon. I knock my first guy out, grab Ioannis by what hair he has left, and shove the piece into his cheek. "Everyone but Mira, weapons down. And I mean all of them."

People comply. Nobody wants Ioannis to be hurt. I have Mira collect the weapons into a pillowcase and sets them by the door. She does it, and then she straightens, looking unsure. Damn. "Rondo, tie Lazarus—now! Hands and feet."

Rondo looks to Lazarus. Lazarus nods. He's unpredictable, but he won't do anything to me while I have Ioannis. I have the room under control now.

Rondo ties Lazarus and then the rest of the guys, hands and feet. They've got enough zip ties around.

That's when things go wrong. Rondo senses Mira's wavering. Senses that it was all an act, probably.

I see it like a slow-motion train wreck. I see him going for his ankle. A third piece. "Don't do it," I grate, trying to be powerful enough for both of us.

I can't stop him. I see it all in slow motion, and I can't fucking stop it.

He pulls out his weapon and goes for Mira—just goes at her, a charging bull. She spooks and shoots. The Beretta she nabbed has mad stopping power—it throws her backwards.

Rondo crumples, holding his belly.

Fuck!

She drops the thing and stares hands out, like she's going to go help him now. Hug him, I don't know.

"Out!" I say. "Go!"

She turns to me. She's not even hearing.

"Out in the hall. For me, baby. Go, go, go!"

She looks back at Rondo.

Movement in the corner. Lazarus is trying to get loose.

She's barely there. She's in shock.

"Mira, don't you fall apart. Look at me. Look."

"You killed him!" Lazarus screams. He's knows she's freaking, and he's pushing her. "How could you?"

"What did you do, bitch?" Ioannis screams.

"Both of you shut up!" I ram Ioannis's head into the wall to make my point.

Mira jumps.

"Hall. Now!"

She goes for the door, and I limp behind, dragging Ioannis, covering her, covering us, covering the fucking world.

It's here that I look Lazarus in the eyes. Mira's out safe in the hall. I have everyone under control. It's my big chance to execute him.

But all I can think of is Mira out there. *You're better than that.*

I'm not better than that, but I want to be. He looks pretty fucking surprised when I back out into the hall and shut them in.

I jerk up Ioannis's arm behind his back, nice and pain-ful. We move past the slumped guys in the hall.

Tito and a few of the Russians come out of the stair-well door. "Fuck," Tito says when he sees the three of us. "Come on."

I hand Ioannis over to him because my ankle is beyond toasted, and mostly because Mira needs me. I grab her, give her a good hard look. We don't have the time, but she needs me. "You're okay."

She's shaking. "I killed him."

"You gut-shot him, nothing more."

"Nothing more? As if that's not enough?"

"We gotta get the fuck out, baby." I pull her. She's coming along.

Three more flights and we hit ground level. Tito leads the way out, right through the lobby. It should be fine—they disengaged the security cameras.

"Hey!" a desk clerk says uncertainly, backing off when gets a better look at us. Guests at the cab stand outside startle when they see the guns and blood. It's cool. It takes people a while to mobilize in the face of something outra-geous, a little fact of life I happen to know firsthand.

"Medical emergency," Tito says. Which explains my bloody face, but not the gun on Ioannis, whose face is also bloody. Sirens sound in the distance. But the real problem will be the Nikolla soldiers. We head down the alley out to the street on the other side of the hotel.

A flower delivery truck rolls up.

Tito opens the back. It has metal coolers along either side with a rubber mat between. I hop up and help Mira up, and he slams the door, enclosing us in cool darkness. He'll handle Ioannis with the other guys. Seconds later we're off with a jerk.

I turn on my phone light. A refrigerated flower delivery truck. The light jumps as the truck pitches, illuminating the crates and metal coolers all around us.

She's crying. "I killed him."

I reach out for her. "Come here."

She pushes me away.

"Mira, you probably didn't kill him. You got him in the gut."

"I know where I got him!" She's hysterical. "It was a bloody fucking hole in him!" She puts her hand to her chest. "My heart feels like it's going to beat out of my rib cage. Fuck, I can't breathe. I can't feel my face."

I go to her and grab her, pull her to me.

"I shot him!"

"You had to, Mira. He rushed you. You get to do that when a killer rushes you. You get to defend yourself."

"I probably killed him."

"Mira—"

"If you say gut-shot one more time..."

So I hold her.

"I'm a fucking..." She can't finish the sentence.

"You're not a killer."

"They lost twenty-one guys because of me tipping you off."

"Guys were going to die one way or another."

"That's twenty-one human beings. Oh my God, what have I done?"

"Fuck, Mira." I hold her tight, wishing I could suck up all the darkness.

"They killed Dad. He's dead, Aleksio. He died—right in front of me."

"I'm sorry," I say.

"Are you?"

"He's your dad."

She pushes her face into my chest. "I don't even know what to think."

"Then don't think," I say. "I'm with you, okay? We can just be here." I flip over my phone light so just a little brightness leaks out the edges, and I pull her into the corner of the truck. A small place in the darkness. It was something that helped me on the run sometimes, being in a small place in the darkness. "You're okay."

"I'm not okay."

I hold her. I suppose she's right.

"Dad...he tried to help me at the end—he really did."

"What did he do?" I smooth her hair off her forehead. "Tell me how he tried."

"He tried to kill Lazarus. To give me a chance to escape. He was...he could barely breathe. He was shot, and his heart..."

The vehicle takes a corner hard. I stabilize her. What the fuck, are we in a chase? I hold her more tightly.

"I know what he was. He killed my mother. He hurt so many people. He didn't tell you everything he knew about Kiro that first day. Like hiding Kiro was everything. But he tried to help in the end—he really did."

"He's your dad," I say. "He loved you." She's lost enough without losing that, too. He did love her in his way.

"They know about Kiro."

I swallow. "But we have the head start this time."

CHAPTER TWENTY-SEVEN

Mira

His phone goes off, and he answers. I lean my head back on his chest and look at the faint shapes of crates and containers and listen to Viktor's rumbly tone on the other end. I feel like I drank a thousand cups of bad coffee. All the death. I used to feel safe and good in the world, and now there's a hole in me that can never be filled. I never want it filled. I shot a man.

"I probably killed him," I say when the call ends. "I need you to hear me and not minimize it."

He tightens his arms around me. "I won't minimize it then. This is a war, and you're right, there's nothing small about shooting a guy. You shot the fuck out of him with a big fucking piece. You maybe killed him."

I sniffle.

"And yeah, you saved yourself, but it doesn't change how it feels."

"Maybe I didn't have to shoot him."

"You think we were getting out of there alive without that?"

"No," I say.

"Fuck no. You saved yourself, and you saved us. I fucking pulled you into this, and you did the best you could."

"Is that what you tell yourself? That you did the best you could?"

"Sometimes."

"Does it help?"

"No, baby," he says. "It's just true, is all."

I suck in a ragged breath. "Does anything help?"

"Nothing helps. I won't lie to you. It's a hard thing— not like on TV or a video game. It's real like nothing else. It's jagged inside you—especially if you never did it before."

I feel a sob come up from my chest. Like my whole body is trapped sobs. I think they might be there forever, like ghosts trapped inside me. All I can see is him doubling over. Lazarus's face when he got that phone call. "I caused deaths today."

"I know."

"It hurts."

"I know, baby," he says.

I love him for being real with me now.

"You stay alive, Mira. It's what we do. It's built in."

"Like animals." I feel crazy suddenly, like everything is upside down. "That's what I am. This is what it really is, isn't it? When you appeared at the boathouse, I thought you were the fucking animal. Child of the Black Lion. But I am, too."

"Mira—"

"No, listen. This shit with me going around putting bullets in people's bellies? Maybe this is the first time I've acted with any real honesty."

"You know that's bullshit. What you did doesn't change what's inside you, Mira."

I feel like it does, though—I feel like things will never be okay again. I want to crawl out of my skin. I flatten my hand to his chest. "Make me forget. Fuck me like an animal. I want you to turn me inside out and fuck me on the dirty floor. Make me feel the dirt."

He takes hold of my hair and turns my face to his.

"Fuck me the way I like."

He sucks in a slow breath, then kisses me long and slow. Much too soft.

I reach for his cock. He's hard. Steely through his jeans. "Tell me what a fucking whore I am until I forget. Until I can't feel."

"Mira." He kisses my ear. Shivers go through me.

"I want you to use me until I'm completely twisted up and worn out. Like a piece of trash for you to—"

He shuts me up with another kiss.

"Harder," I say.

"Baby, I want to just love you," he says.

"Do it, then. Right here on the mat."

"No, I mean, I want to hold on to you and feel how much I fucking actually love you."

My blood races. *He loves me.*

He tightens his arms around me. "I love using you like a whore, don't get me wrong. It's one of the hottest things on the planet, but I only call you that because you're so hot and I'm so fucking in love with you. I'm not gonna call you a whore when you feel shitty and want to feel shittier. Fuck that."

I melt into him. Something falls away. I don't know what. Like ice melting away.

"Okay?"

I close my eyes. "Okay."

"Breathe, baby. You're not breathing."

I suck in a breath, then heave it out. "It hurts to know what I did."

"I know," he says.

"But you're here."

"Always."

"You love me."

"I love the fuck out of you."

I should feel happy about that, but us together is another thing that's doomed. "Sometimes love isn't enough, is it?"

The engine rumbles. There's nothing to say to that. Our lives run in opposite and opposing directions—I care about the rule of law. He lives to break it. I'm all about rescuing kids from a lifestyle he promotes.

The air inside the van is cold except where he holds me. It's like a metaphor: Us together against the cold, dark world.

But his breath is warm on my neck. He kisses me on the tingly, breath-warmed spot, letting his lips linger, hot and soft. He trails a finger down my neck. I stifle a gasp— it's still powerful when he touches me. As powerful as that first day in the boathouse.

"What are you doing?"

"You make me crazy. I can't ever let you go." The fact that he even says it shows me that he knows, deep down, that we're doomed.

My pulse pounds. His hands tremble; his lust is wild as wolves, barely restrained.

I've never had a man want me like this. I've never wanted a man *back* like this.

He pulls down my bra, baring my breasts. The cold air freezes my nipples until he sets his warm mouth on one, his fingers on the other. It's a dark kind of heaven.

He sets his free hand on my bare knee under my skirt. "Baby," he says.

The van shifts as though we took a corner too fast. It feels dangerous in this van. Was I honestly just begging for sex? The phone wobbles, making the light strobe briefly over his cheekbone, his dark curls. He takes my wrists in one hand and pins them above my head, the way he always likes to do. He slides his other hand up my thigh.

My pulse skitters.

He shoves my skirt up and cups me between my legs, hand strong and firm. He just holds me there, moving slightly with the careening van. Everything is falling out of my brain. I'm forgetting everything in the wake of the forbidden sensation of being held and controlled by him.

He finds the elastic of my panties and presses his fingers to my dripping wet pussy.

"Aleksio, we're in a car chase. Be reasonable."

"Be reasonable? Fuck reasonable. I won't be reasonable about you—not ever. That's a promise." Slowly he begins to slide and stroke. "Not ever." He slides and strokes between my legs, and when he hits a certain momentum, I gasp. "You are so sensitive."

To you, I think.

"Jerk your hands. Feel how I'm holding you. Feel how you can't ever get away from me."

I jerk and twist, needing him with a hunger that feels wild and wrong. He pushes a finger into my core, and I gasp.

"Feel how I'll never let you go." He has his hand between my legs, stroking me. "Feel it."

"Aleksio—"

"Say it. Don't let me go."

He tightens his grip on me, and instinctively I try to pull away—but I can't. The way he holds my wrists with one hand while he roams his free hand all over me is intoxicating as pure grain alcohol.

He whispers warm in my ear. "Say it."

Forbidden warmth blossoms inside me. And I want him. "I love you."

His breath hitches. "Mira the rebel." He tightens his grip. It hurts in a way that's beautiful and good, the pressure of him holding me in place.

The van takes another turn.

"This is so wrong," I say.

He strokes me higher, up, up, to the edge of oblivion. He nuzzles the side of my neck. "Nothing's right. Nothing will ever be right."

He slides his finger inside me now, and my laugh turns to a groan of pleasure. He lays me over the top of a cooler and pushes up my skirt and pulls down my panties so that they bunch around my ankles.

"You're beautiful," he says. The freezing air chills my skin except where he puts his hand.

"I need to be in you." He slides his fingers between my legs, and the feeling rises with every stroke. I think to tell him to stop, because it's too much, too good. I'm moving with his fingers, fucking his fingers.

"Spread," he gasps.

I do what he says. A condom wrapper crinkles. His hands are inside my folds, and then the fat knob of his cock is there, penetrating me, filling me completely. He feels huge, and I cry out. He thrusts in again and again, keeping hold of my hair, my shoulder, and I never want him to stop.

And out there is war, but in here I'm lost with the man who consumes me utterly. He thrusts into me, owning me, using me, loving me.

"Aleksio," I say. His name is a velvet glove on my cheek.

He fucks me hard and deep, pushing me over the edge until my mind explodes with color and light. He shoves into me and groans until he unravels inside me.

The van rumbles on. We have this space for ourselves. For now.

Eventually he pulls out.

"Where are we going?" I ask.

"North. Keep an eye on the guy who might have the lead on Kiro. Make sure nobody else is on him."

"Get to him before Lazarus can get to him."

"Lazarus knows nothing about him. It's a good head start that we have here."

"Wait—" I pull away. "You didn't kill Lazarus."

He looks grim. "No, I didn't."

"Lazarus helped kill your parents."

No reply.

"You left him alive. You could've killed him right there."

"Yeah, I might come to regret that."

"Be serious. You spared Bloody Lazarus himself."

"I looked into his eyes, and I thought about killing him. I wanted to. But I didn't."

"Why?"

His face is shrouded in shadow, but I feel his eyes on me.

"I couldn't," he says simply.

CHAPTER TWENTY-EIGHT

Aleksio

I send three of my best guys to guard Konstantin and his nurse. I doubt Lazarus could ever find him, but I'm not taking chances.

Our group waits for Viktor and his guys in a mall parking lot an hour north of Chicago. They roll up in three black Mercedes SUVs, like matched black stallions. Viktor steps out of the lead vehicle.

"What the fuck?" I say.

"I'm done hotwiring cars, *brat.*" He tells me he paid cash for them. As if they were an impulse item, like chocolate mints at a grocery checkout. He's getting into the role of returned prince, a crime royal with bank accounts to rival a small country. The role he was born to—the role we both were born to.

I can't give him shit. Now that we've officially reappeared, we have access to millions of dollars our father hid away—offshore accounts Konstantin helped recover with the aid of our DNA and our fingerprints. It's as if

Dad hedged his bets against people who might betray us, only he certainly never suspected it would be Lazarus and Aldo Nikolla. Konstantin has a lawyer working on unearthing even more money.

Mira rolls her eyes at the flashiness. *Mira.* I love her in a way that feels too vast and huge to explain, and I know she loves me, too, but using the law to help create a more just society is her life. And I'm a mafia prince. Our paths run in opposite directions. I watch her standing there in the sunshine, loving her, trying not to think about that.

The group piles in and heads north to personally protect Noah, the social worker and our only link to Kiro. I have this sense that Kiro is up there somewhere, and I have this vision of riding back with him, three brothers together to finish this thing.

Eight hours later we arrive at the Sky Slope Hotel, a five-star resort outside of Duluth, Minnesota, the only luxury hotel for hundreds of miles. There's a giant pine tree and a waterfall inside the ornate lobby. Light streams in from a sky-high glass ceiling.

We take over the top floor. I grab the best room for Mira and me—all white marble, green linen, and million-dollar views. China cups with fresh hot chocolate waiting for us on the table. She passes them up and goes to the window.

I close the door and walk up behind her, wrapping her tight. The Sky Slope is on a bluff, and you can see miles of endless wilderness with Lake Superior in the distance.

I'm guessing she's focused on the scene out there, but my focus is on our reflection in the glass. There's a haunted expression in Mira's eyes that I've never seen before. Sure, I look like hell—my lip is puffy, and my eye is bruised—but my injuries will heal.

Mira's injuries? I'm not so sure. It's more than her dad dying or what he did to her mother. It's what *she* did. Mira is a woman with a strong fucking code, and she broke it—she shot a guy. He's not dead—we've been getting updates on him—but that doesn't matter.

All those years of watching her, studying her, obsessing over her, I got to know all of her expressions. This haunted look is new. It chills me to the bone.

It comes to me, standing there, that protecting the woman I love isn't about keeping her physically safe; it's about protecting her soul. She can't be in this war, not even on the sidelines. Protecting Mira means letting her go.

The realization is a cannonball in my gut.

It has to be done. I'm not going to execute Lazarus and his guys—I'm done with that old world Albanian mountain vengeance, much to Konstantin's dismay. But I still plan to destroy him and take back what's ours. And I'll break any law to rescue Kiro.

Mira can't be anywhere near that. The look in her eyes tells me that.

She thinks it's too dangerous to go, but I know it's too dangerous for her to stay. I get that now, looking at her when she thinks nobody's watching.

I rest my forehead on her shoulder, trying to get my shit together enough to figure out a plan, because I have the resources to keep her safe now—safe from me and my world.

I suck in a breath there at the window. Maybe this is what loving a person is. Loving them enough to rip your own heart out for them.

She turns in my arms. "Baby? What's up?"

I kiss her. I don't want her to see my face. I don't want her to know I'm dying inside.

I leave her to settle in, and I head down the hall and tell Tito not to unpack. Ten minutes later we have a plan—he's going to fly out to the Bronx, rent her a high-security place near her workplace, and put together a contingency of New York muscle to discreetly watch over her. He'll get it all in place ASAP.

Once Tito's on his way, Viktor and I settle in to plan. We put together teams to watch over Noah the social worker and monitor the area for signs of Lazarus or his guys. We work on our attack strategies. We're like royalty in exile, there in that northern hotel, plotting our siege of the walled city.

The next day, Mira makes me go to a clinic and get a proper X-ray for my ankle. The doctor gives me a medical boot and tells me I'm lucky—I only have a hairline fracture.

We go out for a lavish lunch, and afterward we take a walk on a nearby nature trail, something I'm not supposed to do in my medical boot, but we don't have much time left now. It's strange—going on a date now, after we've been through a lifetime's worth of shit together.

We hike up to a bluff and admire the view. I find a flat, grassy spot to sit on, and Mira settles in next to me, lying back, looking at the clouds, skin glowing in the pale light.

"Sometimes I miss Dad so much," she says. "Sometimes I'm so sad he's gone, and sometimes I hate that I didn't get to make him answer for what he did. And then I feel shitty, because he's dead. And I miss him."

I stretch out next to her and just listen. She talks about how she's been trying to process it. How all her memories seem different now. We talk about people we used to know. About her work. We talk about everything but the future.

When we get back to the Sky Slope, we find Viktor in the waterfall lobby watching his phone. Mira asks him about it, and he starts telling her about Valhalla.

I interrupt, because the less she knows, the better. "It's part of the business that we're going to end."

But Mira sits right down next to Viktor. "I want to know. I want to see."

I'm not sure how I like that—it's a pretty harsh thing, what's happening in that place. Viktor flips through the different feeds showing the women there. He tells her about the pipelines from different countries. He tells her about our plans to figure out where the fuck it is.

Mira takes the phone from him. She scrolls through the different feeds. "What happens to these women when you shut it down?"

"We send them home," I say.

Mira frowns. "Maybe some want to go home, but what if they don't? What if they can't? Some of these women could've come from terrible or even deadly circumstances, and going home could put them in incredible danger. Some of them could even be facing persecution of some sort if they go back. No, that's not how this should happen. You need a system for them."

She grabs a fancy notepad and starts making lists. An entire legal intervention seems to have appeared to her mind the way a criminal operation sometimes appears to mine.

"You need resources, people, and strategies for getting some of the victims asylum and immigration assistance." She has all kinds of ideas. I can't believe I didn't think of it, but that's Mira. It's amazing to see her like this, in her element.

She works on it in bed that night in our own room. Doing research. Discreetly querying colleagues, asking whether they could be on standby. Immigration isn't her specialty, she explains. But she can put the resources together for us.

I scoot behind her, watching her on her laptop. I try to start up some dirty whore action with her, but she's not going for it, so I brainstorm with her on some of the logistics.

It's actually exciting to work together. We bounce ideas off each other—fuck, we're endless with these ideas, like a longtime team. I'm surprised by how natural it feels until I remember how it used to be when we were kids. Plotting various capers.

It feels good. Pure, even, in a way I can't articulate.

Fuck, maybe it's happiness. Probably it is.

She feels me drift and draws me back in. She tells me there'll be a period of time where we need to keep the women out of the hands of the authorities. Can we do that?

Hell, yeah, we can do that, I tell her. I have all kinds of ideas on how to do that.

She laughs. "Of course you would."

"Who says a life of crime doesn't pay, baby?"

She doesn't answer. The question reminds us how far apart we are.

"Is this what life is like for normal people?" I ask.

"Yeah," she says softly. "Maybe even better."

"Eh," I say. Coolly, offhandedly. Like I don't care.

But I do care. Happiness with this amazing woman is the one thing I can't have.

I keep my lips zipped and get us back to the project. She sets it up so that it runs itself—idiot-proofing, she jokes. But she knows she needs to leave as well as I do.

What's that thing they say? Better to have loved and lost than never to have loved at all? Not so sure about that one.

The next morning I wrap her plane ticket in a fucking box along with the key to the new high-security apartment in the Bronx that Tito rented for her; it was delivered via courier overnight. It's her exit visa from my violent life, wrapped up in a bow. I'll drive her out to the Duluth airport. Let her go. I have to do it fast, or I might not be able to.

I think about what I'd do if I weren't in this life. What kind of man I'd need to be to deserve Mira back. What if I took back the empire and turned it over to Viktor and Kiro? Who would I be if I weren't Aleksio Dragusha, head of the Black Lion clan?

I scrub the thoughts from my head. I can't stop being that man right now. Kiro's out there. Kiro needs us to do what it takes.

CHAPTER TWENTY-NINE

Mira

Aleksio and I are sitting in our bed watching TV like a normal couple when he gets the text.

The gleam in his eyes tells me what it is—intel on Kiro. "Gotcha, motherfucker," he says, flipping through a lot of images. A man's face. A man's profile. Full body shots. The man who took Kiro.

I kiss him, hoping with everything that the guy is in some kind of database. If he's not, the road to finding Kiro gets a lot harder. I decide to think positive. I jump out of bed to grab the champagne. I'm considering a toast, but he comes up and takes the bottle from my hand and pushes me face-first into the wall.

"Already?" I joke, because we fucked all morning.

He doesn't answer. He moves my hair aside and kisses the nape of my neck. Just a kiss—a kiss that feels more intimate than fucking.

"This is my place on you," he says, planting another kiss on the curve beneath my hairline. "Sensitive and secret. I love this place on you." He kisses it again, sending shivers up and down me. "Your hair covers it, and nobody touches it, but I do. And it's my place, okay?"

I laugh. "That's a pretty chaste place, baby. Are you sure you don't want to reconsider?"

"I won't reconsider." He turns me to him and cups that place, his secret place, and he kisses me with crazy intensity. Like he's dying inside that kiss. I hold his sweet scruffy cheeks and kiss him back slowly, thinking he's feeling emotional about maybe finding Kiro.

He pulls me onto the bed. I lose myself in him, this man who fits me like no other man ever has.

Sometimes fucking feels rushed and fun and dirty.

Other times, it's leisurely, hedonistic.

And sometimes fucking contains the whole world and all of time. And sometimes that kind of fucking is good-bye, and you don't know it.

We're in the shower afterwards when he tells me we need to go on a quick trip to the Duluth airport tomorrow. Picking up a package? Meeting a guy? He doesn't say what it is, and I don't ask. I know the drill.

The secrecy reminds me of the way I grew up. It's what I always wanted to get away from. My heart sinks at the thought.

We park in the airport lot the next morning and walk into the sweeping glass-fronted building. He pauses near the security line. "Gimme your purse."

I hand it over. "What are you up to?"

He looks through it. Takes out my hand lotion. "Four ounces. No go." He tosses it out.

"What the hell?"

He hands my purse back to me along with a brightly wrapped gift, the size of a book.

My heart begins to pound. "What is this?"

"Open it."

I tear off the paper and pull out a plane ticket and a key ring with a key on it. And a baggie of gas station English toffee. "Aleksio—"

"I'm getting you back home."

"What?"

"Getting you back to your life, baby."

I hold the stuff in my hands, blood racing. I thought we had more *time.*

"You'll be safe. I rented you a new place that's ultra-fortified. Tito flew down yesterday. He's setting up your security detail. You won't have actual bodyguards—don't worry. But they'll watch over you from afar. They'll know if anybody's watching you. We hired the best."

I swallow past the lump in my throat. I know I have to go, but I thought he'd fight my going. I thought I'd wait.

He nods at the departure board. "Direct to La Guardia. It's boarding in ten."

"So...just like that?"

Aleksio kisses me—hard. Then he puts his forehead to mine, and I get the feeling he doesn't want me to see his face. "I love you. I always will."

My throat feels thick. I want to say *I love you* back. I want to say a world of things.

"You wanted to go, right?"

Standing there, I see a possible life with him flash before my eyes. I see a life with a man who sits on top of a violent machine. I see myself looking the other way from a zillion crimes.

And maybe I have my career, but what kind of mockery would that be, involved with a mafia boss? Of course he's right. Of course I have to go. Right?

His dark eyes are deep with soul and sadness. "You need to go rebuild the sandcastles that jerks like me kick down."

My voice trembles. "Right." I kiss him again.

A droning voice over the loudspeaker announces that my flight is in preboarding. I pull out my ID, telling myself it has to be like this. "Let me know what happens with Kiro."

"Of course," he says hoarsely.

I want to say more, but he turns and walks away, dark and lethal in his suit, just the way he came back into my life. But so different.

The security line is short. Before I know it, I'm up at the front, untying my shoes.

CHAPTER THIRTY

Aleksio

I'm halfway back to the hotel when my phone rings. Relief jolts through me for a moment because I have this idea it might be Mira, calling to say she's not leaving.

It's my investigator. *At least I'll have some good news,* I think.

It's not good news.

"I'm sorry, Aleksio," he says. No greeting, just the apology.

"Let's hear it."

"I've been running every image through every motor vehicle database out there. I subcontracted it to my guy in D.C. to run it through the State Department database. I expanded it to my Canadian contact. We're all coming up empty."

"You said we could find him if he had a driver's license or a passport."

"Maybe he doesn't have a driver's license or a passport. Maybe he modified his appearance for those visits. Maybe the software doesn't have enough data points."

The road unfolds ahead of me, a bleak gray ribbon through tall pines. "Okay. What now?"

I don't like the long silence that follows. "All we have is the man's picture," he says finally. "He's a needle in a haystack the size of North America. Worse than a needle. A ghost in the haystack."

"And?" I try not to sound impatient, but he didn't answer my question. "What now?"

"I can keep looking, of course," he says. "I can keep trying new things, but I'm not going to lie to you. We're looking at months, probably years. We may never find this guy."

"Keep looking," I say. "He exists. He's out there. Whatever it takes."

Viktor and Yuri are in the pine-and-waterfall lobby when I get back. Viktor puts away his phone and his strange obsession for Valhalla for once, which I take as a good sign until I realize it's probably because of the torment on my face.

I take a seat and tell them the news about Kiro.

The trail is pretty much dead—that's what the investigator said in so many words.

"No," Viktor says. "He needs to look again."

"Viktor..." I stare up at the shining blue sky beyond the glass ceiling, imagining Mira's plane up there in the clouds. And Kiro...who knows where he could be?

A waitress comes over, and Yuri orders vodka—no, not three glasses; a bottle and three glasses.

"He gives up too easily on our *brat*. He needs incentive, I think."

"It's a computer search of image databases," I say. "You can't just make the computer give better results. And nobody's giving up, it's just..." I'm about to say "more impossible," but I amend it to "harder."

"We will never give up," Viktor says, in a tone like he wants to kill somebody.

"Never," I agree.

"And we will destroy Lazarus without Kiro. I will squeeze his skull until his eyes pop out, and then when we find Kiro, he'll have a place in the world. We take it back for Kiro."

Our vodka arrives. Yuri pours.

Viktor lifts a glass. "We get bloody. Nobody's stopping us now." With Mira gone, he means. "When we're done with them, they'll pray for death." He drinks. Yuri drinks.

I stare into the clear liquid.

"What is it, *brat?*"

"I can't drink to that. Getting bloody just to get bloody. Violence and vengeance."

Viktor looks at me like I just announced I hate vodka and hundred-dollar bills.

"Don't worry, I'm good for my word," I say. "I'm committed to taking back what's ours and destroying the vile parts of it. I'll do what it takes to get Kiro back if we ever—*when* we get a lead. But violence and vengeance..."

I meet Viktor's scowl.

"She thought I was worth saving," I continue. "It did something. It changed something in me..." I'm just as surprised as Viktor appears to be. But it's true. Things feel different.

"Changed something in you?" Viktor spits out. "More like *ruined* you."

I think back to that moment in the hotel, staring into Lazarus's eyes. I could've executed him right on the spot. My greatest enemy. "Ruined me for some things."

He rolls his eyes. "Fine. To *her*, then."

I eye him suspiciously. He shrugs.

"To her." I drain the glass.

He pours another.

"To Kiro," I say. "We'll never give up. And Yuri. To brothers of all kinds."

"Brothers with beat-up faces. The best kind. *Skol.*" We throw back the cool-burning alcohol. I hold my glass out for more. He pours.

"Back to taking the empire the smart way," Yuri says. "More boring. Still effective." Again we drink.

Viktor catches my eye. He looks concerned.

"I'm fine," I say. A lie.

That's when I catch sight of dark hair across the lobby. *Mira.* She's heading to the elevator banks.

She turns to me as if she feels the weight of my gaze. And then she smiles. Her smile is like the sun.

I think it's a dream. A mirage, maybe.

I stand, glass cool in my fingertips, as she turns and starts toward me, past the grand stone waterfall, dark hair catching the light from above.

She looks so beautiful, I think it can't be real. I feel something cool dribbling over my fingers.

"You are spilling it, *brat.*" Viktor takes my glass from my hand. "I would not like you to waste good vodka. Even on a spoiled mafia princess." A joke, I suppose. I'm barely comprehending. I'm already gone, moving across the gleaming marble floor. I stop in front of her, speechless.

She just grins. She's happy. The haunted look is gone.

"What's wrong?" she asks. "I got a bluebird on my shoulder?"

I go to her and yank her in for a kiss. She's warm and real and everything I love.

She pulls back with a mischievous expression. I think she's going to give me shit for drinking vodka at two in the afternoon.

She doesn't.

"You and your fucking English toffee and selfless gestures and you expect me to get on a plane? I love you, Aleksio."

My heart twists. "You said love wasn't enough. The whole thing with the sandcastles?"

"Yeah, you're still kicking down sandcastles, but some of them need kicking down. I want to kick them down with you—like that Valhalla, for starters." She gets a serious look here. "But then let's make our own life, our own rules. Build something better than what our families built. Together. What do you think?"

"Yes. Fuck yes." I brush the hair from her forehead. I love her like this. A rebel and a warrior. I grab her hair and kiss her.

And somewhere out there baby animals are laughing, and it doesn't have to mean everything is doomed. It can just mean something stupidly normal.

Like happiness.

Like forever.

~ The End~

Thanks for reading! I hope you enjoyed your time with the Aleksio and Mira and Viktor and the gang as much as I did!

Viktor's story is out 7/26/16 and Kiro's story is out 9/13/16.

Acknowledgements

I am so grateful to be surrounded by such an amazing community of readers, bloggers, and author pals. You're always there with me in my crazy writer cave, and I want to kiss you all!

Special thanks to author Joanna Chambers, who read this many times and brought so many expansive, creative ideas to it. And to author Carolyn Jewel, who patiently read and helped keep the early draft from seriously going off the rails. Author Katie Reus read it twice and brought her amazing sense of hero goodness. And author Skye Warren was there through early and late drafts with amazing insights, adding immense goodness. Editor Deb Nemeth provided brilliant developmental editing and copy editing. Sadye of Fussy Librarian did an incredible job of proofreading and so far beyond that. (Any mistakes are my own last minute changes.) And thanks to Book-Beautiful for the fantabulous cover, and super gratitude also to Christin Ostheimer, who reached out with much-needed Russian help!

I'm also massively grateful to Heather Roberts of Social Butterfly PR, who came through with great beta-read catches and ideas, not to mention book launch magic and incredible patience with my occasional cluelessness. And BookBeautiful for the fantabulous cover. I'm humbled, also, to all of you bloggers and facebook book readers who got in on this release. You have these amazing communities you have created out of love and passion and friendship, and I'm honored that you'd share them with me.

Last but not least, I want to thank my reader friends in the Annika Martin Fabulous Gang. This is my first year of having a facebook group, and you guys are my bright spot on the web. I'm honored to know you. Seriously!

About Annika

I love writing dirty stories about dangerous criminals, hanging out with my man and my two cats, and kicking snow clumps off the bottom of cars around Minneapolis. I've had tons of jobs: factory worker, waitress at a zillion different places, shop clerk, advertising writer. Animals are a huge passion of mine, especially whales and lost dogs. I like to run and read books in bed, and I spend way too much time in coffee shops. In my spare time I write as the RITA award-winning author Carolyn Crane.

I love hearing from you and hanging out!

• Email me at annika@annikamartinbooks.com

• Visit annikamartinbooks.com to find out about the latest news and to get on my newsletter.

• You are warmly invited to join my facebook group, the fabulous gang at: facebook.com/groups/AnnikaMartinFabulousGang/

• My facebook page is: facebook.com/AnnikaMartinBooks

• And twitter! twitter.com/Annika_Martin

Books by Annika Martin

Dangerous Royals
Dark Mafia Prince
Wicked Mafia Prince
Savage Mafia Prince

Taken Hostage by Kinky Bank Robbers
The Hostage Bargain (Book 1 of Taken Hostage by Kinky Bank Robbers)
The Wrong Turn (Book #2 of Taken Hostage by Kinky Bank Robbers)
The Deeper Game (Book #3 of Taken Hostage by Kinky Bank Robbers)
Taken Hostage by Kinky Bank Robbers: the 3-book set

The Most Wanted (Book #4 of Taken Hostage by
Kinky Bank Robbers)

Criminals & Captives
PRISONER (book #1) by Annika Martin & Skye Warren

Writing as Carolyn Crane

Sexy, gritty romantic suspense
Against the Dark (Book #1 of the Associates)
Off the Edge (Book #2 of the Associates)
Into the Shadows (Book #3 of the Associates)
Behind the Mask (Book #4 of the Associates)

Plotty, twisty-turny urban fantasy
Mind Games (Book 1 of the Disillusionists)
Double Cross (Book 2 of the Disillusionists)
Head Rush (Book 3 of the Disillusionists)
Plus assorted shorts and single titles
More about Carolyn's
books: http://authorcarolyncrane.com

Made in the USA
Lexington, KY
27 March 2017